Miranda Hearn

Miranda Hearn was born in Darlington in 1955 and grew up in Dorset. She worked in theatre before gaining a first class degree in English Literature at the University of London's Birkbeck College, and has since worked in film production. She is currently writing her second novel and lives in London.

Miranda Hearn

A Life Everlasting

SCEPTRE

First published in Great Britain in 2003 by Hodder and Stoughton
A division of Hodder Headline

A Sceptre Paperback

1 3 5 7 9 10 8 6 4 2

A CIP catalogue record for this title
is available from the British Library

ISBN 0 340 82755 6

Typeset in Sabon by Palimpsest Book Production Limited,
Polmont, Stirlingshire

Printed and bound in Great Britain by
Mackays of Chatham plc, Chatham, Kent

Hodder and Stoughton
A division of Hodder Headline
338 Euston Road
London NW1 3BH

For Sue Tabor

Part One

I

Hammersmith

1785–1820

The door opened, and yellow light fell into the room. The darkness, until that moment, had been profound. He heard the skittering feet of a dog on the bare boards, and the quiet again as it reached the ancient rug. 'Not on the bed,' said a man's voice. His father, Nicholas. The old man's shadow slid down the wall as he raised the lamp and placed it on a chest of drawers. The room took shape around him. Mallen looked from the chest to the bed, from the bed to the picture that hung above it, and the small square table that stood beside it. They were the old familiar planes of the room where he had been born, and yet it seemed to him that he was lost. The dog sighed, and settled down on the rug.

Outside, he could hear the creak of boots on the snow. The river had frozen over from Fulham Bridge to Southwark. It was January. He had been looking for months now, and he had not found her. He had searched Hammersmith, Holborn, even Moorfields. Every night he went to her house in Chiswick, but she was not there. Sometimes he wondered if he would spend for ever searching, and still never find her and always end up here again. His father closed one drawer and opened another. Mallen watched the lamp flare in a mirror, and remembered the burning buildings and the din of the crowd, the look on her face outside the Sardinian Chapel. He heard the *twsit* of swallows outside her window and felt the summer breeze on his cheek. He saw the river, and felt the stone come down on his head.

The drawer slammed shut again. Can it be so hard for a man on his own to find another pair of stockings?

His father's shadow lengthened until, for a moment, it lay across a corner of the ceiling, and the whole business started again as the top two drawers of another smaller chest were searched. He was already wearing almost everything he owned. He was nearly seventy, Nicholas Mallen, and grief had slowed him down. At last he found what he was looking for; he lifted the lamp, and shuffled to the door. 'Come on,' he said. 'Out.' The dog got to its feet and followed him.

Mallen remained where he was for a while, then made his way out of the house and down to the river. There he found Franny Bright, walking up and down in the dark. He wasn't surprised to see her. 'Doctor,' she said, and she took his arm, and they walked together on the frozen waterfront, towards Chiswick and Glebe House. It was a promenade of ghosts, beside the river; they passed the houses of royal physicians, men of letters, wealthy quacks. They passed the Creek and the High Bridge, the Dove coffee house, and the house where Catherine, widow of Charles II, spent her summers. At Slut's Hole, a hay barge had frozen to its mooring. The masts of fishing boats stood up out of the ice, silvered by frost and the moon. The ferry was stuck on the other side.

Mallen had brought Franny Bright into the world, and he had known her all her short life. She had died when she was only fourteen, tall for her age, and with an open, intelligent face. There was a scattering of freckles on her cheeks, and a small but permanent smudge under her chin. Her hair, dark and long, fell in untidy curls from a ghostly ribbon. There was a great store of wisdom and chatter in her insubstantial frame, and she talked, even now, non-stop. 'What do you remember about the day I was born?' she asked him, for the umpteenth time.

'Everything, I'll never forget it.'

'Well?'

'I remember a great commotion, and that I said to your mother: Mrs Bright! You have signalled a revolution in midwifery. You have confounded medical science. I told her, as she lay worn out from her efforts, William Hunter must hear of this, and Smellie and Ould –'

'Old and smelly?'

No, not William Smellie, he'd been dead for ten years; never mind. 'My dear woman, I said, you have given birth to something exceptional, if not within common notions of great beauty –'

'*Not?*'

'Mrs Bright, said I, you have given birth to a fat but perfectly formed little pig.'

She knocked him on his arm, *rap, rap, rap*, like a door.

'You came out quickly,' he said. 'I do remember that. Like a champagne cork.'

Glebe House was dark. Its lawns were white with hard, unbroken snow. Inside, the rooms smelled of chalk and logs. The furniture had been covered in sheets, and all the grates were empty. Together they searched the kitchens, the servants' rooms, the reception rooms, the attic. They stood in Augusta Corney's bedroom listening, waiting, but she wasn't there and she didn't come. Could he count on her ever coming here again? Would her ghost return, ever, to sit on the floor in front of the fire, to move through the garden, laughing and calling him a monster? His chest, as he walked from one room to another, was a cavity of loss. He felt, once more, the stone come down on his head. He felt the bone crack, and the wave of terror that had crashed through his body. He remembered the effort, with useless limbs, to struggle free, and the darkness that came down over him that was first red, and then yellow. Who had done it? For what reason? He would not know until he found her.

* * *

He did not find her that night, and not for many years. Death, with its own inscrutable purpose, pulled him back at that point to another, different state. It drew him out of the world again and made him into something almost nonexistent, a shadow in the corners of his father's house. There was nothing he could do, and nothing to understand, only an apparent but obscure necessity. He was reminded of those who, in life, are struck down by exhaustion or illness but not finished off, and at times he was overwhelmed by the fear that this was all there was, that this was the life everlasting. It was not what he had expected. He had expected ... nothing. He was a man of science, and he had found out all there was to know about the anatomy of the human being, by cutting it open and looking. Heart, brain, sinews and valves. He had never found anything there like the seat of the soul, and he had thought that the spirit would cease on the instant that life left the body. It was a matter of reason. He had never believed that there would be more, because to do so was not rational. There is no life without matter, and yet here he was. He had had his chance to find her, and he had failed and it was over and that was that. It was an existence without much to it – only the quiet sift of dust, and creaks and spills in the walls of the old house. Distantly, the sounds of the living. Time had no meaning whatsoever, and he forgot it. Days were marked by light and dark, but they had no other form or length, or more significance than minutes. The old man died and was buried, and for a while his ghost also wandered outside somewhere – in the fields or up and down beside the river – and then he, too, was brought back within the crumbling walls. Outside, the harvests came and went. Church bells rang out birth and death, and various other bits of news. At Windsor, the King came to his senses again, having been, for a while, raving mad. France boiled over into revolution, and revolution into war. The bones were blown out of Europe by cannon fire, but Mallen was none the wiser. When news of victory came from Waterloo and the country went wild, he barely heard the rockets and the yelling and the dancing and the drums. Thirty-five years. The King was buried and the nation mourned, but he had no idea. Really, he might as well have been at the bottom of the sea.

Then a woman with a string of ludicrous and even tragic affairs behind her returned to England from the continent, and Mallen was shaken out of his dormant state, as were most of the ghosts of Hammersmith. Why? She shook them up, for certain. She brought the living out of their houses in their hundreds, the moribund out of their beds, and the dead from their corners and other silent places. Like a force of nature, Caroline, fat and ugly wife of the fat new King, did what victory could not – she woke the dead.

Mallen emerged, like a man emerging from a fever. As a man after a fever feels shaky in his legs, and blinks at the light outside, so Mallen felt shaky and blinking in his heart for a while. He very soon saw Franny Bright, however, and it lifted him and brought him back to himself again. 'What on earth's going on?' he said.

Franny grinned. 'Hello, Franny, how are you after all this time?'

He took her hand, and kissed it grandly. 'Will that do?' It was, after all, as if they had only seen each other yesterday, or a month or a week ago. 'I don't understand,' he said. 'What's everyone doing?'

She shrugged, a gesture that generally indicated that she had a good idea of the answer. 'It's a moment of history,' she said.

'It is?'

'Yes.' She said this with certainty and emphasis and he

knew that, for the time being, he was going to have to take her word for it. 'But Fran,' he said, 'there have been enough of those, I should think –'

'Not in Hammersmith.'

He nodded. There was, he had to admit, an agitation in the air, or in the ground under their feet, a sense of expectation that had galvanised and brought him out. 'But why?' he said. He took her arm, and they walked, once more, along the riverfront.

'It's irresistible. The dead appear in droves.' Franny gestured with her free arm. 'It's a mystery, but it happens. It happened when Anne Boleyn was arrested and taken for execution. They came out then, all over Greenwich and Tower Hill, and up out of the river. And there was a flurry in Whitehall, too, when Oliver Cromwell was about to die. There's a scent in the air of historic change, the smell of a notable death, and it brings out all the old ghosts, like you, who've been hanging like bats in the belfry for years. Some of them stay: some have a look at the way the world has changed and go straight back again. It's like an accident; they all want to have a look, even if they don't know why.'

'I see,' said Mallen, trying. 'But Queen Caroline is not about to die.'

'Yes, she is.'

'Yes?' As a medical man, albeit a dead one, Mallen did not put much store in prescient claims from young girls, even Franny.

She dipped her head to one side, and then to the other. This, he knew, was as near as she ever got to climbing down. 'Anyone can see she isn't well,' she said. 'And besides,' she added, her voice aimed low, for sober and convincing effect. 'In her case it's rather more than that.'

'Now what do you mean?'

'You'll see. You'll find out.'

Mallen frowned. Here, outside in the light, with a breeze from the river that was as familiar to him, almost, as the walls of his house, he knew that whatever reason lay behind this sudden emergence of the living and the dead, he had surfaced again with the same compulsion, the same one thought in his mind. 'And Mrs Corney?' he said.

'Oh, she's here.'

'You've seen her?'

'No, but she's here.'

He first caught sight of her outside Brandenburgh House, where the crowds had come to cheer the Queen. It was October 1820. People stood cheek to ear on the grass above the river – men of property, ladies in sleeves and pleats, porters, spinners, builders and journeymen. They had gathered not just from Hammersmith but from all over London, seething with support. The watermen had come out in their thousands, and the river was corked up with their boats. The numbers were extraordinary – of the dead, as well as the living. Here were Radcliffe and Morland, the brittle shadow, Mallen thought, of Robert Walpole's nephew, Thomas. The royalist, Nicholas Crisp. There were men from one age in black coats and breeches, and from another in long wigs and lace. There were Tudor ghosts in goffered ruffs and some, he could swear, in skirts. Women in damask farthingales, who whispered behind their hands. There were wimples, doublets, and bagpipe sleeves. A confusion, running lightly in the crowd, of manners.

At first she was like a pennant or a piece of trim, and then he saw the line of her face, her dress. She was standing on the slope of the bank, leaning forward and lifted on her toes. Mallen flung himself at the wall of people in front of him, against shoulders and coats, against the smell of shouting, furred with meat and teeth and medicines. He pushed at the solid backs of tradesmen and their wives. He got down and crawled, but it was impossible on the ground, nothing but boots; he kept losing his bearings, and when he did look again, she was further away and fainter. The Queen came onto the balcony to wave, and he saw the blocks of rouge on her face and the signs of disease they scarcely hid. An old ghoul snagged his arm, and hung on like a dog while he accused Mallen of having killed him with a cure for palsy fifty years ago. Mallen shook him off, and then, when he turned and looked for her again, Augusta had gone. He flew round the gardens and into the house, where he lost himself in corridors and state apartments. He ran down passages, up and down stairs, in and out of stale and dusty chambers. He shouted her name in boot-rooms and pantries. He searched the stables, the pavilion. Behind the house, the road was filled with carriages and carts. He saw the corner of a ghostly skirt, but it was some young wraith long dead from dysentery.

Franny Bright found him where he had started, on the lawns. 'She's here, somewhere,' he said. 'I've seen her.'

'I saw her too. She's gone.'

'How do you know?'

She led him to the side of the house, to a stone seat, and made him sit down. They remained there for a long time without speaking. For Mallen, it was very bitter – to have seen her, and then so quickly lost her, and to have no idea where she might have gone, or if he would ever see her again. In the west, towards Kew, the sun fell lower in the sky. Finally, he nodded. Another roar went up from the crowd. The Queen was on the balcony again. 'She's not even beautiful,' he said, lifting his head.

'She's German.' Franny had not been a silent shadow all these years; quite the opposite. While Mallen had been tucked between the layers of lath and plaster in his father's house, she had roamed her haunts in London and Hammersmith, keeping a lifeless finger on the times. She told him now about the battles that had been fought – about Nelson at Aboukir Bay and Cape Trafalgar, and Wellington at Waterloo. About the great upheaval in France; about the King's madness, and his death.

'But why do they love her so much?' he asked her, looking up towards the house. The Queen had gone inside again. 'All these people, why is there talk of nothing else?'

'They love her because the King's a toad.'

'They're on her side.'

'Yes, they're on her side.'

'But it's not because she's innocent,' he said.

'She's the victim of injustice. Everyone knows the King's worse than she is, and if she's bad it's because he made her so. She had the nerve to go off and make a life for herself, and now she's back and, bad luck to the King, the people love her. They should chuck out the Bill, the amount of lying that's gone on, the bloody money it's costing.' Franny gazed at her feet. 'Even so,' she said 'look what it's done. It's brought them all out, and Mrs Corney too. You'll see her again, you're bound to, if you stay near the Queen.'

'Yes?'

'I'm sure of it.'

'You must understand, Fran, I don't have any idea of what's going on.'

'No, I know.'

That night they set out for Westminster, slipping unnoticed onto a boat in the early hours at a mooring on the Lower Mall. They sat in silence as they were rowed downriver, with only the slap of the water, the call of a rattled coot. Franny gazed out over the bows as the dark slid past them. Below the fields of Parson's Green, she spoke.

'It's a shame the Queen's in mourning,' she said. 'I heard she wears dresses that start at her waist. Flimsy silks and masses of bosom.'

'She wouldn't do so at her own trial.'

'She might.'

There were gunboats on the river at Westminster. The barge docked at Lambeth timber yards, and they walked back down to the bridge in a mizzling rain. They made their way to the House of Lords, and drifted through lines of Life Guards and the Surrey horse patrol until they reached the doors. Inside, they waited. The chamber, during the course of the morning, filled. The defence witness wept, and was given lavender water. Stacks of paper spilled from trunks and littered the floor beside quill stands and law books and the thin legs of clerks. Notes were passed up and down, and men leaned over the balcony rails. The Queen's counsel read papers, whispered instructions, stood and sat. Light from the high windows picked out the dust on robes and wigs, and every now and then observers left because of the heat. Mallen watched, but he didn't listen. There were others there, he noticed, not only the living. He made out the shade of Chatham, draped in velvet, and still with his crutches, sitting in the very seat where he had talked himself to death in 1778. Charles Lennox Richmond, looking helpless. Women, too, in the ghosts of precious jewels, but not Augusta Corney. The Queen was in a private room, playing backgammon with Alderman Wood.

They went again to the trial, Franny and Mallen, and then again. They sat through long dull days of perjury and cross-examination, and hours and hours of summing-up. 'It's no use,' said Mallen, after the closing speech for the defence. They were on the river again, this time on a wherry bound for Fulham. It was dark.

'The Bill won't go through, it's dead. The Queen will win,' said Franny.

He shook his head.

'I'm trying to make a point.' She pulled her knees up under her chin. 'If the Queen wins –' They could see lines of light along the great roads of London, their deep dull cast against the sky, and here and there a cluster of lamps around a square or market. 'Did you see Barbara Villiers?' she said. 'Did you? She was sitting in the gallery next to some old duke –'

'I saw her.'

'That woman has not left her house on Chiswick Mall for more than a century. Frankly, you can see why, although I think she should get over it. Nothing and no one in all that time has stopped her pacing up and down, mooing for her beauty. And what has brought her out? What could it possibly be, to get her out of the house, and not only that but all the way to Westminster?'

Mallen shook his head. He had never tried to be as smart as Franny.

'The Queen!' she cried. 'The crowds and the Queen and the hubbub and all of it. If the Queen wins, they'll all come out again. Including Mrs Corney.'

He took Franny's hand and held it. In life, Augusta had seemed to hold one kind of answer; in death she held another. In life, he had only seemed to have no choice; in death he was sure he had none. He would look until he found her. And if Franny thought that his hope lay with the Queen, then Franny was probably right.

Caroline Amelia Elizabeth of Brunswick-Wolfenbüttel had been brought over to England twenty-five years before to marry the Prince of Wales. According to Lord Malmesbury, who was sent to Germany to fetch her, her character lacked both reflection and substance, and she did not wash. She said whatever came into her head, and could not shut up. The Prince, when he saw her, demanded a drink and left the room. On the evening of Wednesday 8 April 1795, they were married in the Chapel Royal at St James's. The bridegroom was so much the worse for drink that he had to be supported, and by the time he arrived at Carlton House later that night, he was in a state of alcoholic helplessness. He collapsed on the floor of the bridal chamber and spent the wedding night unconscious. Caroline – to her astonishment – became pregnant almost immediately, but the marriage was a disaster from the start, and after the birth of their daughter the following year, she and the Prince led completely separate lives. She found a house in Blackheath, where she entertained writers and politicians, musicians and scholars, and every naval officer she could lay her hands on. She was forbidden to attend official functions, and the Prince would not even look at her. She stayed at home, making wax models of him, which she stuck all over with pins and watched melt in front of the fire. Curiously, and perhaps because she was denied contact with her own daughter, she adopted half the local children, and gave them clothes and an education. Her favourite was William Austin, the son of an unemployed dockyard worker, who lived in the house and slept in her bed.

In 1814 she left England to travel to the continent, and for the past six years she had been in Europe; in Italy, mostly, with demented trips to Tunis and Jerusalem. When rumours got back to London concerning her behaviour abroad, the Prince sent secret agents to investigate, and set up a commission to get evidence against her from everyone who knew or met her, but nothing conclusive could be produced. When George III died in 1820, she came back to London to take her place as Queen; her husband promptly instructed both Houses to bring forward a Bill of Pains and Penalties to remove her from the liturgy, from the bonds of marriage and, if possible, from the country; to prove without doubt her licentious and adulterous intercourse with one Bartolomeo Pergami – upstart Italian courier of no rank whatsoever, except for the barony she bought him in Sicily.

There was no real question that she was guilty of adultery, and many times over; she was immoral, unbalanced and shameless, but she was no worse than her husband, and across the country she was hailed and cheered as a heroine. She had become a symbol of injured innocence, of the wrongs of the common people in general, and of women in particular. Loyal addresses were brought to Brandenburgh House from all over the country, from Leeds, Liverpool, from Bristol, Nottingham, Bath. They were brought by the glass-blowers, the brassfounders, the women of Aylesbury. The Navy came onto the streets of London, thousands of seamen blocking the roads, well-dressed and sober, all for Caroline.

Caroline

October 1820, Westminster So boring. Did you see this, did you see that, did the Queen wear such and such scandalous clothes with a mask on her face? This was Italy, and a masked ball you utter dolt. Since July I have been forced to listen to the ridiculous tales from Italy, and even from my own Witnesses. I don't listen, it is so abominably boring, and I go in another room with Alderman Wood. He is my adviser and my only friend, being as how even Brougham, my Attorney General, cannot stand to look at me.

How much did He pay them, those Traitors who spoke against me? When they arrived in England from Italy, the people of Dover threw stones at them and would not let them come ashore, so they had to go to Holland until it was time to give Evidence. Well bad luck to the King, all my servant Theodore could say was *Non mi ricordo*, and half of London is saying it still. It has given them most amusement. Now they are gone back to Italy, good riddance.

The only one who ever said to me good morning my beautiful Highness what shall we do today, take a boat on the lake or go to the ball, was Bartolomeo Pergami, and they want to know did her Royal Highness touch Pergami on the leg or do disgusting things with the man. Did she sleep with him in a tent on the deck of her Boat on the way to Tunis or at Jaffa. Do you know how hot it is in Jaffa? Of course we slept in a tent. Why does not Henry Brougham say your noble lordships I have Evidence from a Physician that Bartolomeo Pergami was wounded in the groin in the Russian campaign and too bad, I rest my case. Never mind he have a daughter, that can be explain.

He hired men to kill me, the King. In Italy and now here. In Italy, if Pergami had been one hour away from me, I would have been murdered. This is why I am in his company day and night, not the other thing. Now Alderman Wood and his sons walk up and down in front of my House armed with pistols to protect me from Assassination.

Still nobody has told me why the Queen's name has been left out of the general Prayer-books in England and why I should put up with it. I did not come back to England for me alone, but for the King and because I must. They said to me here is some money, take it and do not come to England, stay where you are, but I said I do not want the money because it is my duty to be Queen and claim my title.

Everybody must love something in this World. I never had the comfort to have my own Daughter under my care or roof. Not allowed to talk to her. Because the King wanted all control, and said I was a disgusting influence. Instead I always had poor Orphans, or the children of Parents who were poor, to live in my House in Blackheath, of all ages and sizes. I gave them what they needed so that they could grow up to become seamen or industrious housewives. My dear William Austin, my darling who came to me when he was three months old to be like a son. The King told me Billy, too, must go and not live in my House and I must not keep the boy, as he call him, for the reason that nobody knew who he was. If he was my own Child, then might I bring him forward as Heir to the Throne? Even now, they do not know if he is the son of the King or of Samuel Austin or of Louis Ferdinand of Prussia or who his mother is. Ha, ha. I kept him, damn to hell the King. He slept in my bed as an Infant, and is the only one who stayed by me to now.

I shall not see him again in this world, the King. I hope I will in the next, where I shall find justice.

On the third reading of the Bill, on Friday 10 November 1820, there was a majority of only nine votes, and it was withdrawn. The Queen had triumphed, and all London came out onto the streets. There had not been anything like it since Waterloo. All the ships in the river glittered to the mastheads with lights, and there were bonfires, fireworks, dances and parades. Church bells rang out, and cannons and muskets were fired. The Queen celebrated with a thanksgiving service at St Paul's. She went from Brandenburgh House in a state carriage drawn by six chestnut horses, and fifty thousand people came out to cheer her. It was a fine, dry, cold day, and she was met at Temple Bar by the Lord Mayor and the sheriffs of London who escorted her to the cathedral.

In the scrum that lined the route, Mallen and Franny saw Augusta again. They pushed towards her through the horses and the people, but only managed to end up getting lost in the lanes and alleys north of the Strand, where the streets were slick with mud and rubbish, the houses black and dilapidated; they smelled of wet wood and crumbling stone, and there was no real light, and the air was bad. Two small boys sat in a doorway, smoking pipes and watching them with flat and worldly stares. 'What are you looking at?' Franny hissed.

'Come on,' said Mallen, 'we won't find her here.'

'You won't find anyone here,' said the older boy. 'Bugger off.'

'*You* –' spat Franny, pushing her face into his until their noses almost met. His eyes did not move, and he blew out a lazy cloud of smoke. She sighed, and straightened. London, at that moment, seemed to her like an open mouth, with black and broken teeth. It had gobbled up Augusta Corney and stuffed her out of sight. The older boy creased his lips. 'Go on,' he said, 'get lost.'

'She was here!' cried Franny.

'No, we've lost her.' Mallen held a hand out to her, but she spun away.

'She's like mercury,' she said, turning a circle on the grimy cobbles. 'Quicksilver.' She jabbed the air with a finger, and then again, and again. Stab, stab, stab. 'I saw her, she was here.'

'I saw a lady,' said the smaller boy.

Franny twisted round again. 'Where did you see her? How long ago?'

He buttoned his face up like a fist while he thought, and his pipe stuck out of the side of his mouth. 'A week,' he said. 'Or two.'

Franny stamped her foot in fury. 'Where are your mothers?' she shouted. Mallen took her arm, and led her back to the Strand. They had seen her again, at least. They would find her, he was sure, now. In the crowds and the commotion, they were almost bound to be thrown off in the wrong place, the wrong direction. They would find her again, somewhere else, and catch her up. What might come next, he had no idea. The ways of this world could only be guessed at. Perhaps, after all, there might be such a thing as eternal rest. How we cling to that idea, he thought, even here.

2

Mallen

1748–1768

He was born in April 1748. His father owned several acres of good land in Hammersmith, given over to market gardening. Apples, cherries, plums and pears; cauliflowers, currants, herbs. Acres of spinach. A cart left every night to transport the fruit and vegetables to London, to Covent Garden. In the summer, women came in from Shropshire and Wales to carry strawberries on their heads – two turns in the day from Hammersmith, by foot. And at night, from London, in the other direction, came the nightsoil to make them grow. The crops, not the Shropshire women.

On his second birthday, London was threatened with extinction. Three months earlier, at the beginning of February 1750, the people of London had witnessed a cloud of deep dusky red at night to the north-east of the metropolis. Two or three days later, a small earthquake struck the city. Then, on 8 March, one month to the day after the first, came another. It started with a shivering fit between one and two in the morning. Then came a shock that lasted for half a minute. Two old houses came down somewhere near Piccadilly, and several chimneys, but all that anyone lost was glass and china and their senses. The anxiety that followed – that there would be more and greater tremors – was raised to extraordinary heights by a lunatic trooper in the Guards, who predicted that a third, catastrophic earthquake would take place two months after the first, and that the cities of London and Westminster would be totally destroyed; the capital would collapse on itself, and all the outlying parishes, and all the people. This, for the men of the Church, was too good. It brought them together where before they had been at each other's throats; they thundered in to foster talk of judgement and preach reform of moral conduct. Churches filled, language was tempered, and the hand of charity opened. London began to empty – in three days, over seven hundred coaches left the city past Hyde Park Corner. On the evening of 8 April, those who were left abandoned their homes and made for the open spaces, or for boats on the river. The fields and gardens and orchards of Hammersmith filled with Londoners, but there wasn't a peep from the earth all night. Jamie Mallen, however, was suffering from wind, and yelled from dusk to dawn.

He went to school in Hammersmith, where the beliefs and catechism of the Church of England were dinned into his head, along with Latin and arithmetic. The teachers were unintelligent and vain, but he made light work of Pliny, Ovid and Juvenal, and discovered in himself an appetite and bent for learning. When he told his father what he intended to do with his life, Nicholas Mallen went off into the fields and orchards, and did not speak to him for two days. It was not a harsh silence; he was thinking. On the third day, he shut himself in his study and went through his accounts. At dusk, he got up from his chair and stood for a while, looking out of the window at his son. James was outside in the lane talking to one of the men. He was nearly six foot tall, now, with a mild face and even features; with his hands deep in the pockets of an old black coat, he already looked like a physician. Without a wig, his dark hair was blown about on his head, and his ears looked raw. He had his mother's eyes, steady and enquiring. Above all, he looked young, and full of intelligent energy. It would be a shame to see it go to waste, a mind like his, on peas and lettuces. Nicholas shrugged. It took some doing, to imagine a son of his at university, but he did possess imagination, and, thanks to three good years of soft fruit, just about sufficient funds. He walked out of the house, and gave his son a sum of money, and his blessing. And so, at the age of seventeen, Mallen went up to Edinburgh to study medicine.

The school was as good, by that time, as Leiden. He lived in a freezing room that looked out onto roofs and the slate-grey city sky. On a typical day he got up at seven and read for two hours on the lungs or the liver. After breakfast he walked to the university, where he attended lectures and made notes until noon. From twelve to one, he walked the wards in the infirmary in the wake of one of the physicians, along with a crowd of other students who, if they did nothing else, frightened the patients half to death by their numbers. There were strict rules, most of which assumed that the patients were not desperately ill and, far from being bed-ridden, needed to be constrained from wandering out of the hospital and coming back drunk. He observed amputations, the splinting of compound fractures, the removal of bladder stones. This latter procedure they all viewed with their watches in their hands; Cheselden, in his day, had done it in under a minute, and there was always something of a race. One o'clock to three, dissection. Three to five, dinner. Five till seven, lectures and anatomical demonstrations. After something to eat at nine, he worked until midnight on his notes.

He learned natural philosophy, chemistry, physiology and materia medica. He learned the principles of general pathology, and the theory of the practice of physic. He watched operations performed on conscious, screaming patients tied down on a slab of wood, with a channel for the blood, which dripped down into buckets of sawdust. He sat in the crowded dissecting room while Monro, in a filthy apron, cut through the fatty layers of human cadavers. He watched him find the tendons of the wrist and the blood vessels of the lung. He held his nose as the bowel was lifted out. He had made up his mind by this time to be a physician-midwife and to do that he had a lot more to learn about anatomy. The problem, at Edinburgh, was the shortage of corpses. In London, it was a different matter. For a start, there were the bodies of condemned criminals – although they were very few and far between – but the gallows were by no means the only source. The city was littered with burial grounds, and with men prepared to dig. He would go to London, then. 'I'll give you a letter,' said William Cullen on the day that Mallen finished his studies, 'to my old friend William Hunter. He has his own anatomy school in Windmill Street. There's no better man for what you want to do.'

Hunter was at this point the foremost surgeon-midwife of his time.

Mallen found somewhere to live on the second floor of a tall house in Newman Street. It was 1768, October. He was twenty. Again, he had a view of roofs and chimneys. Pigeons sat ragged and blinking on his windowsill.

On the evening of his arrival there, he heard a sound outside his door. He opened it to find an enormous young man standing in the corridor, staring at his feet. He looked up when he saw Mallen, a look of fierce yet sleepy confusion on his face. He was wearing a long green coat and cloth breeches with a narrow stripe. There was a red mark on his brow, as if he had walked into something, like a low door.

'I thought you were about to knock,' said Mallen. 'I heard you come up the stairs.'

'I wasn't going to knock. I was about to let myself in.'

'Do, by all means. Come in.'

The man was at least six foot tall, and broad in the shoulders. His face, though bruised, was freckled and open.

'You shouldn't do that,' he said. 'Not in London. I might be anyone.'

'I know who you are. You're the apothecary, you live upstairs.'

'Upstairs!' His face cleared. Sudden comprehension.

Mallen stood back and the young man came into the room, looking around him in every direction as if he had been sent up from the street to find something.

'Tell me –' Mallen took a pile of his clothes from one of the two chairs, and stood, his mind divided, trying to find another place to put them. Every surface was covered with the things that he had brought with him and not yet put away. Clothes and books, ink, writing paper, wig stand, candlesticks. 'Wait,' he said. He opened the door that led through into the small bedroom, and threw the pile onto the bed. 'I'm sorry,' he said. 'Sit.'

'You're the doctor.'

'I am. James Mallen.'

'Philip Little. How d'you do.' The young man threw himself into the chair that Mallen had cleared, and ran his hands briskly up and down his face. 'The answer to your question is no, I'm not drunk.' He looked up, then, and grinned. 'I was told that you were coming. I remember now.'

'I wasn't going to ask if you were drunk.'

'What then?'

Mallen also sat. He looked into the fire, which wasn't drawing properly, and then at the floor, and then at Philip Little. 'I don't know,' he said. 'It's gone.'

Philip leaned back in his chair and beamed. 'You're as bad as me, and I've been up for two nights. The fact is, I only moved out of these rooms yesterday. I wanted to be at the front of the house. It's noisy, but it's high up so it doesn't matter. I didn't think about the roof, but I'll get used to it. I'll stoop. I forgot completely that I'd moved out; my feet brought me here on their own. It's just as well you were here, or I might have climbed into your bed. I'm talking because I'm tired, take no notice.'

Mallen heated water, and made them toddies. Within five minutes, Philip was asleep. Mallen crept round the room, putting things away and trying to do it quietly. After a while he realised that he could move the furniture from one end to the other and his fellow lodger would not wake up. He found, underneath a crate of books, a box of apples that his father had sent with him from Hammersmith, and he ate four of them, throwing the cores into the fire. After forty minutes, Philip woke up again.

'I've remembered what I was meaning to ask you,' said Mallen.

Philip rubbed his eyes and looked around him. 'Good God. A minute ago, this place was a mess.'

Mallen pulled his boots out from under the table. 'Where do you eat? I don't know my way round. I'm starving.'

'Food!' exclaimed Philip. He slapped his knees. 'Yes, you can have anything you like round here. Give me a minute to get . . . what? Nothing, I don't need anything. I'll show you.'

'But you're tired.'

'And hungry.'

'Help me move this bookcase first.'

Outside, above the stink of soot and horse dung and waste, he could smell autumn. The air had been sliced, and left with a sharp edge. London seemed to him at that moment to be not just a city, but his future. It was huge and filthy, and a building site from one end to the other, but it was alive, it was full of light, the glow from the oil lamps and from the mass of human beings, rich and poor, who stamped up and down its streets in the first cold wind of the season. They went to a chop-house in Compton Street, and sat at the end of a long and noisy table.

'Why haven't you slept?' Mallen asked.

Philip pulled apart a piece of greyish-looking bread. 'A potter's wife who was lethargic, a fellow with dropsy, and a letter-founder suffering from fumes. A man who spent four hours throwing up until there was nothing left to come out and he was practically unconscious. I had to find a physician for him at two o'clock in the morning. Not easy. Two blisterings, one application of leeches, and an old fellow who wanted someone to talk to. They just all came on top of one another. Also I went to the theatre, there is that.'

Apothecaries did as much medical work, in those days, as physicians, and it was a bone of contention between them; generally speaking, they hated each other, but this seemed not to occur to either man as they sat eating chops and drinking watery ale. 'What did you see?' Mallen asked him.

'Not absolutely sure. There was a riot in the first act, and I lost the drift. It begins in the court of some duke, and there's a wrestling match, and the heroine falls madly in love with one of the wrestlers. I know what you're thinking: *As You Like It*. But it wasn't. Everything went to pieces, dramatically, while we were still in Act One. There was a lot of dressing up, but there always is. You never know who anyone is supposed to be, from one minute to the next, and there's always a forest or a graveyard where they get into a worse muddle than you are. And then when someone next to you starts throwing fruit onto the stage and there are fisticuffs, and another fight breaks out in the boxes, and the heroine faints from the heat long before she's supposed to, you haven't a chance, really. It wasn't bad. You should come, one day, though come to think of it, I suppose you won't have the time.'

They walked back to their rooms together, and said goodnight at Mallen's door. That night, and every night for months afterwards, he went off to sleep to the sound of Philip's footsteps on the creaking boards above him.

*   *   *

The first advice that William Hunter gave him, in the anatomy school on Windmill Street, was to find himself a wife.

'But you yourself –' said Mallen, or started to.

'I haven't, and I won't. That doesn't mean to say that you should not. It is a recognised axiom that a doctor who seeks the custom of respectable and fashionable women must first take a wife. With me they make an exception only because I've been doing this for a long time, and because I am a cold fish. But if they – I mean the husbands – think you only know the female body from your anatomical studies, they might very well wonder whether the living reality is going to be too much for you. When they notice that you have direct access to the very citadel of female virtue, they can convince themselves that it's only a short step to the collapse of society and the constitution of the state. A wife is useful against such attitudes. But choose carefully, someone who won't hang round your neck.'

Who would marry William Hunter? He *was* a cold fish, tight-fisted, crabby and cantankerous. He worked all hours, day and night. The smell of death was in every corner, in curtains, in the cupboards – that, and the spirits of wine in which the bodies were kept. There were plugs of mud on the corridor floors from the boots of the resurrectionists. On the shelves, instead of porcelain or novels, there were body parts in jars, specimens injected with spirit varnish, unspeakable bits and pieces. A cyst from the brain of a heifer, which walked for weeks in a circle, then died; the plaster cast of a gravid human uterus, and an ovarian tumour, stuffed with hair. Diseased bones, bits of brain, lungs and livers. At night, all he ate was an egg.

He collected anything he could lay his hands on. Paintings and medals, manuscripts and coins. He had more display cases and cabinets than almost anyone in England. Trunks with dull brass fittings and complicated locks made up a sort of second division of furniture. He had, more by accident than design, an enormous collection of keys. It was like a museum, and one day it would be.

Nobody wanted to marry the man, but there was no one to beat him at teaching. There were others who did it, but Hunter had been to France. In France they understood that in the teaching of anatomy, much more than oratory is needed. You have to see the actual body parts, to handle the bones, to dissect the muscles; to follow the course of nerves and arteries and open the organs. And it is necessary to do these things many times, so that everything is planted properly in the mind and pressed well down. Take Nicholls, who scuttled through the bare bones of anatomy in less than thirty sessions, demonstrating on just a couple of bodies. No, in Paris they did not *watch*; in Paris there was a corpse for every student, and a sharp knife. In Windmill Street, the same. Hunter lectured daily, six days a week, often twice. From time to time he was summoned to the lying-in rooms of the Hertfords or the Sandwiches or the Pitts of this world, to bring their children into the light of day. To her Majesty the Queen, for that matter, of whose health he had the direction when the Prince of Wales was born.

As for his friends at the other end of the scale, God knows how he found them in the first place. They stood at the back door with wooden shovels, an extinguished lantern, a heavy sack. Outside, the night was dark, and a grave lay empty. Like fishermen, they got higher prices in winter, when the bodies were better preserved. Children were priced by the inch. They dug down with their wooden shovels, sometimes meeting straw mixed in with the mud or even guns, rigged with buried wire. A foot down for the poor, deeper for the rich. They broke the coffin at the head end, and slipped the body out. Then the clothes went back. Under law, a body was not counted as property, and therefore could not be stolen, whereas a ring or a shroud or a pair of old pants could put a man in gaol. So the clothes went back, and then the lid, and then the earth. Then off to St Thomas's with the body, or to Windmill Street and William Hunter. Very good, thank you, here's the money, go away. He could do it where others could not. What's that? he might say, as one of them, squinting, brought a small shell out of a pocket and looked at it with dismay. No, no, take it back. Find the grave again and put it back, for God's sake. They'll dig up the whole place if there's the least sign that you've been there. They leave those things on purpose, you should know that by now. He would be almost beside himself, at this point, with rage. All right, you can go now, get lost.

We'll have the sack back, Doctor.

Oh, yes.

They were in the lecture theatre. Hunter – short, slender, with fine and pointing hands and a gouty wince from time to time – stood in front of a skeleton and spoke about bone disease. 'I want you to look at this,' he said to his students. 'It is the tibia or leg bone of a boy of seven years. Notice that it is irregular in contour and broad in girth. The outer casing . . . Yes, what is it?' He put the bone down on a table and took a message from his assistant, William Cruikshank. 'All right,' he said, when he had read it. 'Mr Cruikshank, take over. One of you men, come with me. Jamie Mallen, if you don't mind.'

They made their way out into Windmill Street, where Hunter's carriage was waiting. Night had fallen during the lecture, and a gale was blowing, but Hunter didn't seem to mind the cold. 'I didn't want a crowd,' he said.

Mallen's first thought was that they were on their way to one of Hunter's patients, the lying-in of some lady of standing, in Whitehall Gardens or Berners Street. Then, as the carriage turned past St Giles's, he decided that no, they must be going to the hospital. It came as a shock, then, to hear that this was not a mission to bring another child into the world, but to fetch a dead one. 'The woman's name –' Hunter placed his spectacles on his nose and looked again at the document in his hand. 'The woman's name is Coffey,' he said. 'Hannah Coffey.' Hunter saw his student's confusion. 'There is some suspicion,' he said, 'of murder.'

'She killed her child?'

Hunter didn't answer him at once. His eyes were still on the paper, but the light in the carriage was bad, and the page leapt at every rut in the road. He gave up the effort and put the document and his glasses back into different pockets. He sat back and pinched the top of his nose. 'Who knows?' he said. 'The main point being not to jump too quickly to an opinion.'

'Has she been examined, the woman?'

Hunter nodded, then shook his head. 'I don't know,' he said. 'In any case, she doesn't deny that she has given birth.'

'Why are they so certain that she killed it?'

'The child was found wrapped up in rags, beneath the bed. I'm not sure in my own mind that this is the same as attempting to hide it, but that's what they will say. And concealment of the body is seen, nine times out of ten, as a sign of guilt.'

Hunter put his head out of the window to peer at the dim lights of Great Wild Street. A hawker appeared from under the carriage wheels to thrust a fistful of flowers in his face. He threw the window up again. 'Where does he get those from,' he said, 'at this time of year?' He sat back against the burgundy leather. 'I have heard a lot of perfectly ordinary prejudice passing for expert opinion in a court of law, especially when the woman is poor and the child has no father. The coroner has asked for my opinion, and I shall give it to him only after a great deal of thought and a proper post-mortem examination. This woman –' He frowned, and his hand went to the pocket of his coat.

'Hannah Coffey.'

'Coffey, yes. She's been thrown into Newgate, Dr Mallen, and it is up to us, you and me, to find what evidence and expertise may be offered in her defence. Or otherwise.'

'She might hang,' said Mallen.

'She might.'

The child was in a locked room in a public house behind Clare Market. The street underfoot was scratchy with fish scales, and there was a strong smell of old meat by the shambles. The tiny body was wrapped in sacks. Hunter pulled them open, looked briefly at what they contained, and folded them again. 'You take it,' he said to Mallen.

'And even supposing,' Hunter said, the following day, 'that the child was born alive, we cannot conclude that it must have been murdered. We know that if a child takes only one breath, the lungs will swim in water as readily as if it had breathed for five minutes, or an hour.' Hunter, Mallen and William Cruikshank stood either side of the table in the dissecting room. In front of them lay the body of Hannah Coffey's child. 'Observe,' Hunter went on, prodding a small grey mass in a metal basin, 'that they do.' Mallen forced himself to look. 'We still have to be sure that the air is not there because it has been generated by putrefaction, and that it is in the lung vesicles and not due to an emphysema of the cellular tissues. Remember, it is perfectly possible for a child to take one breath and die, particularly if the labour has been long and if there is no help to hand.' Hunter scratched his face, and leaned forward again over the table. 'Also, it is generally known that a child may be brought to life by inflating its lungs, and it seems that the mother herself or some other person might have tried to do this after the death of the infant. This I am going to try to find out today or tomorrow.'

'How?' said Mallen.

'I'm going to ask her.'

The prison stank. It was in the walls, it had rotted the floors, and it would never ever come out. A human muckheap built over years of rot, a bog of past and present infection. They were led through alleys and slime-paved passages by a gatesman in a wide coat that billowed with the stink. It was pitch-black everywhere, and he carried a link to show them the way. In one of the yards, men and women stood together, drunk and freezing, playing skittles and mississippi. From the cells on the common sides, hands reached out from behind bars and brushed them as they passed.

Hannah Coffey wouldn't look at them. They found her in a female ward where their breath, in spite of a small fire, stood frozen in front of their faces. There were no beds, only raised platforms around the walls, where the prisoners lay on rotting blankets. Some of the women seemed stupid or senseless, others chattered like birds, wicked and outrageous. They hugged themselves, their voices shivering, or lay in awful heaps. Hannah Coffey sat without moving, without even lifting her head. Hunter took her hand and lifted the rat's-tail hair from in front of her face. He sat on a wooden pallet and leaned forward over his knees. He spoke to her, and she looked aslant into a solitary distance. She didn't speak, not once. Mallen wanted to shake her, to shake down all the blankness and silence into her feet. He felt the prison walls all round him, and a pulse began to jump in his throat. What if they forgot to let them out? Hunter sat with his head bowed beside Hannah Coffey's, talking into her lap, as if leaving the words there for her to look at later.

'Well?' said Mallen, on the steps of the prison. Hunter's carriage was waiting in the yard.

'Well,' said Hunter. He shouted an instruction to the driver, and climbed into the carriage. 'Tell me,' he said, settling back in his seat. Mallen was caught on the door, and fumbled to free his sleeve. 'What did you make of her?'

'She is . . .' Mallen struggled to find the word. 'Unbalanced,' he said, though it wasn't the one he had wanted. 'Her mind has been overcome.'

'I agree. But by what? By grief, would you say, or by guilt?'

He took so long to answer that Hunter had his head out of the window again, yelling at the driver to back up out of a crush in Clements Lane. 'I don't know,' he said, eventually.

'No, nor I. And if she won't speak, then there's no ready way of finding out. There's only one way to account for the air in the lungs, but I must have it from her own lips. She has to speak.'

'But she hid the body, what about that?'

'She only put it under the bed. It was dead, Jamie, she had to put it somewhere out of sight. I wish to God, however, that she had not.'

'And if she did kill it?'

Hunter held on to the strap inside the carriage door. 'The mind of a woman about to give birth . . .' he said. 'I'm telling you, they live in a different world. You have to look very deep. Try to imagine the thoughts and feelings of a woman like Hannah Coffey. She has no husband, not much money, names thrown at her, probably sick. And she's alone, through it all. Any woman who commits such a crime should be the object of our greatest pity. It isn't evil that makes her do it, but a sense of shame which has been taught her over and above the laws of nature. God forbid, Jamie, that killing should always be murder.'

3

Coronation

1821

Mallen and Franny kept close to the Queen, and to the people close to the Queen. They hung about in the paths and gardens of Brandenburgh House and watched the coming and going; they drifted under the windows like scraps of frost. The days were high and clear and cold. Franny slipped off to haunt the kitchen yards. 'We've got an invitation,' she said one day.

They went in through the back of the building. Their guide was the same wraith Mallen had seen in October on the road behind the house – a ravaged child, brittle and restless. 'You think she's so bloody marvellous,' said the wraith, 'you look at the state of the carpets. Wax, ink, oil, food. It's not even her house, and she's broken every chair in it. The keys are all lost, and the beds stink. So does she.' Franny said nothing. She slipped upstairs to watch the Queen prepare for bed, bare-breasted in front of a mahogany mirror, her black wig on the floor like a dog. Pots of rouge and powder spilled everywhere, and a curtain tassel sat amongst dried-out laurel leaves and earrings on the dressing table. The room smelled sour. Franny let the door bang shut behind her, and the Queen shrieked.

For weeks, they walked the floors of the state rooms and lingered under ornate ceilings. They watched from every window for a sign of Augusta Corney on the lawns. They saw carriages arrive with dinner guests, and go away again. The Queen struggled around the house, half-dressed and shipwrecked, or lay in bed complaining about the weather and writing letters to Lord Liverpool. The struggle for victory was over. Now came all the difficulties over details. Money, a house, the liturgy.

'I wish they'd passed the bloody Bill and sent her back where she came from,' said the wraith, flitting, like a duster, up a long, curved banister. 'She wants a palace, so she can wreck that, too. She could pull Hampton Court to bits in a week. She should lay off the booze, in my opinion.'

'She's miserable,' observed Franny.

'Drunk,' said the wraith. 'It's over, and no one can be bothered to like her any more.'

Spring came, and then summer. Mallen went out every night and walked the path to Glebe House, or to Holborn. He could not understand what it was, if indeed there was anything, that linked the ghost of Augusta to the Queen. Perhaps it was not the Queen herself at all, but the crowds. He remembered again the scenes outside the Sardinian Chapel, and the look on Augusta's face as the people streamed into Duke Street behind them. Perhaps there was no real link at all, and he was waiting in the wrong place. Perhaps she had gone again for good. What am I doing here? he asked himself. What were any of them doing, in this strange place, this strange existence. It was a life without the structures of life, an existence without the familiar means of survival. Only the living need to sleep and eat. Hunger was something wide and vague, and weariness was of the spirit. Patience no longer relied on time, but still demanded the same sort of effort, and waiting produced a similar ache.

'Trust me,' said Franny, whenever she saw his mood dip.

One day, the Queen vanished completely, and half her household. They found her, after a lot of trouble, in a house in South Audley Street, in Piccadilly. 'You might have told us,' said Franny.

The wraith shrugged. 'She only came to spend the night.

She's got to get up at three, as it is. If you're going to the coronation, good luck to you.''

'Why?' said Mallen.

'Riots.'

The crowds began to build before daybreak. At four in the morning, South Audley Street and the streets around it were thick with people. Soon after five, the Queen came out and got into her coach, with Lady Hood and Lady Anne Hamilton. They set off for Westminster with a mass of men and women running after them, yelling and shouting and splitting the thin air of dawn. Mallen and Franny followed, scouring the throng. Each time a white ribbon blew in someone's hair, or on a hat, Mallen's eye was drawn to the place; each time a piece of harness flashed, or smoke rose from a pipe. For forty minutes, he followed a lace veil at a distance, thinking it was her. Horses threw their heads up, eyes rolling back and veined with brown. Then Franny had him by the hand. 'This way,' she hissed, and dragged him out in front of the Queen's carriage. 'There!' she cried. 'No, not yet.'

They ran the length of Constitution Hill, until the Queen was way behind them and the noise had gone, or hadn't started, the streets still lined with waiting, with people on their feet since dawn. 'There!' shouted Franny, in Birdcage Walk.

Mallen swerved round. 'Where?'

She grabbed his hand and patted it. 'I'm sorry, I'm sorry. It's only Barbara Villiers.'

The old Duchess, once beautiful, illustrious and beloved, was struggling, disfigured and ugly, towards Storey's Gate. Franny dragged Mallen along to catch her up. 'Your Grace,' said Franny.

The old woman started. 'Oh, it's you,' she said. Barbara Villiers, Countess of Castlemaine, Duchess of Cleveland and mistress to King Charles II, had died in 1709, aged almost seventy, blown up and bloated by dropsy. Mallen had often seen her, a distracted ghost, standing at the window of Walpole House on Chiswick Mall, her face not only fat but pulled apart by grief. In her day, she had been the most powerful woman in England, demanding the complete submission of a king, but since her death, and until the arrival of the Queen in Hammersmith, she had not left the house in over a hundred years, pacing its floors at night and mourning for her beauty. Now she stood in front of them in a silk dress with a straight bodice and open skirt. In spite of her ruined body, and the fact that she was dead and Caroline was still alive, the Duchess was much more regal in her demeanour than the Queen. 'And Doctor Mallen,' said Franny, introducing him.

It was the first time Mallen had met, formally, anyone from another century. He made a small bow, putting some flourish into it, a gesture that made him look, more than anything, as if he were trying to get the old woman to hurry up, or move out of the way. He earned himself a thin look of scorn from Franny, who then began to talk to the Duchess at a great rate, throwing her own hands out to point this way and then that. 'Augusta Corney?' said the Duchess, interrupting her.

Mallen swerved again, pivoting on one foot. 'You know Mrs Corney?' he said.

'Well, I know her, I've seen her, yes,' said the Duchess. 'She has walked up and down in front of my house often enough.'

He frowned, and knocked his fist against the bridge of his nose. It was impossible; he'd beaten that path repeatedly, night after night for years, and he had never seen her.

The Duchess took Franny's hand, and dropped it again. 'Well,' she said, 'that's quite a story, though I find it extra-ordinary, really, that you didn't notice her in the House of Lords, at the trial. Admittedly, she wasn't there every day, but I saw her more than once.'

Franny spun round with a look of triumph in her eyes, but Mallen only shook his head.

'Come,' said the Duchess, 'we might as well go inside and see what there is to see, including Mrs Corney, if she's here.' She looked up at the building in front of them. 'I hardly know my way around London any more,' she said. 'It's very easy to lose one's way. I tend to stay as close as I can to the river. It means going out of one's way, of course, but it's better than getting hopelessly lost. I know where I am here. You know that Cromwell's army camped in there, in the Abbey? They made an awful mess.' She shook her head, and the flesh trembled under her chin.

At that moment, the Queen's carriage arrived. It drove through the cheers and waving hats into Dean's Yard. The gates were closed behind it. The carriage stopped and the Queen looked around her, as if she had left something behind at home and just remembered it. The soldiers outside the Abbey presented arms, and there was a scattering of applause from the seats. It was still only six in the morning. She stepped down from her carriage, but the doors of the Abbey were shut in her face. She went from one to another, on the arm of Lord Hood, but no one would let her in. Lord Hood produced a ticket, but that was not enough. The Guards were called out; they closed ranks and waited for her next move and whichever way she turned, the doors were barred.

She left. As the carriage pulled away, to return to Hammersmith, the Duchess appeared at their side again. 'I shall go in,' she said. 'This is something I want to see. They might not let the Queen in, but his mistress is there, done up to the eyes, of course. I haven't been inside myself for a very long time.' Mallen considered this: no doubt she had been in the congregation when Charles II was crowned. It made him for a moment humble, not because of her status in a royal household, but because of the weight and the generosity of time, and of stone. 'As for your friend,' said the Duchess, 'did you see her? I was right, she was here, but she's gone, now, I'm afraid. I'm quite certain you're right, however, she won't be far from the Queen, poor woman.' And with that Barbara Villiers, Duchess of Cleveland, was gone.

'What did she mean?' Mallen turned to Franny, but she was already moving off, with the crowd.

St James's Street was a mire. There had been a lot of water on the road, and it had turned to mud. People picked up handfuls of the stuff and threw it at the windows of some public offices, illuminated for the King. Small boys rolled in it and were covered from head to toe. The Duchess was wrong, however. Augusta, if she had ever been there, had vanished. Mallen felt his patience turn to something small and hard, like gravel. Every time that he saw or heard of her, she turned away and disappeared, as if a force independent of them both had been commissioned to keep them apart. Why, for God's sake, could she not stand still?

Within three weeks of the coronation, the Queen lay dying in Hammersmith.

Caroline

20th July 1821 They would not let me in. They do not say oh Lady Conyngham you are only the King's mistress, we must bang this door in your face and let the rightful Queen come in and take her place with the Royal Person. No, they let her in so that the King can make faces at her and send her kisses in the ceremony like some boy. He is nearly fifty-nine, for God sake. To me they say show us your ticket, please: sorry, no admittance. I should have been crowned as a right. I should be Queen of this Realms.

There were no riots. Everybody said so, that there would be, and there was a man of war and armed boats in the

Thames, and thirty thousand soldiers in the town and what happens. Nothing. The cheering was not so great, and even some people hissed. *The Times* today says great crowds and cheering and a multitude of people to cheer me, but it was not so much. One day they love you, and then they do not. I wish I was still merry and in Italy.

Did they really think that I would go to the banquet, to see all the Nobles and Personages of the land decked out in robes and coronets and magnificent dresses and dripping in diamonds? Did they think I would watch them eating quail and turbot and salmon and trout and venison and veal and mutton and beef and geese and lobster and jellies and pastries and butter sauce? I wish I had not thought of that just now. I am not well, and it makes me vomit.

31 July 1821 He must let them Pray for me now. I am sick. I knew it when I was in the theatre. Lady H tried to persuade me to retire, but it has never been my line of conduct to Disturb any public Assembly by retiring earlier than was positively necessary. I came back here to Brandenburgh House and vomited. I took a great deal of medicine, laudanum and nervous medicine and feel no better.

August 3th 1821 I have still much pain in my bowel, but Doctor Holland says I am not Poisoned. He send for more Physicians which I consider a waste of Time and Money as I have confidence in him. The doctors say that things will turn out all right, and at the same time that if I have any Papers of Consequence I should dispose of them since everything must go to the King or ministers if I die. So I sit up all night with only Brunette, my maid, burning letters and papers. I am tired of this life.

August 4th I cannot go back to Italy. Pergami no longer loves me. And now I think I am Content to Die because nobody ever did. My own daughter, only some, a little. If I could have found only one person to love, if I might have found one man, not

Pergami but maybe like him, who will have said come your Royal Highness, do that or this with me and come by my side away from this stinking weather, the rain all the time and fog so you cannot see the front of your nose.

August 5th They will not give me the Sacrament. So be it. I do not doubt but that my Intentions will be accepted by God the same as if they did. I am going to Die, but it does not signify.

Mallen stayed in the Queen's apartment during the last hours of her life. There was a serious obstruction of the bowel, and inflammation. The doctors gave her twenty grains of calomel which she threw straight up again, and then another thirty-five, as well as quantities of laudanum which only made the constipation worse and didn't ease her pain. They took sixty-four ounces of blood, and dosed her with enough castor oil for ten men. Perhaps she was right, perhaps this was murder. From time to time she cried out, 'I know I am dying, they have killed me at last!' And then she wailed, 'Where is my William, why doesn't he come?'

All the time, outside her door, the young Billy Austin was weeping bitterly, asking over and over to see her and being told either that she was too ill, or asleep.

'Has she gone?' whispered Franny, appearing at his side.

'Very nearly.'

'What's she saying?'

'Nothing, Fran.'

She lay in state in Hammersmith. The King was in Ireland; his only instructions were to prevent all honour being paid, and to stop the funeral procession from going through the City to avoid the danger of demonstrations. Take it round London to Harwich, he said. Put her on a boat, they can bury her in her own country. So the troops were brought out.

The wraith stood with her hands on her hips, and tears streaming down her face. 'Good riddance to fat rubbish,' she sobbed, as the heavy coffin was manhandled down the stairs.

As soon as word got out that the cortège was not to pass through the City, the crowds began to gather at Hammersmith, on foot and on horseback, determined to get it through and onto the road to Temple Bar. Before they reached Kensington they saw Augusta. She was a hundred yards ahead of them at the front of the procession. 'There!' yelled Franny, but Mallen had seen her too. 'I told you,' she yelled. 'I said so!' They ran, charging through the crowds, dodging the horses and making, sometimes, progress. It was like running through mud, and indeed, in places the road was inches deep. All the time, the front of the procession seemed to make a better pace than the rest, and however much they advanced, they were somehow further behind. At Kensington, they met the first contingent of soldiers, who forced them through Hyde Park and turned them north towards Cumberland Gate. In the panic, Mallen and Franny fell back again. Shots were fired, and two men lay dead, but the crowd broke through the cordon of troops, and carried the coffin through. Franny pushed a way forward, and Mallen scrambled after her. Horses reared and screamed, and the soldiers hit out with batons and rifle butts, their plumes and capes turning dark with rain. It was pouring. 'This way,' said Franny.

Oxford Street was choked with troops, and the crowd turned off into Edgware Road, where progress was better, quieter. From there they turned into New Road, which was almost empty. The procession was made to go at a round pace, to get to the City before the soldiers.

'Can you still see her?' said Franny.

'I can, just there.'

Augusta had stayed close to the coffin, half-hidden by the shining flanks of sopping horses.

'I don't understand,' said Franny wearily. 'Why can't we get any nearer? To get this close, it's madness.' She twisted, banging the air with her fists. 'Damn.'

The hearse continued eastwards until it reached Temple Bar, where it turned into the City. There were hundreds, thousands still following it, and more lined the streets and the windows and the tops of houses. All the way out of the city, and along the road to the coast, Augusta stayed ahead of them. They reached Harwich on Thursday morning. The rain had stopped in the night, and it was a glorious day. The sea was as still and smooth as glass, and covered in boats of every sort and size, their colours at half-mast. The yards of four ships of war were all manned, and minute guns fired from ships and shore. Everything was done, however, in a disgusting hurry. The coffin was taken to a quay and lowered by a crane into the barge. Four men rowed the boat to the side of the schooner, *Pioneer*, and even before the corpse was safe on deck, the ropes were being hauled, and in minutes the *Pioneer* was under sail, to join the frigate, *Glasgow*. By this time, the velvet that covered the coffin was shredded. The mariners got the body on board the *Glasgow*, as well as the mourners, who had come out in smaller boats: Lady Hamilton, Alderman Wood, Billy Austin. The ghosts watched from the cliff-top, where gulls hung, canted and lifted, over their heads. Augusta had gone down to the quay, and they lost sight of her in the breeze of shawls and dresses, the handkerchiefs. The sea was bright and still and blue, and the sky was blue and bright above it.

The wraith lifted an arm and pointed. 'There,' she croaked.

Mallen looked. Augusta was with the party of mourners out in the bay, climbing on board the *Glasgow* from their boat. Bound for Stade, and Brunswick. She was mad. What on earth could make her want to follow this stupid woman's bones through London, through the length of Essex, and across the North Sea? Surely, he thought, if nothing else, we should be more rational in death, not less.

He felt a wave of the greatest sorrow as he watched her vanishing form, thought of their vanished years. There had been time enough, and yet so little. He remembered the streaks of soot on her face, the shine of moisture on her lips. He would not now forget these things, not ever. Death had made great alteration, but these and sorrow would always stay.

'Well,' said a voice beside them, sad but firm. 'So that's that.'

'Yes it is,' said Franny, quietly. She did not know who had spoken, and she turned. 'God almighty, your Majesty!' she shouted.

There stood Caroline, late and uncrowned Queen of England, not yet buried, dressed in velvet, lace at her bosom. Franny dropped into a full curtsey, and the wraith collapsed.

'Not even this, they do right,' said the Queen, her eyes on the small flotilla. 'To me, it doesn't matter. For the people, it's a shame.'

'But you –' said the wraith, pulling herself to her feet. She turned and looked out to sea.

'Oh, Brunswick, yes,' said the Queen. 'They can have my bones. For me, I don't know. I will never see that place again. Being as I have no choice, and also I don't want to. I know you,' she added.

'Me?' said the wraith.

'You, all three of you.'

'Not us,' said the wraith.

'But yes.' Caroline stood without moving until the boats were out of sight. Finally, she sighed, and turned to them. She lifted a hand to her face. 'Tears,' she said.

'It's sad,' said the wraith.

Caroline put an arm around the child's shoulder. 'It is,' she said, 'though that is not what I meant. My body is on its way to Brunswick, and yet here I am, and these are tears.'

The wraith dipped her head from side to side, as if to say: well they are, and at the same time they aren't.

'What is this place?' said Caroline.

'Harwich, ma'am.'

The Queen sighed. 'When I am come to England from Brunswick,' she said, 'I sailed up to Greenwich in the royal yacht, *Augusta*.'

'And now,' said Franny, '*Augusta* has gone off on a frigate to Brunswick.'

The Queen didn't hear her. 'What a journey,' she said. 'So cold, and Napoleon's army everywhere. We heard at night the guns and have to wait while he conquered Holland or was driven out. Lord Malmesbury is come to bring me to London, and we wait and wait, and in the end we went not to Holland but Stade. In Osnaburgh I lost a tooth. I give it to Malmesbury, very funny. And all the time it was seventeen zeroes below. Before ten weeks, we still haven't reached the coast. Finally, we come to London and I meet the King.' Her eyes were on the sea again, the water darkening under the falling sun with chips of shadow like schools of fish. The others listened. They too remembered talking, that long thread of words between one world and another. They had all talked for hours across that divide. They were sitting now, the Queen's arm still around the wraith, Franny leaning on Mallen's knee.

'I thought the King would be sick,' said Caroline. 'Malmesbury told me this is a word not to use in England, *sick*. But that is what he looked, when he sees me, sick, sick, sick. But no, he was not the King, he was Prince of Wales at that time. We come to St James's, and I curtsey to the ground in front of him. He lift me to my feet again, and give me like so on the cheek, not a kiss, something like it, then he ask for Malmesbury to bring him something to drink. Brandy. Then, immediately, he run away. This is for who I am come to marry.'

'He was already married,' said the wraith, from the Queen's armpit.

'That is so, he was. Maybe this is why he appeared so sick. Or maybe because he didn't like the way I look.'

'You were young and beautiful!' cried the wraith.

Caroline gave her an unhappy smile. 'Then come the time when we get married,' she said. 'Again, sick. At one point, he get up from his knees on the floor and try to walk away. Well, I am sorry for him.'

'Sorry!' yelled the wraith.

'Nobody love him, either, the Prince.'

'Oh, please,' said the wraith. 'He already had a string of women. He had married Mrs Fitzherbert, in secret. He broke the law of the land to do it.'

Caroline sighed. 'You know he had to force her. He have to threaten to kill himself, blood and everything. He stab himself one night at Carlton House, and send for her to see. When she come, he put a ring on her hand.' The wraith made a sound of disgust. 'And so, what does she do? She flies to France, to Holland, to Switzerland. She goes as far as she can to get away. This, my little girl, is not love. And the Prince, because of the pain that she is gone, he drinks. He roll on the floor and tear his hair and swear that he will sell his jewels and go with his love to America.'

'Tragic,' said the wraith.

'Yes. He want only someone to love him as much as that. Not even the King and the Queen loved him. They said, oh George, for God sake he is such a fool, and fat.'

For a while, no one spoke. It was almost dark.

'You say you know us and yet you never met us,' said the wraith, who had been trawling back through the conversation and the events of the day in her mind.

'But I do, of course. While I was dying, and only the doctors came to me. And poor Billy Austin, but I never saw him. Only you, standing by my bed. I knew then that I was over, but also not so alone.'

The stars had come out in a clear, cold sky. Caroline of Brunswick sighed, and then they heard the thick and guttural sound of her weeping. 'There, there,' said the wraith.

The Queen went back to Brandenburgh House. She tramped its rooms in trembling boredom and almost complete isolation. When, after only a short time, the house was knocked down and a distillery put up in its place, she wandered in the gin-soaked air and sat on the rims of the stills. The place was like a cathedral, with soaring columns and echoing chambers. The halls smelled dry and dusty, like worship. By day, there was the echoing racket of cogs and wheels and the sour smell of men at work. The wraith was her only companion; the place was a lodging-house for ghosts, but they slid away like trays of light from under a door.

'You see,' said the Queen, 'how they love you only a short time when it is such a case as mine. Now, yes; now, no.'

4

Julia Neville

1768

'She will have to swear to it in a court of law,' said William Hunter. 'That she tried to breathe air into the child.' They were on their way to Earl's Court, to have dinner with Hunter's brother, John. They had spent the afternoon looking for marks of violence on the body of Hannah Coffey's child. 'I don't think I can do any more,' he said.

'I'm afraid she barely knows where she is.'

'That's my fear, too.'

John Hunter's house was set in grounds with gardens and dens and conservatories, filled with creatures from opposite parts of the habitable globe. They passed, in the darkness, small herds of buffalo and deer, as well as outbuildings housing leopards and lions, wolves and snakes. 'Come in, come in,' said John, not really looking at his brother. Things hadn't been completely straight between them for years. There was always something to be chippy about, although they had not, at this time, had their great falling out over the structure of the placenta. They did quarrel, but between times they consulted together, and helped one another at post-mortems and operations.

He took them first to a room on the ground floor. 'Give me a hand,' he said. There was little left of the corpse on the dissecting table. It had done its work – all that remained was a gaping chest cavity and deep layers of whitish fat, the vessels tied off with string. It was not, however, a human cadaver, but something that smelled disgustingly of brine. It was, in fact, a small whale, or part of one. 'She won't let me upstairs until it's out of the house,' he said, pulling a guard in front of the fire.

Together they packed the pieces into sheets, and took them down through a dark subterraneous passage into a covered cloister that ran all round the house. At the end of the burrow, he led them through a door into a small room, half-filled by a huge copper boiler.

'You're going to do this now?' said William.

'No, no. Put them down. Now we are going to go and have a drink and something to eat.'

Upstairs, the house was a different place, as if they had in fact quitted one and entered another. There were cushions everywhere, and fabric on the walls; in the drawing room there were moveable panels painted with the story of Cupid and Psyche. There were half a dozen other people there, holding glasses to their lips. Talk moved back and forth between the state of the roads and the price of land for building. 'Dr Mallen,' said Anne Hunter, taking his arm, 'I don't think you have met Miss Julia Neville.'

No, he hadn't. How do you, excuse me. He was much more interested, just then, in John Hunter, famous for his temper, for his work on the organ of hearing in fish, for his recent treatise on human teeth and his knowledge of gun-shot wounds.

They went through to dinner in another fine room, done up to the gills. He noticed a couple of sober portraits, mostly shadow. There was a leafy decoration in the centre of the table, and a draught from somewhere that made the candles gutter. More leaves on the dinner service, and a delicate tracing in gold. 'Naw, ya dinnae want to hear that again,' said John, placing himself at the head of the table. William grimaced at the Lanarkshire vowels, thinned by a single drink. Everyone had heard the story of how John had tackled two of his own leopards in the yard; now they were hearing it again from the man himself.

'Your family lives not far from here,' Julia Neville said to Mallen.

'At Hammersmith.'

'Hammersmith is pretty, especially near the river. I have an uncle –'

Mallen nodded, and turned his head towards the end of the table. 'Not at all, far from it!' John Hunter was saying. 'I had no idea that they were out. The first I heard of it was the dogs!'

'With a view across the river,' said Julia Neville, 'as far as Putney.'

Hunter's eyes were intelligent and bright; he had high cheekbones, and a thin but expressive mouth. 'Of course I did, I rushed out there. One of them was half over the wall, and the other was spitting like Christ at the dogs –'

Mallen laughed with the others. Septimus Neville, Julia's father, slapped his leg and made a corkscrew sound that began high and ended on a deep note.

'He reads, nowadays; his library is full of Hobbes and Locke –' He hardly heard her. Julia Neville scowled, and turned back to her food.

'I got them back in the den,' said John Hunter, 'and tied them up, and fell down in a dead faint. One of the servants had to bring me round.' There was a yelp from one of the women that gave everyone at the table, though they were expecting it, a fright. Septimus Neville shook his head, as if it were just too full of mirth. Neville was a senior partner in a firm of bankers in Lombard Street, though he chose not to live in the City. His wife had died some years ago, and he and his daughter lived in a large house near St Mary Abbots, in Kensington.

The soup plates were taken away, and they helped themselves to poached trout, quail, loin of veal and fried celery. After that came crayfish, a casserole of beans and bacon, strawberry fritters and jellies. William waved these away. Two courses were more than enough for him. True to form, the two brothers began to argue, this time over some piece of gossip about a colleague and his affair with a woman in Hatton Garden. Keeping the mood light, Anne Hunter laughed at the first few twists of the story, then turned to her neighbour with another, probably truer, version. Talk went on between people sitting next to each other, a genial murmur while they ate. Mallen watched William stab at crumbs in irritation while his brother made a point.

'But enough about me,' said Julia Neville.

She had a pale strong freckled face, framed by reddish hair. Mallen noticed the small flare at the side of her nose, the shape of her eyebrows, strangely dark. He blushed, and reached for his glass of wine.

'Tell me about your work,' she said.

He opened his mouth to speak, and hesitated. He was fairly sure that he could still smell decay on his hands. 'I'm afraid –' he said.

'That I wouldn't find it interesting?' She tilted her head, and dared him to say so.

'I am a student of anatomy, Miss Neville.'

'Yes, I know that.'

Unconsciously, he picked up a fruit knife and turned the blade to catch the light from the candles. His mind struggled to find something to say, but it was full, that part of it, with tiny organs and specimen jars. He tried to smile. She arched an eyebrow, waiting for him to speak. At the end of the table, John Hunter was now telling his neighbours about his experiments with ducks. He had fed a number of them on nothing but sprats for a month, and when they were killed and cooked, he told them, they were hardly edible, they tasted so strongly of fish. Mallen laughed, and felt a sharp pain in his ankle. Julia Neville leaned back in her chair, and lifted the cloth to peer under the table. 'Oh!' she exclaimed, 'that was you! How awful, I'm so sorry.' She put a hand to her mouth, and lowered her chin. Mallen felt the pain travel up the back of his calf. 'No harm done,' he said.

She studied his face. 'So, tell me. You must do a lot of reading.'

'Actually, no.' He read hardly at all. Hunter did not let them read – he demanded constant practical application, during every waking hour. He shook his head, and toyed with his wine glass.

'But how do you learn anything?'

He was nearly rigid with discomfort. He could not talk to her, he possessed no opinions, no curiosity, no charm. His hands did, quite definitely, smell. He was, socially, of no more use to anyone than the small whale they had just taken down for rendering. Beside him, she continued to stare. Septimus Neville roared with laughter again, and Mallen's eyes went again to the end of the table. John Hunter had cleared a space, and was sketching something out on a piece of paper. Perhaps, when the meal was over, he would take them, the men, to look at more of his specimens. There were pigs fed on madder to make their bones go red; bats and snails and vipers, somewhere, which he used for his work on torpidity, and rabbits that had their ears frozen, to prove something to do with the circulation of the blood.

'Dr Mallen –'

She had only said his name, but it made him jump like a fish. His hand flew up, and the wine glass tipped and fell. It made little sound and did not break, but a large red stain spread across the tablecloth between them like a huge red shout. It seemed like an hour before he could move. He righted the glass, and muttered something that even he could not understand.

Anne Hunter stood up, signalling that it was time for the women to leave. Julia Neville took her napkin from her lap, and placed it over the stain. She made a point of not noticing the vermilion spots on the skirt of her dress. He could not look at her.

'So,' John Hunter said to Mallen, when the women had left them, 'I understand you are going to join the venerable and growing ranks of physician man-midwives in the city.'

'Soon, yes.'

He went back to the prison alone. 'Please talk,' he said. Behind him, a condemned woman let fly a string of oaths and spittle through the bars of an iron grate. Hannah Coffey looked at him. She frowned, as if she had forgotten the day of the week, and shook her head when it still wouldn't come. No, can't remember. Mallen, who had been full of words, full of care and warning, found that he, too, was mute. He sat on a wooden pallet and said nothing, stunned and useless. At last, he spoke. 'You must tell them what you tried to do,' he said. 'Listen to me. Tell them that you tried to give it life, how you breathed into its lungs. The evidence isn't enough on its own, it won't get you off. If I could do it for you, I would, but no one can; it's up to you and you simply have to do it. If you don't tell them, you may die. You will, almost certainly.' He looked around the ward, met the ratty eyes of inmates, watching him. 'And if you were to die,' he said, 'though I hardly know you, I don't think I would forgive myself.' On his way out of the ward, he heard the lice crack under his feet, like shells on a garden path. By the time he got out of the prison doors, his pocket had been picked.

Hunter's lecture course ended in May. In April, he had

invited Mallen – along with a fellow student whose father Hunter had known in Glasgow – to have lunch with him in a nearby coffee house. Afterwards, he asked Mallen to walk home with him.

'I have been approached by a colleague,' he said. 'This is his name, and this is where you can find him.' So it was that in the summer of 1769, Mallen found himself working as a medical officer at the General Lying-In Hospital in Quebec Street, London.

The wards smelled rancid, of mutton and blankets. They were loud with the groans of women in labour and thick with the fusty air of patched-up poverty. It was a place of blood and fluids and language Mallen had never heard before. He went every day in the early morning, and often during the night. He had never, until this time, performed or even seen a delivery but, though the rules and orders of the hospital stated that medical men in theory attended only complicated cases, he spent his first weeks doing the rounds of routine births. These all took place in open wards, and most were straightforward. Sometimes it fell to him to show subscribers round the hospital, the men and women who financed it out of the kindness of their hearts or out of concern about the wastage of life and the shrinking population of London. Then it was Mallen's job to impress on them the medical setting, the clinical competence of his colleagues. This is Matron, he would say. These are the kitchens, this is the laundry. These are our rules regarding personal conduct and religious observance. The patients must obey both the doctors and Matron, and show the right degree of gratitude. Any irregularity, and they are out on their ear.

It was at this time, too, that he was summoned to his first private patient. One night in the first week of September, there was a pounding at the door of his lodgings. Forty minutes later, he was being admitted to a house in Clerkenwell, his hat and stick whisked out of his hands, his shoes loud on the floor.

'For God's sake, go up,' said Percival Drake, the gibbering father. 'She's got a madman with her.'

The lying-in room was like a cave. It was hot and airless and smelled of liquor, dust and wax. The curtains were tightly drawn, and even the keyholes had been stopped up. Several women stood on either side of the howling mother, holding her hands and pouring the caudle down her throat. Dr Cryer – a man Mallen knew to have started out as a pork butcher – stood at the foot of the bed, spitting with effort. He had drawn back a sleeve, and his arm was slippery with hog's lard. Beside him, on a chair, lay his forceps.

Mallen threw everyone out except for the woman's sister, who looked level-headed and strong. He opened a window, spoke to the mother, pulled her into a sitting position in the bed and examined her. The cervix was not even dilated – Helena Drake was still in the first stage of labour. And, thanks to her gossips, drunk.

'What in God's name are you doing?' she said, as Mallen pulled a chair up to the bed and sat.

'The same as you,' said Mallen. 'Waiting. Unlike a hackney, I don't charge any more for it.'

'*Waiting?*' Another wave of pain overtook her, and she strained against it, red and rigid. 'Look at you,' she said when it had passed. 'You must be mad. I don't call this *waiting*, Dr Cryer did not tell me to *wait*.'

'It may be tedious, but it is normal,' Mallen told her. 'Nature, generally speaking, has a better sense of timing than you or me or anyone on the other side of that door.'

'For God's sake, it isn't coming. Dr Cryer said I am in the utmost danger.'

'Well, you're not. Everything's in the right way for a safe delivery, and Cryer used to make sausages. If you want to help it on, then the best thing you can do is get up and walk around a little.'

She looked at him with eyes slung between fury and despair. Mallen took his opportunity. 'Let's say that here, at the start, we are in America. If we make a fairly straight line to the chest, and turn in good time, we can reach the European continent in a few steps. I suppose you would rather he was born in Europe than America? If things don't come on too quickly, you may yet get across this rug and make the coast of England.'

'Mad,' said Helena Drake, but she let him help her off the bed.

For more than seven hours, throughout the night, he stayed with her. He sent for water and syrups, and told the women outside on pain of death not to bring up any more liquor. They looked at him with the sterile fury of the usurped, the dispossessed. Dr Cryer had long since gone home.

Finally, as London began to wake outside with the rattle of wheels and starlings, the head began to emerge. Now Mallen placed a finger into the birth canal and lifted the cervix, pressing back to support the perineum until the next pain came. The mother heaved and swore and kept up a low, wild groan. The tendons in her neck stood out like hawsers, and her face became furious and blue. She smelled fat and slick. Straining forward over her belly, she hit Mallen hard on the side of his head and called him something unspeakable. The child was delivered, a squall of blood and lungs, and Helena Drake fell back on her pillows, drenched. Mallen wrapped the infant lightly, and put it in her arms. Then he dived for it once more, and passed it to the sister. Mrs Drake had started again.

Later that day, he went to Hammersmith. In the afternoon, his father lit a pipe and sat down in his study with his ledgers. Raspberries, plums, walnuts, cherries. Beans, the last of them, the bill for the seed still outstanding, how did that happen?

Mallen took himself off for a walk. He had not shaved, and wore old clothes. He made his way down to the river, and strolled beside it, under the trees. The water was dark and sliced by boats. The sun was low but warm, and a strong breeze fought against the currents, ridging the water and making the rigging tick on the fishing boats moored to the wall. He passed the houses where Moreland and Radcliffe had lived, and Catherine of Braganza. Further on, he paused in front of the house where Barbara Villiers was still supposed to pace the rooms, up and down, up and down, mourning for her beauty. Mallen looked up at the walls of the house, but he didn't believe in ghosts.

Gates hung half-open onto gardens and private moorings, and reeds waved at the water's edge. He looked down and watched his feet for a while, then lifted his face.

He stopped so suddenly that he felt as if he was going head-first out of a window, or over the side of a boat. It was *her*, barely thirty feet away, walking towards him in the middle of the path, arm-in-arm with a man old enough to be her father. He must be fifty at least, thought Mallen. But what in heaven's name was she doing here?

They were getting closer – very slowly and with heads bowed, thank God, in conversation. Something snapped at the back of his head. To meet her now was out of the question. He lunged towards a low wooden gate on his left; it gave about twelve inches before sliding into leaf-rot, but he got through, grazing his face on an arching branch. He was in a small garden, hedged on two sides and dropping in front to the river. The grass was long, and overgrown with mint and straggling roses. A boat lay keel-up, half-covered by brambles. Mallen cut off to the right, behind the boat, but it was useless, stupid, it would not hide him. *Was* it her? It wasn't her father, anyway. Mallen made for the end of the hedge, turned, slipped, and understood a moment too late that the hedge only stopped because at this point terra firma stopped too.

He was up to his thighs in the brown mud of the steep bank, stuck but somehow still sinking, on the point of losing his balance, and with nothing to hang on to. He put out a hand to steady himself and found that, too, plunging deep into soft mud. Briefly, he saw the image of William Hunter, up to his elbows in a stinking corpse. He wiped off what he could on the front of his shirt and leaned slowly forward. He rested for a moment, his head bowed into one shoulder. His right foot was stuck; he could move it up and down from the ankle an inch or so, but at the very least he was going to lose the shoe. From the road he heard a single peal of laughter. He closed his eyes and waited, and heard a voice, hers, low with narrative then briefly emphatic. He looked down between his legs and worked out where to put his foot should he ever get it out. He clenched his toes like a fist inside the shoe, then shifted his weight and lifted his head. Droplets of mud swung from his hair into his face. His hat had gone, was floating towards Fulham.

When he looked up again, Julia Neville was standing above him. 'Dr Mallen,' she said. 'Are you fishing, or drowning?'

He groaned, and looked down into the water around his feet.

'If the latter, you must let me know and I shall go and tell John Hunter. He has a great interest in drowning; he has written quite a lot about it. Did you have a hat?'

'Miss Neville –'

'So you know who I am.'

'Of course.'

She nodded. 'What I am trying to work out, in my own mind, is whether we should try to rescue you from the water, or from land.' She raised an eyebrow, and leaned forward a little, over the bank. 'Tch,' she said. 'Perhaps a block and tackle? I've seen it done with horses.'

Mallen felt his left leg sink another inch.

'Or again, it might be more sensible if I simply gave you a push and got you off, like a boat. You could swim round to the mooring outside my uncle's house –'

'Your uncle.'

'My uncle, yes.'

'Hobbes and Locke.'

'Very good, Doctor. However, I only mention him because he has easy access to the water or, in your case, to land. He's at home, I have just now seen him to his door.'

'You're very kind, but I can manage.'

'You're sinking.'

He wished for a moment that he would, that the mud would swallow him with a loud and ugly sound, that he could disappear into the riverbed and never have to look again into those supercilious eyes. He could see the silk toe of her shoe, the hem of her dress.

'Look!' she said. 'Fish.'

He felt the lap of a small wash lift the back of his coat.

'Have you read any Locke?' she said, looking out, for the moment, over the top of his head.

'I . . . some, yes.'

'I've been having another look at him. Interesting.'

'Yes.'

'Did you know that there is a race of people who profess Christianity and yet bury their children alive?'

'No,' he said.

'It goes to show the variety of human beliefs.'

His left foot had now become lodged in something that felt like a rat hole. 'I suppose so,' he said.

'Though I think that is where I would probably draw the line at religious tolerance.'

He made one more effort, and reached for a tuft of coarse grass on the bank. It was only inches from her shoe, but she didn't move. 'You're going to have to stand back,' he said. 'I am covered, Miss Neville, in mud.'

'I can see. And if you're going to try to pull yourself out like that, I wish you good luck.'

For a moment he thought that she was going to leave, that she was on the point, with these words, of turning her back and letting him shift for himself, but she remained where she was, looking down on him, shielding her eyes from the sun on the glinting river.

There was nothing for it but to seize the moment, before he fell back into the water with a fistful of grass. He would have to trust to Julia Neville's instincts to get herself out of the way. As he pulled himself forward, his left leg sunk backwards again, and what leverage he had in the lower part of his body was lost. A hand came down to take his.

'No!' he yelled.

'It is only mud, Dr Mallen. I am strong enough, take my hand.'

She was strong. Strong legs, strong shoulders. She hauled, while he scrambled, and within a few moments he was on the bank, stumbling, blind with shame and loss of balance. She caught and righted him, then pushed him gently onto his own two feet.

'There,' she said.

He was covered. From his feet to above his knees, stockings, breeches; the front of his coat and shirt, and up to his shoulders. And Julia Neville, too.

'You're bleeding,' she said.

He wiped the back of a hand across his face. 'It's nothing,' he said. 'It's mud.'

'You're the doctor, but it's blood.'

5

The Service for the Dead

1829

'Follow me,' said the Queen.

'If you believe her, you're off your head,' said the wraith, lifting her nose in the air and turning a circle on her toes. 'It's only for the attention.'

'Grow up,' said Franny, then bit her lip. 'Listen,' she said. 'Stand still, can't you?'

The wraith collapsed her arms at her sides and stood. 'All right, it's true.'

'Then why don't you tell the doctor?'

Mallen stopped at the distillery doors, and waited for them. The Queen stepped past him and continued on, but slowly. The light was wide and empty towards the river, and streaked with shadows, all odd angles and brightness. It seemed to him that this was how, if anything, he had imagined the world would be after he was dead – a sense that it was always dawn, with a huge peripheral darkness at its edge. He saw Franny put her arm around the wraith, and felt a soaring, awful pity. He turned again, and watched the Queen make her slow way down the steps. Why was he again following the shape of this fat creature, this old ghost in her shivering velvet? For eight years, since watching her board the frigate at Harwich, he had not laid eyes on Augusta. She had been nowhere near the Queen. He had roamed London, grazing on rumour and following old and papery clues. He had found himself, again, roosting in the walls of his father's house. His son's house, now. He had begun once more to believe that this was the end, and that the end was long and inconclusive, a dull and intolerable paradox. Even so, the years had passed, as they always did, like months, or days, or weeks. Then Franny had come to find him, once again, with news that the wraith had something to tell him.

It appeared that, like the rest of the world, Augusta had long since lost interest in the Queen. Whatever it might have been, it seemed to have vanished with Caroline's death, but she had now found, if the wraith was to be believed, an interest in someone else, someone still living – still living, but under sentence of death – and was following his progress just as she had followed the Queen's.

Mallen had begun to shake. 'Why didn't she say anything?'

'Who? Don't shout.' Franny scowled at him.

'I'm sorry.' He pointed at the wraith, his chest full of fury. 'Why was I not told?'

'Don't look at me,' said the wraith. 'If you want someone to blame, you can blame the fat bitch Queen. It's only been a few days, anyway.'

'Days?'

'Oh, God, what's a day here or there to you?'

Mallen had no answer to that. He turned his back on them, and gazed again towards the river. Though time might have little meaning, that did not remove his sense of urgency; perhaps it was still a residue of life, a habit of thought or feeling not yet extinguished. He was coming, as the seasons came and went, to accept that the ways of the spirit world were different and unfathomable, but his mind sometimes still struggled against them.

'I bet you never been to Newgate, Doctor,' said the wraith.

'Bet you he has,' said Franny. Mallen drew a finger across the bridge of his nose. He had never, not once, spoken to Franny of what had happened to her mother before she was born, of how he had come to know her, or where. It made no difference that it was all a very long time ago now. It had never been his secret to tell, not while they were alive, and not now.

'Bet you he's never seen a man hang.'

'We are not going to see anyone hang,' said Mallen.

'But he will,' said the wraith. 'He is condemned.'

'But not today.' Weariness crept through Mallen's fury.

'An innocent man!' cried the wraith, dancing around the Queen. 'Thrown without mercy into the stinking cells of Newgate Gaol, made to suffer the greatest indignity known to human man, brought before a judge and jury and made to swing for someone else, for another man's evil crime.'

'How do you know he didn't do it?' Franny was on the steps, translucent in the thin, low sun.

'Oh, Christ, he did do it. Her Majesty thinks he didn't, but he did. She gets things arse-backwards, in case you didn't know. Guilty is innocent, in her book.'

Snow lay on the road, carved by market carts. Sheep on Kensington Common turned their backs on the phantom group, as if it were a wind. The Queen moved with purpose, if not grace, with Mallen beside her. 'It is just the same thing,' she told him. 'Like me, a victim of injustice, and with little time left to live. This, I think, is what draws Mrs Corney to the place.'

There was a good deal of difference, to Mallen's mind, between Westminster and Newgate, between a man accused of murder, and a Queen accused of adulterous intercourse.

'Perhaps she is looking, like me, for justice. For herself, but also not so direct. I mean to say, if she cannot have justice, she can see it for other people. Like when I come back to claim my rights as Queen, and am a wronged and persecuted victim. Like me, she suffered too much, and no one to pay for it.'

Mallen wasn't even listening. Her guesswork did not interest him. He found himself thinking, however, that perhaps there was some company in being lost, a sort of confederacy of the dead. He saw Augusta's face, the last expression he had ever seen on it, a look of pain and love and astonishment. He saw the Queen, as she lay dying, and Billy Austin weeping outside her door. He saw the bloated, grief-stricken face of the Duchess in the window of Walpole House, and Franny, slipping out of life. Something had brought them together, he thought, with nothing more than the logic of sorrow. They were all searching for something, even though some of them did not know, after years or even centuries, what that might be.

Hyde Park was a field of white, with magpies chattering in the trees, and the muffled sounds of horses being exercised. Fence posts leaned on their own shadows, and a bell rang out from the barracks. The wraith became moony. She sang quietly to herself, a roaming, lonely tune. 'How come you know so much?' Franny asked her. 'How did you find Mrs Corney?'

The wraith shrugged her shoulders. 'The Queen saw her going past the distillery every day for a week. Up and down, and onto the London road. I followed her, and saw where she went and made *enquiries* in the *vicinity*, and now I know everything.'

'And?' said Franny.

The wraith thought, then shook her head. 'He's not innocent, that's for certain.'

'Who?' said Franny. The wraith chewed her lip and said nothing. 'Who? you little squit.'

The wraith laughed. 'Arthur Lempson,' she said. 'They picked him up with his floozy in Kennington.'

'Never heard of him.'

'You have now.' The wraith stopped still. 'Look!' she said.

A flight of geese came in low over their heads, towards the Serpentine. One after the other, they landed on the ice, skidding and slewing, their feet in the air like paper fans. The wraith smiled. 'First,' she said, 'they find the trunk of the body, near some new buildings on the Edgware Road. Then they find the head, jammed in the lock gates in Stepney Fields. One month later, someone comes across the legs near Cold Harbour Lane. Perfect fit, everything. Who is she? Nobody knows. They do now, they didn't then.'

Franny leaned down as she walked, and scooped a handful of snow. A young dog, leg cocked against a chestnut tree, dropped to its belly and cringed.

'She was still alive when he took off her head. They're so clever, they can tell. He took it with him under his coat and dumped it in Regent's Canal. Floated all the way to Stepney.'

'There's no such canal.'

'Oh, keep up, Christ! There is now.'

'And you found all this out, where, exactly?'

'Exactly outside the prison. *Exactly*, outside the Old Bailey. I just so happen to know a number of . . . nobody, people.'

'Felons,' said Franny.

'Maybe.'

'Hanged?'

'Not all of them, no. They found who she was when her brother came from Curzon Street to view the head, which what was left of it was preserved in spirits of wine.' By one of the park gates, a young girl blew on her hands to warm them before she started to milk her cows. They left the park, and followed the doctor and the Queen into Jermyn Street.

'And Mrs Corney,' said Franny. 'She was at the Old Bailey.'

'Yes.' The wraith looked suddenly glum again, and slapped her wrists against the pockets of her dress.

'Her interest being what, exactly?'

'Christ knows. I reckon she's backwards and forwards to that place all the time. Lempson's just one more fool she likes to look at.'

'But *why*?' The wraith's lack of any sort of logic infuriated Franny. 'And why did you wait until now to say so?'

'Oh, oh, oh. Nobody says I'm obliged to tell you anything. It's the doctor's obsession to find her, not mine. And obsession,' she said, pointing her little finger at Franny's chest, 'eats the soul.'

Franny bit her lip, and scowled.

'There's going to be a crowd,' said the wraith. 'Lords and ladies and God knows what.'

'There won't, they don't allow it.'

'Well, there will. The sheriffs have had that many applications for admission, they're letting them in. For this day only! Due to popular demand! Hear the Ordinary speak his sermon to the condemned!' The wraith swivelled and turned and dropped into the slush-filled gutter of the Strand.

'Get up, what's the matter?'

She shook her head. 'What's the point?' she said.

'The point of what?' said Franny.

The wraith spread her hands.

It was not the same prison where Mallen had come to see Hannah Coffey. The old building, the old stink and overcrowding, the old muckheap had been pulled down, and a new one put up, with its own squalor and vermin. That too came down, burned out fifty years ago in the riots of 1780, but here it was again, with strong new windowless walls, and a strong new windowless stink. All that, and no improvement.

The avenues to the prison gates were blocked by ticketholders – the wraith was right, lords and ladies, doctors, politicians. Inside, the chapel was full of prisoners, coughing with a sound like shovelled grit, playing catch-eye and scratching. The ladies and peers of the realm, clutching rue against the fever, talked in churchy tones. There was no sign, yet again, of Augusta. Barbara Villiers was there, and Chatham again, in velvet, but Augusta Corney, no. Mallen felt a fool. It had been a pack of lies. The wraith was right, the Queen had only done it for the attention. At the same time, part of him believed that it was true, that she had been here, and in the relentless way of things in this other life, he had missed her once again.

The condemned men entered the chapel. There were four of them – a boy of eighteen, sentenced to death for stealing goods to the value of more than five pounds; a sheep-stealer who had been transported to Australia and returned without pardon. A clergyman, condemned for forgery, who looked half dead already. He flung himself to the floor before he reached the pews, burying his head underneath his body. The peers of the realm craned forward to see, but nobody tried to move him. The last to come was the murderer, Lempson. Apart from his chains, he looked as sane and normal as anyone outside on the street; he did not look like a man who had gone round London with the various parts of a murdered woman under his arm.

Barbara Villiers appeared beside them. It had not occurred to Mallen that until now the two women, she and the Queen, had not actually met. They did so at this moment with, on the Queen's part, a sort of dance that seemed to come from nature, somewhere, like the darting movements of a large water bird. Her eyes narrowed, and for a moment it even looked as if there might be a fight. The Duchess resolved the situation by making a curtsey, inelegant but correct. Never mind that rank, like property and the fear of fire or poverty, had been cancelled out by death. With this formality, the two women knew where they were. They settled, side by side, into a corner with a view.

Mallen watched them. Here was Barbara Villiers, mistress of King Charles, a woman who had dominated the Court and amassed a fortune and left behind a dynasty, and here was Caroline, wife of King George, who had had to put up, even on her honeymoon, with a string of royal mistresses, and who never had a home to call her own. Caroline, who was loved by no one, and Barbara Villiers, who had had men dreaming of her up and down the country.

'I take it,' the Duchess said to the Queen, 'that they do not draw and quarter people any more. Or stick their heads on posts.'

The Queen turned briefly to peer at her. 'They do not,' she said, 'no.'

'And they are no longer burned at the stake.'

'For heaven's sake,' said the Queen. 'Of course not.'

'Another thing I notice,' said the Duchess, as if one thing followed the other, 'is that gentlemen wear their own hair nowadays.'

The Queen understood that she was being appealed to as an authority. 'They do,' she said. She could find, however, nothing of value to add to that.

'I would prefer to see a man in a full-bottomed periwig, and petticoat breeches, with a doublet and coat.' The Duchess signified, with her hands, the assembled gentlemen. 'They look, to me, untidy. Half-dressed.'

The Queen, though stupid, was not unaware that an effort was being made. She nodded her head in agreement, and her own wig slipped down over her eyes.

'King Charles was always exquisitely dressed. Sober colours, but always elegant.'

'King George –' said the Queen, in the same proprietary tone. The note of fondness, however, was absent. 'He have vile taste in clothes. He go out in a purple waistcoat with a gold tree on it, and monkeys running up and down the tree, and he have silk bathing gowns and Polish caps and Muscovy sable muffs and he wear pantaloons under his kilt. In his cupboards he have dozens of everything. Now I think he just wear an old dressing-gown.'

The Ordinary stood. 'Now for you, my poor fellow mortals,' he intoned, 'who are about to suffer the last penalty of the law –' The chapel was hushed, and though he hardly spoke above a whisper, he could be heard by all.

'Of course, for many years,' said the Duchess, 'King Charles lived in poverty. His shirts were rags, and he could hardly afford to have them washed.'

'King George,' said Caroline, 'in nine years, when he is Regent, he have more than five hundred new shirts.' She was not sure, in her own mind, whether she had trumped the Duchess here or not, or even whether she had intended to. 'He have one dozen pairs of riding breeches made for him a long time after he gave up riding and didn't go near any horse.'

'Royalty,' said the Duchess, 'can be very profligate.'

'Hmn. I think so. He never give me any thing. Not for my birthday, even.'

Wisely, the Duchess decided against mentioning the great riches that she had been given, the house, the titles, the jewellery. 'Of course,' she said, 'given your . . . situation *vis à vis* the King, the ladies of England have for some time had no outstanding royal figure whose fashions they could imitate.' She produced an inscrutable smile, and turned to bestow it on the Queen. 'It is to their immense disadvantage that you, with your exquisite taste, should have been prevented by the King's behaviour from leading the way for them.'

The Queen smelled a rat. She was well aware that her costume, throughout her life, had not been immune from acid criticism. However, it had been cleverly put by the Duchess, and she had no choice but to concur. 'They liked my crimson morning dress, and some others. They only came all over shock when I appeared *en Vénus* in Geneva and waltzed the whole night. Too bad, I sat in the same clothes for my portrait at Catania, which afterwards went to Milan and for a long time stayed in the Villa Barona, but I do not know what has become of that now.'

'No doubt you looked lovely.'

Suspicion and pleasure were mixed in the Queen's response to this remark, which expressed itself in a wild grin.

Having got here by way of capital punishment, the Duchess returned to it. 'I believe that before the heads were displayed, they were taken by the hangman who put them in his kettle and boiled them with bay-salt and cumin seed, to keep them from putrefaction, and to stop the chickens from eating them. It's a morbid thought, I know, but it occurs to me that in some ways these poor men are better off now than they might have been in my day.'

The Queen was in two minds about this woman. She might have been illustrious, once, but clearly she had lived in barbaric times, and it had rubbed off on her.

'It was excessively cruel,' said the Duchess, 'and quite unnecessary.'

Now she was merely being confusing. 'Do you see Mrs Corney?' said Caroline.

There was no sign of her. When the sermon had been preached, the sheep-stealer threw up his hands and cried for mercy from the Lord God, while the young thief clutched the back of the pew and passed out, hitting his head as he went down. Lempson alone sat still in his seat. The forger uttered a scream, and the chapel fell into a deadly silence. Then the women prisoners set up a yell, an awful noise that mixed with the sound of rustling as those who had fainted were taken away. The sheriffs covered their faces, and a Member of Parliament blew his nose into a glove.

Then it was over, and the congregation began to disperse. The clergyman forger was picked up by the arms and legs and carried off to his cell by turnkeys. Lempson's face was set in a thin and disturbing smile as he made his way out of the pew. The young thief was brought round with a rag soaked in water, and began to sob his eyes out. The wraith fell to her knees and wouldn't be moved. She was smitten, and anguished. The sheep-stealer shouted something about the Lamb of God as he was carted off, and someone laughed. Augusta Corney stood in the main door to the prison chapel, looked without expression on the shifting crowd, and turned and left.

'Doctor!' yelled Franny.

Mallen was already gone.

'Get up!' said Franny to the wraith.

'For stealing in a dwelling-house goods valued at above five pounds,' blubbed the wraith. 'For this he has to lose his life.'

'Stay there then.'

A tremor went through the crowd of shades and, amongst the living, women pulled their cloaks around them. 'Move!' yelled Franny at the Queen.

'I shall stay and talk to the Duchess,' said Caroline. '*She* may stay with me,' she said, pointing at the wraith.

'No she bloody may not,' said the wraith. Franny grabbed her hand, and they ran.

They ran into Ludgate Hill, the wraith swivelling on the corner to cast an eye back towards the chapel. They turned into Fleet Street, Mallen fifty yards in front. 'He's lost her!' cried the wraith, but she didn't stop, didn't slow. They ran through Temple Bar into the Strand, where there was a smell, in the cold air, of China tea. 'Where is he?' said Franny, in the shadow of St Clement Danes. She looked in every direction, but Mallen had vanished.

The wraith turned a shimmering circle. She stopped, and flung out her arms, then dropped them to her sides again.

Franny sighed. 'What *is* the matter?' she said.

'Nothing.'

Franny nodded. Beside her, the wraith looked like something cold and poor pegged out on a line to dry, snapping in the wind of the living world and shivering at its heedless touch. Her eyes flashed with a winter light. 'Why can't we lie down and die?' she suddenly cried, with the tones and strength of a bell.

'Never mind,' said Franny. 'Come on, keep up.'

Mallen was standing in the Strand. 'She's here,' he said, when they reached him.

'She isn't,' said the wraith, looking one way, then another.

But the doctor was certain. From behind them, near the doors of the Exeter 'Change, came the thin shriek of a capuchin monkey. The animal, dressed in a suit and ruff, chittered with fear on the pavement. Mallen looked up. Above the door of the 'Change, between Corinthian pillars, hung a sign: *ED^wd CROSS, Dealer in Foreign Birds and Beasts*. He turned on his heels.

They ran through the long gallery of shops and auction rooms on the first two floors of the 'Change. From above them, on the third floor, came the drilling cries of startled birds. 'Oh, Christ,' said the wraith, as they flew up the stairs. The rooms of the menagerie were packed, stacked high with animals in narrow pens and cages, one on top of the other. There were mothy, gap-toothed tigers, and lions twitching with dusty instinct; a zebra, monkeys. Around the cages, exotic foliage was painted on the walls. 'Don't!' screamed the wraith.

'Don't what?' said Franny.

'Don't go in. We'll drive them mad, we'll send them all off their heads.'

'We won't. How do you know we will? We won't.'

Londoners roamed the rooms with their country cousins, children dressed in Sunday clothes, and squires with bellies and waistcoats. The smell was rank. Mallen ran from cage to cage, looking, flying. The sound of fear grew louder. At the end of the long gallery was the cage – hopelessly small – that contained the elephant, Chunee. Through the wooden bars they could see the great grey flanks, the white flash of a short tusk, and what might have been the twisting, disappearing shadow of Augusta Corney.

'Bitch,' said the wraith.

'She's gone,' said Franny, but she could not be sure, and it was too late. The elephant lifted its trunk and screamed, a trumpeting bellow of fear. A stream of piss sluiced down into the straw. It charged the small cell, throwing itself against the walls, slamming its sides against the wooden bars. The keeper shouted. Men came running, with staves and sticks and, for some reason, a bucket. Someone yelled for the owner, Edward Cross. Mallen climbed into a window frame, and crouched there, watching and still, like a hawk. The wraith, exhausted from weeping for her thief, wept for the elephant.

The visitors were driven out. Most had fled, but some remained, sick with the thrill. There was a loud crack as the elephant's foot came through one of the lower bars and smashed it into pieces. The wraith threw herself at Mallen's knees. 'She's killing him!' she yelled. 'Look! She's made him berserk.'

'Hush,' said Mallen.

'Is she still there, is she?'

He didn't know. Sometimes he thought he saw her behind the maddened animal, but it was only spit or straw. Chunee had turned, and his head filled the bars of the top half of the cage door. His trunk snaked out with another yell of terror, and with it a sweet, fermented smell. Ropes and hinges strained and another bar began to splinter.

Through the din of panic came a stamp of boots on the stairs. A civilian firing squad – ten or fifteen men in shirtsleeves – tramped with their muskets into the great long room. The men formed up in front of the cage, and raised their musket stocks to their shoulders. 'God almighty!' yelled a man in a velvet hat. Edward Cross. 'Not like that! Make a line. Fire and then move back. The next line, fire and then move back. You're going to shoot each other, for God's sake.'

There were five reports, with a deafening noise and gouts of smoke. Then five more, and five more. The men who had fired reloaded, and formed up again behind. The bullets thudded into the animal's sides, explosion after explosion, but though the elephant still roared and slammed, it did not even bleed.

Cross sent to Somerset House for a party of soldiers. They came in their red coats, with boots and epaulets and bandoliers. They lined up with the other men and fired, two and three and five at a time. Mallen felt, again, the stone come down on his head. He felt the shattering surprise, the long, stunned moment of disbelief. He remembered how he had tried to twist, to see the face of the man behind him. How he had thought of his children and tried to run. He felt the stone come down a second time, and found it unbearably strange that he should die like this and not know why.

'Send for a cannon,' said Cross. 'And men to get it up the stairs.'

For an hour and forty minutes the guns were kept constantly firing. At last, a bullet found its way to the brain. A flowing gush of bright arterial red poured from behind one ear. Chunee folded his forelegs under him, dropped and curled his trunk around them, and began to die. Silence rose like the smoke. A cloud of sulphur dragged around the rooms, and boards and leather creaked as the firing squad shifted on its feet.

'You!' said the wraith to Mallen. But whatever else she wanted to say was shovelled too high in her throat. He looked at her, but only for a moment. His eyes were still on the cage, the massive, lifeless form inside it. What would John Hunter have given for that, he wondered. Five tons of skeleton and flesh, a heart the size of a child; you could spend a fortnight picking out the shot.

'Very well,' said Cross. He looked shattered, grey with shame.

'Will we move it, sir?'

'How? No.' The windows had grown dark and below them the lamps had been lit on the Strand. Cross stood with his hands behind his back and looked out over the gully of the street. Franny appeared at Mallen's shoulder. 'She's gone,' she said.

'Yes.'

'What a sad and bloody mess.'

6

Hannah Bright

1769

'Matron, I need some space here. What is all this?'

'Linen, Doctor.'

'I can see it's linen. What's it doing here?'

'I'll have it moved.'

'If you would. Now, Mrs . . .' Mallen looked up as if he were peering over a pair of spectacles, though he was not. It was the autumn of 1769. He had been working at the hospital for a matter of months, and was into his stride. 'Mrs Place can go home later today. Make sure she's fetched. There's a brother, if you can't find the husband. These others . . .' He looked down at the book open on the desk in front of him and scowled. 'Whose writing is this?' he said. 'I refuse to believe that Mrs . . . who is this? She can't be sixty-five.'

'Mrs Andrew. She is twenty-five, as of last week.' Matron was a widow, with short impatient legs and a long straight back. 'She was admitted this morning by Dr Wren.'

'His writing's worse than mine. Never mind, we'll get there in the end. Mrs Andrew. I shall see her in a moment. The one I'm looking for . . . here. She came in yesterday and there's nothing to her, no strength. She should be given beef tea, mutton, puddings. Whatever you can get her to eat.'

Matron lifted her chin and stretched her neck. They were always coming in half-starved, needing a fortnight's solid food before they had the strength to do what they had to do. Matron fed them like pullets, and if she didn't make them sleek, she got them stronger. She had the feeding-up of hungry women screwed right down, but she nodded and said, yes, Doctor. 'There's another new one in Canning Ward,' she said. 'Mrs Bright.'

'Very well, I'll see her, too.'

The ward was a flotilla of rounded bellies, stretched like sails. Those who were not in bed sat and sewed. Sally Andrew was the biggest of them all, and she was scratching.

'Vermin?' said Mallen.

Matron looked daggers. The doctor knew very well that not a single parasite was allowed past the doors, and anyone found to be crawling was sent back home again. 'A rash,' she said.

Mallen, behind his grave face, was grinning. 'Let's hope it isn't a fever,' he said. 'How do you do, Mrs Andrew, I am Dr Mallen. Stay where you are, don't get up.' As if she could.

There was no fever, just the rough weave of her clothes and a skin singing with tenderness. Mallen ordered a compress of elecampane root.

They moved on towards the end of the ward. Matron pointed out the next newcomer, and Mallen's jaw fell open. 'Mrs Bright,' said Matron. Hannah Coffey, thought Mallen.

It was Hannah. But it wasn't possible; Hannah Coffey was in gaol. There was still the inquest, and Hunter's testimony. Where had the time gone? The weeks had slipped out from underneath each other like cards. It was nothing, no time at all, it was . . . a year, at least. He stood on the bare boards of Canning ward, feeling light-headed and robbed. He felt the ordinary terror that the legs had gone out from under his life, that time was sliding downhill. He remembered making some kind of vow, in the prison ward, and yet he had forgotten her.

'Mrs Bright,' he said.

She smiled, and Mallen nearly choked. The face of this woman, surfacing into a pretty and brilliant smile, a woman he had feared would hang, would go to the scaffold without a word to help herself.

'At last I can thank you, Doctor,' she said.

'But I have done nothing for you, not yet.'

'Why do you say that when you know you have? You saved my life.'

Mallen shook his head. Briefly, he smelled the vinegar stink, saw the black passages lit by smoking links.

'I have not forgotten it,' said Hannah Bright. 'I never will, either. I had no other friends.'

For Matron, this was cryptic, and she bristled. 'The husband is an upholsterer,' she said, 'address in Holborn. First child, thirty-eight weeks, no disease.' All business, Matron. When she had moved on to the next bed, Mallen took Hannah Coffey's hand and held it in his own. Bright, Hannah Bright. To his distress, he felt like weeping.

She went into labour when no one was expecting it – before she had even been in the hospital a week. Matron sent someone off to find Mallen, who came from home with his stock untied, his shirt buttons wrong. Matron took one look at him, and he ducked into an empty board-room to straighten himself. She would not lose this one, he would make sure. That, at least, at most, he could do for her.

Her face was grey with fear. She was riding against the back of the bed as if she would push herself into a standing position against the wall; for a moment he was afraid that the child had not turned, that it was breeched and obstructed. He threw back the sheets, pulled up her gown, prodded her belly. She yelped. Cold hands. The cervix was fully dilated, the pelvis seemed wide enough, and this, that, was the head, thank God. 'A good strong push, Mrs Coffey,' he said.

'Mrs Bright!' yelled Hannah Bright, and she pushed.

It was one of the quickest deliveries he had ever seen. If she had not been in the hospital, she might have had the child in the street, in a pastry shop. 'A little girl,' he said. Small but sturdy. A lot of noise.

Mallen stirred his coffee. His friend Philip Little was reading the newspaper. 'If you want a life of venesection and clysters,' said Philip, 'then you're in the right way for it. Hunter was right. They won't let you near their wives until you have one of your own.' He didn't take his eyes from the paper, and might have been reading aloud from it. They were in a coffee house on Fetter Lane, out of a driving, soot-stained rain.

Philip had a point. Mallen was making his way – with fevers and rashes and worms – but he had not studied under William Hunter merely to make his way as a physician. The Drake twins had set him up, but as a family doctor, not as an *accoucheur*. His chosen field was still obstetrics, but almost the only work he got of that kind was in the hospital. 'I haven't the money,' he said. 'I'm too young.'

Philip scowled at the newspaper print. 'Just do it, James.'

'Just *do it*? Put the paper down. I need to know if we're talking about the same thing.'

Philip lifted his head and gave his friend a look that was both studied and indulgent. 'Find someone to marry,' he said.

Mallen nodded. 'You're right.'

'I'm serious. I want you to become a famous man-midwife so that you don't always depend on physic, and complain that I poach all your custom.'

'You do poach my custom.'

'Find a woman, James. You don't make the smallest effort.'

'I called on Mary Chalmers fifteen times. I took her to Vauxhall Gardens. I talked to her father about trout ponds. I drank tea with her mother. Not Chalmers, Chambers. I tell you, I can't afford it.'

'It was nothing like fifteen times. If it was, it was only because the mother had something unspeakable wrong with her.'

'Foot-rot.' Mallen watched the steam run down the inside of the window, the almost empty street beyond it. Perhaps the rain would clear the air, if it didn't only turn it into paste. He leaned against the wooden panelling between the seats and studied his friend. Philip looked damp, but handsome. Mallen wondered why he wasn't married himself. His shop on Cursitor Street was always full of the mothers of the young and hopeful. He sat forward again, and reached for his coffee. This was where Mallen did all his work; it was here that patients sent for him, and it was here that he returned when he had treated them. Behind Philip, on the other side of the room, a preacher from St Dunstan's was writing furiously, dipping his pen sometimes into the ink and sometimes into his cup. 'But you say I should marry her anyway, in order to get on,' said Mallen.

'The mother?'

Mallen sighed. 'Mary.'

'It wouldn't be a bad idea. But no, I agree. Much, much, better to marry someone you like.' Philip tapped on the table-top with his coffee spoon. '*Much* better. And as you are already in love, and as her father has a pot of money, I fail to see the problem, or why Mary Chambers has even been mentioned.'

'I am not in love.'

'You may think what you feel is humiliation, but it is not, it is love. There is often very little between them.'

Mallen lifted his cup and squinted over the rim. 'I've no idea who you're talking about,' he said.

Philip looked up again from the newspaper.

'No,' said Mallen. 'I don't think so, not Julia Neville.'

Part Two

I

Holborn

1780

Julia Mallen lifted a book of poetry from the table and dropped it again with a low slap. 'I shall need some money,' she said.

He was sitting at his desk, near the open window in his study, writing. It was not yet dark, but the lamp on his desk had been lit. It was hot still, in spite of a massive downpour earlier in the day, and the skies were heavy. He frowned at the papers in front of him. This was wrong, Philip must not have charged him for something. Valerian, album graecum, bark. 'Money, yes. Sorry.' He unlocked a desk drawer, pulled it open and brought out several coins and a banknote.

'Will you come home tonight?' she said.

'I don't know.' More to the point, would she? He did not ask her.

'Mrs Trent has gone out.'

His wife was dressed in dark blue satin. Her hair had been curled and piled on top of her head, and there was a deep blue jewel at her throat. Her mother's. 'You could occasionally come with me,' she said. 'It never hurts to have your face known.'

A breeze lifted the corner of one of his papers, then dropped again. A clock chimed the half hour. 'I'll get something to eat later,' he said.

'She's left you some lamb.'

He shook his head. 'I have to see Philip anyway.'

They were living in Holborn. The house was not far from

the fields of Finsbury, and they could walk into the country in fifteen minutes. It was well placed for Mallen's private work, and only a mile and a half from the hospital, which had moved to St George's Row. They had been married in 1771. Since then, his practice had grown; on top of his work at the hospital, and the growing demand for his medical services, he was now, at last, becoming popular as a man-midwife amongst the professional classes, attending, in their own homes, the wives of attorneys, of magistrates, coach-builders, merchants. Tea, calico, palm-oil, hemp. The wives of literary men and painters – not yet famous, but not unknown.

Philip had been wide of the mark, in the coffee house in Fetter Lane, when he said that Mallen was in love with Julia Neville. In fact he had been more afraid of her than anything at that time, but Philip was also right: Mallen was badly in need of a wife. He set himself to the task without any real conviction, but Julia had let him court her with a mixture of amusement and disdain and then, to his astonishment, had agreed to marry him. He never thought very much, in those early days, about their happiness. To his surprise, however, after only a short time, he began to worship the ground she walked on. It was, for both of them, a great stroke of fortune. Over the years, time had done what time does to love, but he was devoted to her still, and she to him. They fought, they irritated each other to the point of screaming, and sometimes, because of his work, they did not see each other for days on end, but they had found a constancy, companionship. Their only real sadness was that they had no children, yet.

'How's your back?' he asked her.

'Better. Stiff, but only because I've been out so long. Louisa Grey is still beside herself. She misses her father; I spent the day with her to get her spirits up.'

. 'I didn't know her father was dead.'

'Dead? James, he isn't dead, he's gone abroad.' Julia lowered her head as she looked into a mirror on the far wall. The glass was old, the silvering cracked and flaked. She frowned at her reflection.

'Did you get caught in the rain?'

She lifted her hands, and dropped them again. 'How is it possible that hailstones can form in this heat? I don't understand. A man was killed by lightning in Bethnal Green, apparently. No, we weren't caught; we were in Henrietta Street. We bought gloves. It had stopped when we came out.'

Mallen took up his pen again, and wrote in his regular copperplate. His wife's friends interested him very little, though many of them became his patients. It was enough, it seemed, that Julia's own face was known in rooms that glittered with names and candles, rooms where tea and wine were drunk and money lost or won at cards. The men whose pulses Mallen took, the women whose puckered, bloody babies he held, had usually won several guineas from his wife at the tables. Such is the strength, he sometimes thought, of beauty and losing. Thanks to his wife, Mallen was becoming known in circles of property and even power.

She brought them to him, but it was up to Mallen to keep them, and he knew very well that physicians won their reputation primarily for their bedside care. In the lying-in rooms of women all over London he was considered careful and pleasant and to have unimpeachable integrity. His other patients liked him not because he carried with him any wonder drug or because there was something miraculous in his touch, but because he was recognised as an expert bedside doctor, whose clinical judgement was reliable.

She was beautiful, but she was tired. Her face was chalky, and a faint smell followed her, of powder and fatigue and wine.

'It won't get better unless you rest,' he said.

'What won't?'

'Your back.' He might as well talk to his desk. Julia could look down on him from that great height of her vitality and make him sound trifling. Although she was dressed now to go out, she seemed in no hurry to do so and in fact it was still, for her, early.

She moved nearer to look over his shoulder, and he took her hand and held it to his face. It smelled of money, a brown tang caught in the moisture of her palm. When had he last held her; had they completely given up? The hand he caressed seemed to contain the whole message of her body, and he was staggered by its nakedness. How could he allow it, how could he let her out of the house like this? The bluish hollow of her elbow, the tremor of her arms, the pale lift between her hips – it was all here, in the shell of her hand. It felt like memory, the silent appetite of undressing, his anxious affection for her wrists, the dark hair on her shins. In the last months, when they had reached for each other, their sadness had been unbearable. It pulled them down as if their clothes were wet and heavy, it extinguished the familiar astonishment of their bodies. That, and those weeks when he could not touch her, the tender misery of healing after every loss. Each time she conceived, he felt the thin ache of hope in his throat, the desire to run somewhere, anywhere, fast. Then, always, the horrible mess of sudden blood, the jaw stretched open in gaping failure. He longed to touch the fragile skull of his own child, to hold its slick knees and punching fists. More than once he had found himself appalled by the fury he felt at his wife, had lifted a hand to find it shaking with hatred. It would never happen now, not after all this time.

She came home, as often as not, when the night was almost over, but she did not play for high stakes, and she didn't always lose; more than once he suspected that she had made herself, though briefly, quite rich. It was not a vice in her, it was not going to lead to ruin.

'So they intend to present this petition tomorrow,' she said.

'Do they? Who?'

'Read it. Forty thousand men to assemble in St George's Fields.'

For some months, notices had been appearing regularly in the newspapers advertising a monster petition calling for the repeal of the Catholic Relief Act. This petition lay waiting for signatures at Lord George Gordon's house in Welbeck Street and was said, by some, to be a mile long. Gordon, as far as Mallen knew, was a madman. He was also the parliamentary representative for the pocket borough of Ludgershall, and president of the London Protestant Association.

The Act was not much, but for some it was clear evidence that soon the Pope would be in Westminster. It was a limited piece of legislation, passed two years previously, and removing three mainstays of the laws against Roman Catholics, who had been subject for years to restrictions so severe that they had been largely ignored anyway. Now, Catholics could purchase and inherit land, they did not have their property taken from them if they were educated abroad, and papist teachers and priests were not thrown into prison. This small dent in the law, however, was a sure sign that the streets would soon run with Protestant blood. There was rumour everywhere: twenty thousand Jesuits were hidden in a network of underground tunnels on the Surrey side of the Thames, waiting for orders from Rome to blow up the banks and flood the city; Benedictine monks, disguised as Irishmen, had poisoned all the flour in Southwark, so that no man could eat his bread before giving it first to a dog to try.

'It's the war,' said Mallen.

'The war is in America, James.'

'But now that the French and Spanish have joined in against us, we have a new excuse to hate and despise the Papists. It's mad, all of it, and I have to go out.' He stood up and pulled his coat from the back of his chair, smacking out the creases. As he did so, the maid, Ellen, came in with a message.

'Is this someone you know?' he said, when he had read it through. 'Corney?'

'In Chiswick?'

'No, Bedford Row.'

'It's the same people. They have a house in Chiswick as well. He's a Member of Parliament.' Julia lifted her shoulders. 'I know her, I don't think I have said more than two words to him. Is he ill?'

'His servant's having some kind of fit. I must go.'

The man was in agony. He bucked like a landed fish, his face wet and green, his lips flecked. His pulse was all over the place and he was in a cold sweat. 'What has this man had to eat?' said Mallen. 'Find someone who knows.'

The housekeeper was a west country matron, wall-eyed with terror and smelling of sweat. Her name was Mrs Vance. From the kitchens at the end of a corridor came the cymbal clash of salvers and a yelp. 'He hasn't eaten anything,' she said. 'Not since I don't know when. Only the salts he took for feeling bad to start with.'

'Get them,' said Mallen.

She stared at him, or past him, uncomprehending and rigid.

'The salts, fetch them! I must know what they were.'

'Dover's Powder, sir.'

Mallen straightened and turned and spoke low. 'I cannot help this man until I know for myself what he has taken. Find the paper that they came in, the powders, and bring it to me. Do it now, please.'

'Down by his bed,' she whispered.

Mallen found the screw of paper on the floor. He picked it up and licked it. It had a pungent, saline taste. He swore and spat. 'Bring me a cup with water in it,' he said. He dug in his medicine bag and brought out one phial and then another. Ipecacuanha, senna, calomel, something else – liquorice, anything. He took the water from Mrs Vance, gave the mixture a vigorous stir and emptied it into the mouth of the screaming man.

'Basin,' he said.

She placed the basin near the man's head, and Mallen grappled with him, turning him half upside-down and holding him by the neck. He shoved his fingers into his throat. An elbow struck him on the chin and made his teeth slam.

'What is his name?' he asked the woman.

'Holman. Frank Holman.' She was, he could see, on the edge of tears.

'I shall want you to make up as much as you can of warm milk and water,' he told her, more gently. 'We'll need another basin, first.'

Holman threw up everything but the lining of his stomach. He moaned like a bull, and his eyes and nose streamed. The veins in his arms stood up and the sweat poured off him. Each time the retching slowed, he fell back, blowing, but the contractions of his stomach threw him forward again almost immediately. Outside the room, the normal sounds of the house continued, as if in another world. At last the heaving stopped and he took gagging sips of milk and water. When he was able to keep some of it down, Mallen released him and straightened his own clothes. He bathed the man's eyes and hands. 'Mrs Vance,' he said. The housekeeper stopped in the doorway, the cloth-covered, stinking basin in her arms.

'You'll need another one of those.'

'Yes, sir.'

'And shortly, a night-stool.'

She nodded, and he saw she was trying not to breathe.

'Where did this man get his medicine, do you know?'

'No, sir. Apothecary, I suppose.'

'Thank you.'

George Corney met him at the top of the back staircase and took him up to the library on the first floor. The evening was too warm for a fire, but lamps and candles had been lit. As well as a library, it was a dressing-room, and the smell of vellum and morocco leather in it was mixed with that of boots and hair powder. Apart from themselves and the servants, the house appeared to be empty. 'I'm hugely grateful,' said Corney. He was a man of forty or so, with a distracted look and a high stomach. What hair he still had stood up from his scalp in short, ashy twists. 'Your colleague, Dr French, has been shot.'

Mallen put his bag and his cane down beside a writing desk that had been brought from France or Italy. A tall leather chair stood near it, and the walls were covered with glass-fronted bookcases of different sizes. Encyclopaedias stood on the lower shelves, and there were drawers for maps and manuscripts. Everything was clean, and the spines gleamed brown and gold and red behind the glass, a sort of standing army of books. The room was stifling. 'Shot?' said Mallen.

Corney lifted a decanter and sniffed it. 'There are, as far as I know, at least four versions of what happened. Do you know him?'

'Not personally, no.'

Corney poured dark wine into glasses, and gave one to Mallen. 'The one thing they agree on, these reports, is that he isn't badly hurt. A flesh wound, and upwards of thirty guineas gone, as well as his horse. Poor man. Anyway, Holman –'

'He'll live.'

Corney looked at him with a frown of concern.

'A few more minutes,' said Mallen, 'and he would have died. He had taken two ounces of saltpetre.'

The other man nodded, as if to say that he understood, then shook his head because he did not. There were men in London of every rank who could tell you the composition of any proprietary nostrum, and the benefits of one above another, but George Corney was not one of them. However, the point was a simple one. 'He was poisoned,' he said.

'Small amounts are used in many medicines, but more than that can be dangerous.'

'Yes, of course. This is unbelievable –'

'I'd like to come back tomorrow to see how he is,' said Mallen. 'He's weak now, and there will be further purging in the night. For the time being, he must drink milk. He should be given some brandy, later.' There were small crusts of vomit, he noticed, on his waistcoat.

'Poor man.' Corney rubbed a hand across his face. He had picked up a sheet of paper from his desk, and was rolling it into a twist. Then, seeing that it was from the House of Commons, he put it down again. 'Holman's not an idiot, he wouldn't do that to himself; his head's screwed on too tight. I'll try to find out what happened.'

'What has happened?' The voice came from the door, and Mallen turned. He had not heard her approach, and did not know if she had only just arrived, or had been standing there like a pale sentry all the time. There was little light behind her, in the passage, and little reached her from the room, so that he could not properly make out the line of her dress, her cheek.

'My wife,' said George Corney, also turning. 'Augusta, this is Dr Mallen. Mallen, my wife, Mrs Corney.' She looked at him without moving her head. 'Dr Mallen has just saved Holman's life,' he said.

She gave her husband a long and level look. 'But there's nothing wrong with Holman,' she said, entering the room. 'I saw him this morning.' She was a tall woman, her eyes in this light as dark and flat as a bird's. She looked well proportioned and strong, but when she lifted her hands, they trembled. She crossed the room and pulled apart the curtains to open a window.

'He had taken something,' said her husband.

'Holman?' said Mrs Corney. 'A thief?'

A lamp guttered. Her husband lifted his glass and looked into it. 'He took something that made him ill,' he said.

'I see. Where's Dr French?'

'He has had an accident.'

Her back was still turned to them. She pulled a light shawl from her shoulders and placed it over the back of a chair. 'How can you stand it in here without a window open?' she said. 'It's hot enough to send one mad. There's more lightning, look. What did he take, Holman?'

'Saltpetre,' said Mallen. 'Two ounces.'

Augusta Corney turned, and it was now as if she had only just truly entered the room. Some other part of her had caught up and made her, finally, present.

'He nearly died,' said her husband.

'Good God! Who's with him?'

She was, in this light, older than Mallen had first thought, though still considerably younger than her husband. Her eyes were not flat after all, he saw, but deep and black. Her hair was reddish-brown, and piled on her head, with strands falling loose on her neck. Her skin was flawless, and the lines of her face were both bold and graceful. They were filled with a strange and searching energy that made her beautiful. Her face, at that moment, was grave, but there was a rare quality in it, a quality he had not seen before but which, it seemed to him, he recognised instantly. A strong face, with a measure of expectation in it, he thought, something avid and alert. Above the bodice of her dress, he noticed the white skin over her collar bone, and at the hollow of her throat. Under her glance he felt himself quizzed, felt that he had been asked something that, though difficult, he could answer. 'I gather he thought he was taking Dover's Powder.'

She examined the surface of a small table. 'I suppose it's possible,' she said. 'With half these things, you don't know what you're taking.' She looked as if she was waiting for someone else to speak. No one did. 'Is there anything we should do?'

Mallen put his glass down on the lower platform of the library steps and shook his head. It was George Corney, though, who answered her. 'Nothing,' he said. 'He must drink milk, that's all. Mrs Vance is taking care of him.'

Mallen heard the hour strike. Perhaps it was only the heat, but the night seemed to him to be dancing, hovering a few feet above itself, like midges over a stream. Sounds outside – carriage wheels, laughter – were all struck out of glass, and broke like small windows. Mrs Corney seemed to study him, and for a moment he had the peculiar impression that she was trying to remember something that she had known about him, once upon a time. Even more strange, he was certain that he was about to reach and touch her sleeve, her naked arm. Suddenly he could not bear to be in the room any longer, with the smell of leather and furniture wax. He was already long overdue at the hospital, and supper with Philip was out of the question.

'Thank you, Dr Mallen.' She looked at him for a long time, and then she smiled. George Corney put down his glass and clapped a hand on Mallen's shoulder. 'This way,' he said, 'I'll see you out.'

At the bottom of the steps, Mallen almost ran over a cripple, dragging his leg along the street. He was a man of considerable size, loping like a swift but injured wolf in the dim circle of light from a street lamp, his head swaying from side to side. His face, for a moment, loomed in front of Mallen with small but clever eyes and a long chin.

2

Here So Far

The wraith was creating a family where in life she had never had one. God only knows what happened to her mother. Gin, or transportation. Her father was a tanner, but he had died of drink when she was seven, hawking his life into a midden in Bermondsey. She was taken in by a porter's wife, then passed from pillar to post. How she ended up in Hammersmith was anyone's guess; when she did, she was given work in the household of the Margravine of Brandenburg, where she remained for three years, until she died. There were thirty servants in livery, not to mention cooks, scullions and grooms, but she never had a family.

Now she had an eminent physician-midwife, the daughter of an upholsterer, and the estranged wife of King George IV. The distillery was dark and quiet; the wheels were still and men had gone home.

'He is nearly blind,' said a voice from the other side of a mashing tun.

'Oh, here we go,' said the wraith. 'Let me guess: Sir Walter Scott, no. Wellington, no. Lord Byron? No, dead.'

'He has cataracts in both eyes,' said the Queen who, after the service for the dead at Newgate, had gone to Windsor with the Duchess, where they had seen the King and gossiped with ancient shades. 'He don't get up until six in the afternoon. They come to him and open the window curtains in the morning early. He has breakfasts in bed, he read the paper, he says hello, go away to some persons, not many. Then he for three or four hours sleeps, gets up in time for dinner and goes to bed again. He rings his bell forty times in the night for his *valet de chambre* to tell him what time is it.'

'Hasn't he got a watch?'

'Yes, of course.'

'The man is a spoiled, selfish, odious toad,' said Franny. She was sitting on the rim of the tun, dangling her feet in the mash. 'He has no idea of doing anything but what is agreeable to him, which is spending money and ordering people around.'

'He is sick,' said the Queen.

'In his head.'

'It take them three hours to dress him, and he bulge out like a sausage.' The Queen sighed. Needless to say, in the corridors of Windsor Castle they had come across the King's current mistress, fat but beautiful. She had walked through them, oblivious.

'I got practically next to nothing from him,' she said. 'She is no one. Her father was a clerk.'

'If you are talking about Lady Conyngham,' said Franny, 'that is true. But he made himself a bloody fortune by work and scraping.'

Caroline waved away this piece of pedantry. 'I had nothing begiven to me, while she has diamonds heaped every day on her. Also a golden melon, that comes apart like an orange into four pieces, each one with a different perfume –'

The wraith put her head in her hands. 'Oh, oh, oh,' she wailed.

'She has made the King's house a desert and driven his friends all away from him and what is more,' she shouted up at the wraith, 'the King is bored with her. He is very ill. His doctors are idiots. I want you to go and see him,' she said to Mallen.

Mallen didn't look up. He had not been listening. He had

been thinking once more about how he had lived with death all his life, and yet his thoughts had come nowhere, ever, near to this. He had seen death almost on a daily basis, and had known only that it was unfathomable, a great mystery that people met sometimes with fear, sometimes with an extraordinary and moving indifference. And still, even now, he was at a loss. He came back to it time and time again: where were the others, everyone else? Where were his mother, Julia, the countless thousands who were not here? Nobody knew where it was that they went, or if they had gone anywhere. However much they asked, there was never any answer. And this hovering world, this place to which they were attached like so many pieces of fluttering paper behind the indifferent living – it stretched in front of them, but it was not eternity. We are here, so far, and then where?

He had gone to Edinburgh. He had studied Boerhaave's philosophy of dualistic mechanism. He read the men – de Bordeu, Whytt, John Hunter – who said that mechanics were not enough, that there was more to health than a balance of internal fluid pressures, and that the body was more than a hydraulic system of vessels and pipes; that there had to be some vital force or organisation in it. He had considered the astonishing powers of living things to regenerate and regrow, and asked himself, how is this explained? He had learned anatomy under William Hunter. Skeleton, sinew, blood vessels; tissue and fat – he knew, as precisely as it was possible to know, what we are made of. He had cut through it, he had revealed the organs, and then cut through the organs, too.

And what is it that we are made of now? I can walk through closed doors.

'Doctor.'

He heard his name and looked up.

'Oh, you deranged, stupid woman,' cried the wraith. 'What can he do?'

The Queen lifted her chin, and glared at her. 'I am the Queen of England,' she said. 'You cannot speak to me like that.'

'No you aren't and yes I can. *The grave, great teacher, to a level brings . . . something and something, queens and kings.*'

Franny turned, her mouth hanging open. 'Poetry?' she said.

'Shut up.'

The Queen opened her mouth, too, to say something cutting, something to knock this little brat down to size, but on reflection, the wraith was right. Death removed all social status, and most of the rules that went with it, and there was no point in arguing. Thank goodness for people like the Duchess, who strove to maintain some standards, and some manners, even in the afterlife. 'Not for the King,' she said. 'For me. I want to know. I want to know what it is what is wrong with him.'

'I am afraid I have no idea,' said Mallen.

'But you must see him.'

'I don't think that would do any good.'

'For me it would do some good. To know what his illness is.'

Mallen shook his head. Yes, it was unfathomable, and so often the imperatives of death seemed to him to be meaningless. What possible good could it do the Queen to know what her husband was dying of? It was she who was haunted, in every hall of this ringing, steamy place, and through every street she walked. He no longer felt any pity for her; at first he had thought her someone robbed by fate and the monarchy of a happy life, but now he saw her as a woman who had grubbed for love, raking through a thin soil of unintelligent men and settling time after time for insincerity. She had become a prurient, jealous ghost, dragging with her everywhere horrible rags of memory and resentment.

He felt the stone come down, again, on his head, and the staggering sense of grief when he knew that he was going to die, the awful sadness. He recalled the useless regret that he had not put things right, and that it was too late for that, and for everything. 'Well, perhaps,' he said to the Queen.

'Yes! Thank you.'

They could not go immediately, there wasn't time. They made their way back in dull procession to Newgate, Mallen dreading the spectacle, even though he fully expected to see Augusta there. The street outside the prison was crammed with spectators. Many had been there for hours, pressed against the barriers and nearly fainting from exhaustion. Every shop window and every roof was packed with fat placid faces; every gin shop and coffee house with a view. Above the roar and murmur they heard the lowing of cattle being driven into the stalls at Smithfield.

The condemned men emerged from the prison door. Lempson, the young thief, the cringing figure of the clergyman forger. The sheep-stealer, weeping like a drain. There was another roar, and cries of 'Hats off!' and 'Down in front!' Then came the deep ringing of the death-knell from the church of St Sepulchre. All the men removed their hats, and the murmur of the crowd became almost inhuman. Mallen left the others and went through the crowds on his own. It was a cold day again. Behind him a woman's voice, throaty and maudlin with gin, raised itself in an ugly prayer. More and more old shades and phantoms sifted the living crowd, but the one person he had been certain to see was the one he could not find.

'James.'

The tears started before he saw her. They streamed, improbably, down his face. The bells tolled with incalculable seconds between them. Something laden in him lifted and rose; all his hope reversed and settled. He would know now, and it would be over.

It was Barbara Villiers.

He turned his streaming face back towards the scaffold.

'I was hoping to find you,' said the Duchess. 'I have been here all morning, and have found out a great deal, but there is no one I know, and this crowd is very rough. Are you weeping?'

'Your Grace. I thought –'

'That I was Mrs Corney? James, I am sorry. For me, that is very flattering, but I know what it means to you. I haven't seen her. However, you must come with me; this particular hangman, William Calcraft, is said to be inefficient.'

Another ghoul, thought Mallen. It was another hammer blow of disappointment. It did not mean, however, that Augusta was not here.

The Duchess led him towards the scaffold, through the crush and the din. She was right, the crowd was appalling. Fists slammed and noses poured blood, young boys flung obscenities and thieves wandered everywhere. They had all come to roll in it, to go away smelling ripely of funk or courage. It was not so much the snap and choke of violent extinction that filled Mallen with horror, but the multitude that massed like crows, black and open-beaked, snaffling fried fish and ginger beer.

'I know all about him,' said the Duchess. 'By trade he's a lady's shoemaker. He is a devoted rabbit-fancier, and fishes in the New River. Shall I tell you more?'

'No. Thank you. He is a man like any other, the point is not lost on me. He is employed, like any other, so that he may feed his children.'

The Duchess nodded. 'Do you suppose he has killed more people in his time than you did in yours?'

Something had changed in the Duchess; each time he met her, usually with Franny, she had altered. Her voice had lost some of its edge, and her eyes no longer seemed like black pebbles in her great fat face. Mallen felt a sudden trepidation, though not because he was fond of her, that Barbara Villiers would very soon leave them. 'No,' he said, 'not by a long way.'

'But you, unlike him, were not trying to do so. You were doing your best for the opposite result.'

'Of course.' Though not always. There were a few that he had hastened out, nudged over the shelf of death when it was coming too slowly or with too much pain, whose fingers he had lifted and straightened as they clung on; not to mention those he had killed in the act of trying to cure them. Mallen turned away. He heard the signal given, and the drop falling. The quay-like sound of straining rope, and silence, for a moment. Then the cries, again, of the sellers of pies and fish.

'She liked crowds.' Enough was enough, apparently; the Duchess had turned, too, and was letting him lead her away. He did not know, immediately, who she meant.

'Yes,' he said, 'she did.'

'It's a great shame she wasn't born a man, or she might have gone to war. If you think of it, enough men have made it their obsession. In any case, she would have had her crowds. And the drama of sword and crossbow. I am thinking back, of course, with crossbows. Before my time, even.' She hurried them past a gang of phantom beggars. 'One wonders what it is that so intrigues her. I think she must be morbid. I always hated crowds, they frightened me. There was the threat of assassination, of course – not me, King Charles. But again, if you are looking for drama, all human life is there. Perhaps that's what she is looking for. It must be something, after all; she never stays in one place for a moment, she moves like only someone who is searching moves. Each time you see her, she vanishes, and it is not because she has seen you, and is running away.'

'No.' This much, he knew, was true.

'She cannot stay still, any more than you can. Surely you must have thought this too, no?'

Mallen lifted his hands, and dropped them to his side again. 'But for what?' he said.

'What is she looking for? Well, that I can't tell you. Not you apparently. Forgiveness, I rather suspect. Don't look at me like that. You can't be completely stupid, James, even if you loved her. She must have done something wrong at some point in her life. Ask yourself what she did, and then think what it might be that she's in search of.' She paused. Behind them, a pie-seller slipped and fell. 'It might not be that, of course. We also look for the things we have lost, or never understood. She seems to me to have been a strange woman, if not slightly mad. Very selfish, clearly.' The pie-seller had not yet managed to get up. Each time he tried, someone pushed past and knocked him down again. 'She was never very easy to find, was she?' the Duchess went on. 'Not for you, much of the time, and not for her husband who, as far as I can tell, never had a clue where she was. She must have been doing something all that time, she must have had her wants and needs. She hardly knew her own sons, and not just because they were sent away to school. She neglected them dreadfully.'

'You've been talking to Franny.'

'I have, yes.'

All our lives, he thought, we are looking. All of us, for something. And if we never find it, we go on looking, after the grave.

The Duchess moved serenely through a fight between two screaming women. 'Do you know, I sometimes used to long for death. To put an end to what at the time seemed unendurable.' She laughed, a flat and meagre sound. 'I used to think, let me die now, let me walk out into the river and be dragged down by my own clothes, and I shall no longer be ruined, I shall cease to be monstrous and repulsive. I didn't know, of course, that we do not cease to be what we are. What I wonder, however, is if it is really Augusta Corney for whom you are searching.'

A sound escaped him, nipped and baffled, like a dog astonished by pain.

The Duchess raised her eyes above Mallen's head, above the crowd, and frowned. 'The question occurred to me only recently,' she said, 'but with extraordinary force.'

'But if not Augusta, who?'

'Yes, of course. Or what? Perhaps you are not looking in the right place at all, or for the right thing.'

He saw her old beauty then, a smile both tender and lazy, a dreamy light of promise and of care. He, too, lifted his eyes. A man was hanging on the young thief's legs to end his suffering.

'What else?' he said. But Barbara Villiers had gone, she was no longer by his side. 'What else?' he roared across the snivelling, gawping crowd.

A face appeared in front of him. It was a face he had known in every detail once, briefly, a long time ago. The eyes peered into his with a look of great personal curiosity, then momentarily closed. Their lids were thin with age, the lashes short and white. The cheek on one side was swollen, and the mouth was grey. Then with a nod of either pain or recognition, the face slid away and vanished in the scrum. Yes, he remembered. The body had been brought in from the scaffold, in the middle of winter. Thirteen guineas, cash. His hands had been freezing when he made the first cut. There had been a tumour in the jaw. Well-formed, the size and shape of an unripe apple. William Hunter had ordered it to be preserved. It was probably still sitting somewhere, in a glass jar. No, possibly not.

Even now, at the foot of the scaffold, agents from the anatomy schools were fighting with the families of the hanged for possession of the bodies. He could hear the jagged cry of a wife or mother above the sounds of the crowd. There was half a chance, when they got them down, that the men were not truly dead, that they could be brought back with a lungful of air and a thump on the chest. In Mallen's day, and even now, establishing death was an inexact science. There were stories of bodies flinching on the table, under the anatomist's knife. If they were truly dead, the families fought for them for the sake of their souls; a hanged man who was cut up in the name of science would be chained to the earth, or go to hell. Whatever that might mean, thought Mallen, looking around him.

What had the Duchess meant? Her words had hooked themselves under his ribs, but he could not think where they had come from, or why she should have uttered them. He was looking for Augusta, and for one reason. Who else, what else? No one, nothing.

By the time he found the others, Lempson had also been hanged. 'Buck up, Doctor.' It was the wraith, looking strangely reserved, a smile of maternal calm on her face.

'We can stay for a bit,' said Franny. 'She might be here, and we haven't seen her.'

'Tuh,' said the wraith. It was then that Mallen noticed the young thief, hovering behind her like a shadow, his shirt buttons open and his neck black with rope-burn. Even as a medical man, it always astonished him how quickly the body responded with bruises, with death. He found it almost impossible to believe that the brilliant machine that is the body could stop on an instant, that life could be separated from death by such a thin blade of time. Nothing can stop so quickly as life; there are laws which make things slow before they stop, but not life. In fact this boy had had his few years squeezed out over minutes, slowly choking before his neck was broken. Even so, minutes ago he was alive, and now he was dead.

'No,' said Mallen, 'she isn't here. We can go.' Lempson, it seemed, had been forgotten by them all, including Augusta Corney.

The young thief looked around him, trying to fathom where he was.

'His name is Dick Grace,' said the wraith.

Mallen nodded. He wanted to go home. 'Come,' he said.

Dick Grace began to talk in Broad Street. He talked all night, lying in the vaults of the distillery. Above them, pigeons roosted on the cast-iron beams that supported the ceiling.

3

A Surging Sea

1780

He had returned in the early hours from the hospital, and Mrs Trent, the housekeeper, had let him sleep. It was noon before he finished dressing and looked through his post. Julia had not emerged from her room by the time he left the house; he thought about leaving a note for her, then didn't know what he would write. He rubbed his face in his hands, and held them over his eyes until the colours swam. He felt like a man who had seen some great event in recent hours and who could remember nothing about it, or even what it was. Our lives can change in a matter of seconds, he thought. His own had not, but the back of his neck was raw with expectation. He let himself out of the house and made his way to Cursitor Street to visit Philip Little at his shop.

The apothecary was grinding scilla bulbs for oxymel of squills. In the window, syrups stood like beacons in crystal vials with cut-glass stoppers – emerald, plum and saffron. In the centre of the shop stood sacks and casks of senna, gum arabic, peruvian bark and myrrh. There were more casks behind the two counters, as well as drawers containing dry goods, weights, labels and containers. There was a bookcase, a safe, species glasses and more drawers, all lit by a brass chandelier with two sconces. 'Saltpetre?' said Philip. 'I don't know anyone that stupid. Not an apothecary, not round here, James. Some itinerant quack, more than likely. It is not up to you, however, to discover who or how.'

'No. What I came to find out was why I never paid you anything in March.'

Philip nodded. 'Have you eaten?' He tucked a few papers under his arm, and pulled the blinds down over the window. The shop, when they locked and left it, seemed heavy-lidded, half-asleep. All of London leapt with the heat and smelled of straw and stables and human sweat. Horses drenched their heads in troughs of water, and lifted glittering sprays. The two men pushed their way through a scrum of carriages on Chancery Lane towards a chop-house in Portugal Street. 'You know,' said Philip, 'there's some poor fellow supposed to be lost amongst these streets, someone who came up years ago from the country. He started one night from Portugal Street to get to the Strand, and he's been wandering round and about ever since. On foggy nights, you can see him in Clare Market holding his bag and looking, I suppose, rather sick. At any rate, no one has yet heard that he ever reached the Strand.'

'I didn't know you believed in ghosts,' said Mallen.

'Did I say he was a ghost? No, the poor man is not only lost, James, but alive.'

The talk in the chop-house was about Lord Gordon and the crowd that had gathered that morning in Southwark. News from the streets came in each time the door swung open, and each man who brought it demanded a drink and spoke of a sea of people.

'I think we should see this,' said Philip. 'We can both be spared for half an hour. No one's going to die. James . . . what is it, what's the matter?'

'The matter? Nothing.' He made himself smile, and his face felt like paste. He was trembling and his skin was too tight, but what could he tell his friend? In the course of a few hours, it seemed to him that he had had something poured into him that was either misery or joy, and so far he did not know which, or what to do with it. He kept seeing

Mrs Corney's face, and the fact that he seemed to be able to remember it, in every detail, made the day seem all the more extraordinary. 'They're in Southwark,' he said. 'They'll go over Westminster Bridge. If you want to see them, you'll have to go to Westminster, and I haven't the time, not this afternoon.'

Philip leaned back in his chair, something that always made Mallen expect the pistol-crack of breaking wood, and took the arm of a passing clerk who had just come up from Temple Bar. 'Where are they?' he asked the man.

'Blackfriars Bridge,' said the clerk, draining off half his mug of beer. 'And London Bridge, and Westminster. Three divisions.'

Philip bought the man a drink, and by the time they went back out into the scorching light, Mallen still didn't know how much he owed his friend for medicines in March, or why.

The streets south of Lincoln's Inn were a maze of dark and narrow alleys, made darker by bulkheads and overhanging eaves, and what with being overtaken and slowed by small crowds of people, and the carriages that had backed up into the side streets, it took them twenty minutes to reach the Strand. What they saw when they got there was, indeed, like a sea, and sounded like one, like the quiet drag of waves across the shingle on a beach.

The marchers walked behind their banners, talking softly, six to nine abreast. They filled the street, a mass of steady unsmiling faces, and the only sounds were the tramping of feet and the murmur of their voices. There was no beginning to them, and no end, and every one of them, wave after wave, wore a blue cockade or knot in his hat. Mallen watched, mute at the sight of so much mustered piety. Up and down the Strand, people stood on the house-tops to watch. Behind him, from a side street, there was a sudden drunken current, with bullying laughter and a bloated, incoherent shout.

Philip stood with his back against a wig-maker's shop on the corner of Catherine Street. The people in front of him parted like water around St Mary's church, then slowed and shuffled for the narrow channel where the Exeter 'Change projected into the street. As they went past the church, they cheered. Philip's face was very still, very sober and impressed. How could a big man look so young, thought Mallen. He felt a thud of affection in his chest for his friend. Philip caught his look, and grinned. 'Best-dressed mob I ever saw,' he said. Mallen had noticed too. From the menagerie on the third floor of the 'Change came the low roar of a lion. The ranks of marchers bulged in front of Mallen, and he stepped back out of the way. 'Extraordinary,' said Philip.

'Come on, you've seen enough, and I have to go to Bedford Row.'

Philip pushed himself away from the wall, and squinted at the sun. 'I could come with you,' he said. 'I shouldn't mind taking a look at your man.'

'No!' Mallen spoke too quickly, too loud. 'No,' he said more gently. 'There's nothing to see, now. If he's still in pain, I can give him something. I have everything with me. I would much rather you went back and wrote me out a proper bill for March. And one other thing, I shall need balsamic syrup.'

They parted company in Cursitor Street, but Mallen didn't go straight to Bedford Row. Instead, he made his way to the house of Patrick Bright, a stone's throw away in Dyer's Buildings.

The workshop door was open, and all the windows, but there was no sign of the upholsterer. In front of the house, an old dog lay under a small tree.

Mallen knocked but didn't wait. The workshop smelled of

sun-hit wood and glue. The bench was laid out with tools and needles, gimp pins and buttons, and a crate of sunlight lay across it, squared by the window panes. He could hear the gentle racket of family life, a spiralling shriek, a chair being dragged. Hannah's voice, square and low. He knocked on another door, and went through.

Hannah Bright was waving her arms and shouting. An orange cat went flying in one direction, out of an open window, while a tall but vivid child flew past him in another, yelling, apparently, for a certain radical alderman. After some negotiation under a wooden table, the child stood up. 'Mince got Wilkes,' she said, with serious self-possession.

'Hello, Franny.'

A small grey face looked out from between her fingers. She bent her head and blew at it. 'I think his back is broken,' she said.

'Wilkes and Liberty!' came a voice from the corner.

'Good afternoon, Patrick.'

'Doctor.'

Mallen put down his cane and took off his hat. He could feel the rim it had left around his head. Hannah wiped her hands on her apron and smiled at him. 'Sit down,' she said. 'I'll get you something to drink.' She moved round the table, straightening the chairs.

'Nothing for me,' said Mallen.

Another child lifted itself off its backside with the help of Patrick's trouser leg and used this added height to scrutinise Mallen with big and steady eyes. It was pink from crying; a leftover sob took it by surprise and it staggered on its feet. Mallen took a chair on the opposite side of the empty grate from Patrick, and Franny climbed onto his lap. Her bare feet were filthy, and her legs were brown beneath her skirts. Nothing ever stayed in her hair, and it fell down over her shoulders in fat curls.

'I can't leave you for a minute,' said Mallen. 'Look at your scratches.'

'Mince,' said the girl.

'In my day,' said her father, 'we never kept vermin in the house. That is the purpose and function of a cat like Mince, to keep them out.'

'In your day!' said Hannah. 'You being so excessively old.'

'He isn't old,' said Franny. 'When you're old, you die. Who will die first, me or Pa?'

'Pa,' said Patrick. 'At this rate, all too soon.'

'Dear, oh dear,' Franny whispered into her fists. 'So very, very soon, such a terrible tragic shame.'

Mallen leaned back in his chair and shifted Franny's weight. She was eleven now, and getting heavy. 'And how is the patient?' he said. Richard, Franny's brother, had been in bed for a week with a fever.

'Scratchy,' said Patrick. 'He is sat up there in his bed like a little Indian prince. He's been out the window twice, and onto the back roof.'

'Good,' said Mallen. 'I expect he can get up.'

'I'm going to tell him,' said Franny, nudging herself forward onto Mallen's knees, both fists lifted in front of her.

'You'll do no such thing,' said her mother, 'not until Dr Mallen has seen him. And put Wilkes back in his box, please. Really, it's a losing battle.'

To this day, Mallen did not fully know the circumstances of Hannah's life before her marriage to Patrick Bright. It was never talked about – not the house in Clare Market, not William Hunter nor Newgate Prison. It might have been possible to believe that it hadn't happened, any of it, except for shadows sometimes in Hannah's cheeks, hollow pouches holding secrets, and pauses where she stood for minutes and then came back with a baffled start. Though he had not been the father of her first child, the child that died, Patrick had taken Hannah home when she came out of prison, and Franny was born at the end of the following year. He was a good man and, since Franny, Mallen had assisted twice more in the increase of his family. He had done it not at the Lying-In Hospital, but in a room above this one, while Patrick ripped apart horsehair stuffing in the workshop. Twice, the doctor had gone downstairs to announce to a room full of dust and splinters a new addition.

'His back might be broken,' said Franny, remembering that Wilkes had not been examined, and gazing into Mallen's face.

'I'm a people doctor, Franny, not a mouse doctor, but I can say with certainty that if that were the case, Wilkes would be dead and you would be crying your eyes out.'

'But you haven't looked, you don't know.'

Mallen lifted her fists and peered through the small fingers. Franny scowled and waited. 'Well?' she demanded.

'He's all right. Unscathed.'

Franny pulled the sides of her mouth into her cheeks, less than satisfied. She smelled of dust and sun, a sparrow smell. Her hair fell across her face, and she puffed her cheeks and blew at it.

'Poof!' said Patrick, plucking the other child from his trouser leg and holding him up in front of his face. 'We need changing, we do.' The child's eyes widened in placid astonishment at finding itself in the air.

Mallen reached into his pocket. 'This is for Franny,' he said. 'I almost forgot it.'

Franny's face lit up. She dug her elbows into her stomach, the mouse cupped under her chin, while Mallen brought out a small book. '*The Top Book*!' she yelled.

Patrick tutted. 'No need to shout,' he said.

Franny subsided briefly, then sat up, still twisted, on Mallen's knee. 'Read,' she demanded.

'You can read it.'

'Open it.'

'I haven't heard a thank-you, yet,' said her father.

'Open it.' She held out her clenched hands, with a cripple's importunity. Mallen opened the book. 'There,' he said. '*A gaping wide-mouthed waddling frog.* Too difficult for you.'

She held the book open, on her lap, with her wrists, and scowled at it in silence, her lips just moving. She looked up and grinned at Mallen. 'Thank you,' she said, planting a kiss on the side of his face. He held her waist and lifted her down. He felt their safeness, the tidy coolness of the room, the muscular and watchful presence of Patrick, idly thumbing the naked spine of the child on his knee. Extraordinary, really, he thought. Sometimes I lie in bed at night and worry myself sick about the children of an upholsterer. I go half mad when I hear that one of them is ill; I forget completely that I am a physician and am certain that they will die. I am aware of every risk they run across, speared by broken glass, cracked open on cobbles, crushed by hooves. Yes, Richard can get up today. It must be hot in his room, I should have thought of that.

'Oh, God, damn and blast,' hissed Franny, as Wilkes slid out from between her fingers. At the same time, there was a loud yell from upstairs, and a string of indistinguishable words.

'I'll go up,' said Mallen.

It was after four when Mrs Vance let him into the house on Bedford Row. Frank Holman was white and weak, but on his feet. His hands were red and itching from contact with the saltpetre, and Mallen gave him a salve. George Corney had gone to the House of Commons, and his wife was not at home.

4

Windsor

1829

The countryside was black and cold. The snow had not lasted, only in small clumps under the hedges. At Osterley they found something else under a hedge, a man passed out with drink. His lips were almost black. 'Get up!' the wraith yelled into his ear. 'You are going to die. You damn bloody drunken tosspot, get up, stand on your feet!'

'He's only passed out,' said Franny.

The wraith kicked him uselessly. 'He's a soak, and he's frozen solid. Get up *now*!'

The man's eyes shot open, pebbles of white under the morning stars.

'He's all right,' said Mallen. 'He'll live.'

'What is the bloody point of being bloody useless?' complained the wraith.

Franny peered at the man and shrugged.

'Not him, us. What good are we to anyone, nothing, none. We may as well not be here, we may as well just not exist at all. Whooh!' she wailed into the man's ear. His eyes opened again, and he saw on the road above him the frosted outline of a skinny child, the glassy and quizzical face of a strangled boy. His legs began to run before he was standing.

'Better,' said the wraith. 'Good.'

Windsor was wreathed in mist. The castle rose up out of it, heavy and newly Gothic. Smoke curled from its kitchen chimneys.

'He has rebuilt it, like one from Wales,' said Caroline. 'Like for the olden times. Up there is for to pour boiling oil on the enemy. This way, keep up.' She led them through the castle as if, by dint of her marriage and background, she knew every inch of it. 'It is not so big as it looks,' she said, dragging them from chamber to chamber and tower to tower. The renovations had been going on for some time, and were not finished. The vast reception rooms were still filled with ladders and scaffolds; dust sheets covered the precious furniture, and chandeliers sat like huge skirts in white canvas sacks.

'Whoa,' said the wraith. 'Ghosts.'

Sarah, Duchess of Marlborough saw Caroline and fled. Queen Anne, sad and fat, swung from the ropes and pulleys that had been used at the end of her life to hoist her from one floor to another. She leapt off, however, when she saw the late wife of the King, and also disappeared.

'Popular, aren't we,' said the wraith.

'We are in the wrong part of the castle,' said the Queen, padding in front of them along the length the Grand Corridor, where misty light pooled down through skylights onto the rich crimson carpets, and onto the clocks and busts and chairs that lined the walls on either side. Everything smelled of thick wool and new paint. Eventually they came to the King's lodgings, on the east side of the castle.

King George was in tears. He sat in a dirty dressing-gown with an envelope in his hands, which he lifted now and then and kissed. As far as they could see, the envelope was empty. His face was plastered with greasepaint, which the tears had chased into streaks of oil and chalk. 'Well?' the Queen said to Mallen.

It didn't take more than moments to see that the King was up to his eyeballs in laudanum and cherry brandy. Whatever the underlying illness, the man was maudlin and half-stupefied. 'On the high ground behind the farmhouse,' Mallen heard him whisper. The only other living person in the room was a page, sitting sideways on the edge of a large, decorated chest, with one foot on the floor.

'He's stewed,' said the wraith. 'Another bloody soaker.'

'The papers give him a new disease every week,' said Franny.

'As if you know,' said the wraith.

'If it's mortal, so much the better. He would like everyone to think he's dangerously ill.'

'He *is* dangerously ill!' shrieked the Queen.

Dick Grace, having talked himself across the great divide between life and death, had said little since. Most of the time he watched, gawky with change and new information. Now he stood with his eyes on stalks. He found the King's bath, a square structure covered with a piece of marble, and he crossed himself, thinking it was an altar.

Mallen closed his eyes. The King had cataracts, yes. And all the symptoms of dropsy. Gout in his right hand, a hugely swollen arm, inflammation of the bladder. Oppression in the chest, pericardium slightly swollen; ossification of the valves of the aorta, heart greatly enlarged. It was precious information, and of no use. If he could tell the King's doctors, then yes, but all he could do with what he knew was feed it to the Queen. We are all so hungry, he thought.

'Well, Dr Mallen?'

He opened his eyes and sighed. To his horror, the wraith was leaning over the King, screeching into his ear. 'You will die of drink before you have a chance to die of anything else,' she shouted. 'And everyone will hate you.'

'Stop it,' said Mallen.

'They do hate him,' said Franny. 'At least he isn't mad, like the last one.'

'But you will go mad,' hummed the wraith. 'You will go mad with drink, won't you, fat old King?'

The fat old King, strangely, had a smile on his face. 'They

had the advantage in numbers and artillery,' he said to his page. 'Don't look at me like that, you squit. You don't believe me, I'll show you.' Galvanised, he swept everything from the top of a writing desk. 'This!' he said, squinting. 'What is this, boy?'

'It's your stamp, Majesty.'

'Never seen it before. And this? No, I can see what it is. Pay attention. This is the farmhouse.'

'It'll fall off if you put it there.'

'The French here, here and here. This is Kempt, and Pack up here is threatened.'

'I told you it would fall off.'

'Well, put something under it to stop it sloping. No, under the leg, boy. Good. D'Erlon is over here on the left flank. Wait, I need those. This will be d'Erlon.' The King picked up a pair of spectacles with pebble lenses, and put a rouge pot down in its place. 'Now,' he announced. 'The Earl of Uxbridge.'

'What?' said the wraith.

Franny shrugged.

'Uxbridge sees the situation at once,' said the King, peering through the spectacles. 'Very grave. He gives orders for the charge. We need something for the Second Life Guards.'

'No room,' said the page.

'Waterloo,' said Mallen.

'Perfect timing,' said the King. 'Trumpets sounding the charge, through the hedges, over the road, smash through the French here and here. Damn. No, leave it. Drive them back across here, chase them over the drop over there, frightful mess in that direction. Yes, yes, above the farmhouse. Now, the Scots Greys, up here behind this . . . whatever it is. This is a muddy field, and here is the 92nd, giving way and unable to open ranks. Advance the Scots Greys, and hack the French to pieces, here.'

'Your Majesty wasn't there, though, was he?'

'I was right here!' said the King, slamming his fist down behind Uxbridge's charge. 'That is what I am explaining to you.'

Caroline was looking on with a grin of satisfied fury. 'Doctor?' she demanded.

Mallen lifted his head. 'No, he was never at Waterloo,' he said. 'It is a fantasy in his mind.'

'That is not what I'm asking you! I know he was not at Waterloo, he was by his house, he was all that time making more restrictions on me and on my daughter. He was forbidding me to come inside this castle and making me investigated by the Privy Council. I know all that. You, I want to tell me what is wrong with him now, today.'

Mallen sighed. 'He is certainly ill,' he said. 'His heart is weak. He may live, however, for another two years.' This was ungenerous – not to the King, to Caroline – but Mallen was not inclined to give her all she wanted.

'Two years?' said the Queen, with a small and quizzical frown.

'It seems to me,' said Mallen, 'that he is keeping himself alive. He has a strong will, and also a remarkable constitution.'

'He is pickled,' said the wraith, 'like a walnut.'

At that moment, Sir William Knighton, Keeper of the Privy Purse and the King's confidant, entered the room. 'The Duke of Wellington,' he said.

'Wellington,' said the King. 'Yes, Wellington is up here, somewhere, north of Mount St Jean.'

'He is waiting,' said Knighton, 'outside.'

'Arthur is?' The King groaned and turned slowly towards Knighton. 'I'm not signing anything. I can't see and I can't write. I am worn out, for God's sake. Where are my teeth?'

'Supporting the left flank,' said the page.

The King's face assumed a weary scowl, directed at Knighton. 'Tell him I am ill.'

'He said he only wants five minutes.'

The King breathed out in a long, stertorous sigh. 'I never get any pity, only demands. By the way, where is my brother?'

'Somewhere, I don't know; I believe he went for a ride.'

The King put his great head between his hands, and his sleeves became smeared with greasepaint. He swung his head slowly from side to side. 'They are tearing me apart, those two,' he said. 'Arthur on one side and Ernest on the other.'

'Your brother is going to bring down the government.'

'Oh, he is not. Cumberland is a man who knows very well what the feeling is in this country; he knows there is little support for Catholic relief, and he knows that my father would have laid his head on the block rather than let this through.'

'He has only made you more intransigent. He bullies you, and works you into a frenzy. He is, at this very moment, planning to get together a mob of twenty thousand Protestants to march down here and frighten you into refusing any concessions with regard to the Bill.'

'You have just said that he went out riding.'

'You know what I mean. Are you going to see the Duke in that old dressing-gown?'

The King tried to raise his hands, but the movement gave him pain up and down his arms, and he laid them back over his great stomach. 'I shall go to Wiesbaden. I will not be driven mad by all this. Tell them to start packing, and remember that it is *very cold* at this time of the year in Wiesbaden.'

'Calm down.'

'What on earth am I to do? I've made it perfectly clear that this is not a Cabinet matter.'

'Perhaps it should be.'

'For heaven's sake, William. I am a Protestant King, a

Protestant upholder, and nothing on earth will shake me on that subject. Not even Arthur.'

'Of course you are, and truly faithful and a marvellous example. On the other hand, you know very well that he's right. There's growing support everywhere for relief. If you got out more, you'd see it for yourself. But quite apart from the question of moral justice, if you don't do something soon, you're going to have a serious problem in Ireland. The Catholics will carry a large number of constituencies at the next election, and it won't just be supporters of emancipation who get in. You'll have to deal with a lot of radicals, who are going to threaten the government's authority in the Commons.'

'Shut up, shut up, shut up.'

Knighton let out a long sigh. 'I'll show him in, shall I?'

The young thief at that moment collapsed on a Louis Quinze chair and put his head in his hands. Yesterday morning he had been in the company of a murderer, a sheep-stealer, and a clergyman forger in the condemned cells of Newgate. Now he found himself in a suite of rooms filled with marble and bronze, surrounded by goods five hundred times the value of five pounds. The King of England was playing with an army of false teeth and paperweights, and the Duke of Wellington was at the door. 'And who,' he asked quietly, 'is that woman following us?'

'Following?' said the wraith. 'Nobody.'

'All day, from Hammersmith.'

'No.'

'Who's that, then?' he said, motioning with his head towards the door.

Mallen looked up. A woman was standing in the door to the King's room, with one hand on the jamb. 'James,' she said. 'Could I have a word?'

5

The Sardinian Chapel

1780

It was almost eleven. Mallen heard the knocking, and went to the door himself. 'Is he worse?' he said to the messenger.

'It's not him, it's Mr Corney.'

'I know the way.'

'I'll wait, sir.' He wasn't much more than thirteen, and his shirt was black with sweat.

'Give me five minutes.'

The streets were still hot and close. In the short walk to Bedford Row they encountered knots of men, venomous-looking and two-thirds drunk. Some carried pickaxes on their shoulders, or crowbars. The boy trod on Mallen's heels all the way. 'Are these Gordon's men?' said Mallen.

'Don't know who they are, sir.'

'Has there been trouble?'

'You could say so.'

Corney had a wide gash on his cheek which had dried into a messy scab, and his chest and back were covered in bruises. He was shirtless, sitting in the leather chair, a glass of brandy at his side. 'I'll be downstairs,' said his wife. She was wearing yellow silk, with half-sleeves trimmed in lace, and there were jewels at her throat and wrists.

'This thing runs very deep,' said Corney. He reached for a decanter on the desk top, and flinched. 'My carriage is in splinters, destroyed.'

Mallen found somewhere to put his bag, and opened it. The same smell, everywhere he went, released each time; senna and foxglove, cinnamon, musk. 'Let me see,' he said. He made Corney take off his belt, and found more bruising beneath it. 'I saw them marching this morning,' he continued. 'I went down to the Strand. They seemed a sober crowd. Mostly tradesmen, mostly well-dressed and decent.'

'Any man may be sober at breakfast and out of his senses by twelve, especially when he is drunk on righteousness. Ouch!'

'It's the rib, it may be broken.'

'I made the stupid mistake, with Charles Turner, of helping Bishop West to escape. This' – he put a hand to his cheek – 'was a horsewhip.'

'It needs a stitch.' It needed several.

'There were people running for their lives, Mallen. Welbore Ellis was badly beaten. I got away, he didn't. There were peers of the realm with mud and shit all over them, dragged from their coaches, kicked and pelted . . . Ellis had to go over the roof.'

'Lean forward, please.'

'Gordon could have sent them all home with a word. He pretends to give out Christian injunctions for peaceful behaviour, while doing everything in his power to promote a massacre. I swore to his face that I would kill him if one of those men got into the Commons. You will not survive, I said, to recount your exploits if the people force their way into this House.'

'All right, you can lean back.'

Corney stretched an arm behind the doctor's back to fill his glass. 'More than half of them were street boys and bullies picked up on the way from Southwark. We were barricaded! Every one of us thought we would have to fight our way out of the House, sword in hand.'

'Tell me if this hurts. Here?'

Corney said nothing, but his body jumped when Mallen

pressed. A jug of water had been placed in the room, and a wide bowl. Mallen soaked a cloth and wrung it out.

'It lies very deep,' he said again. Every time he reached for his brandy Mallen was forced to step out of the way. 'I don't suppose any of them out there knew the terms of the petition, or even that there was one. No, this is something else, it has come up out of the night-cellars and the rookeries. For the love of God, they took my wig!' Finally, petulance. It sat badly on his big frame, an angry, twitching little creature. Mallen addressed himself to the wound on his cheek. The brandy, at least, was doing something for the pain. 'Had they ordered the civil power to be prepared and the justices to be out?' said Corney. 'No, they had not. A crowd of forty thousand, and six constables. They didn't call the Guard, Dr Mallen, because the Prime Minister forgot.'

'Keep very still.' Mallen took the man's chin in his hands and set his head, like a brick in mortar. 'This is going to hurt,' he said.

'What I don't understand –'

'Don't speak.'

The room seemed accustomed to silence; a clock ticked, and something creaked above them. Somewhere out in Holborn a shout went up. Mrs Vance appeared with more water. Corney's eyes were closed and his face held a checked and sliding concentration. His head bobbed once, like a man fighting sleep. Mallen finished the stitches and began to dress the wound. There was nothing he could do for the chest beyond strapping it. Some would let blood for the broken rib, but Mallen reckoned in this case the blood was better in than out.

'The Horse Guards!' bellowed his patient, suddenly. 'The Guards,' he said more quietly, 'rode into Palace Yard and held up their swords –' Speechifying, now. Corney must have heard it, too, because he looked confused and dropped the tone. His eyes were still closed. 'They did nothing, Mallen. They stood around on their arses. Horses. They were laughed at, roundly.'

'Sit forward,' said Mallen.

'For God's sake go and talk to my wife, will you? She'll be anxious.'

Augusta Corney lifted her head and smiled. Then, quite suddenly, she gripped his arm. 'Come,' she said, 'you have to come with me. Leave your bag.' She had put a lace shawl over her shoulders and she had, he noticed, removed her jewellery. 'There's no one else,' she said. 'Please.'

Where? He did not care where, anywhere. 'Your husband –' he said. It sounded dreadful; too urgent, nearly breathless.

'I've sent Holman up to him.'

As soon as they were in the street, he smelled the smoke. 'This way,' she said. She pulled him through a narrow court at the bottom of Bedford Row. Lights burned in high windows, but doors were shut and barred and the lower floors were dark. Soft white ash brushed their faces and landed on the shoulders of his coat. Her face was bright, a light and vibrant fever in her cheeks. 'Did he tell you he saved a bishop?' she said, steering him with her weight on his arm. In spite of the heat and the lack of rain, High Holborn was laced with streams of mud. She must have sent the boy back out to bring her news; she knew where she was going, at any rate. The streets were alive with news and rumour, and she led him through them without a moment's doubt.

'He told me, yes.'

'Ha!' She gathered her dress as they stepped up over a drain. 'Well, never mind.'

'He acted bravely,' he said, understanding in the same moment that no, George Corney had run for his life and went head over heels in Parliament Street or Palace Yard and got himself run over. He had never spoken two words to Lord George Gordon. Mallen started to turn towards Lincoln's Inn, but she stopped him. 'Not yet,' she said. Women ran against them, dragging grimy children, looking backwards and shouting. It was as if the city was screwing itself up against an invading army, down to the smoke and the gathering roar and the light of burning staves.

They came out into Great Queen Street and saw the first fires – four, five of them, and the glow of more beyond. They passed the flaming ribs of an empty birdcage; lintels, mantels, a Hepplewhite chair. Men, rangy and livid, patrolled the flames, their figures bright and then dark, lit and then hidden, while others threw furniture from the windows. Drawers exploded and boys on the ground ran whooping at them, shouting anti-papish jibes. Augusta Corney's face was brilliant. I must get her home, he thought; I should never have let her do this. Someone above them yelled, 'Heads below', and he pulled so sharply that he feared her shoulder would come out of joint. A huge gilt mirror slammed into the pavement and shattered. A young boy smacked a hand to his cheek and started to bleed through his fingers.

She swung round, and put her arm through his. 'Come,' she said. He dug in his heels, but she insisted. 'Leave me if you want to,' she said. 'I'm going this way. I want to see it.'

Lincoln's Inn was an ocean of faces, hollowed and yellow. Mallen looked round, once, and saw the man he had almost fallen over outside the house on Bedford Row, on his first visit there. The cripple met his eyes, and lifted his chin, as if to swing his whole head into the air. His mouth fell open, but no sound came out of it. Then he vanished. They pushed through the shoving crowds on the west side, until they came to Duke Street. I'm going to lose her, thought Mallen. If I let her out of my sight, I will never find her again.

In the street outside the Sardinian Chapel, anything that would burn had been piled up and torched – vestments and altar ornaments, pews and benches, smashed to bits. Even now, more was being passed out over the heads of the mob. Boys of no more than fifteen ran riot with flaming brands and threw hassocks and dead cats at each other. Strangeness settled on Mallen like the ash from the fires. He thought briefly of his home, and it seemed to him that it was a place a hundred miles away, instead of just a few streets to the north. Two men in leather waistcoats, their hands bleeding from jagged cuts, knocked him against Augusta Corney, making him stumble to avoid her toes. How insane to think that he might protect her, if it came to that.

'Doctor!' said a voice behind them. Mallen turned, while Mrs Corney continued on. 'Stop,' he said to her. 'Wait.'

It was Simon Greville, a coppersmith whose wife had brought one dead child after another into the world. 'What are you doing here?' said Greville. He was a man of not more than thirty, though tonight he looked ancient. His hair and beard were green with copper, and his mouth was a black hole. He swung an arm at the fantastic dance of boys and flames. 'If they take you for Papists, they'll break your bones. If not that, you'll get arrested. Rainforth has sent for the Guard.'

Mallen's jaw worked like a fish. 'Greville, listen –' he said, but the man had gone.

'What's wrong with you?' said Augusta Corney. 'This way.'

She was a salamander, a seraphim. She led him closer to the flames, her elbow wedged in his. He found himself praying let this moment never end, let it last and go on for ever, but let us be somewhere else and not here. Her dress was torn at the hem, and filthy with soot and lime. Her hair had begun to come undone, and a pin was dangling under her ear. It looked somehow disgraceful, and he turned her towards him and lifted a hand to draw it out. Have I gone mad? he thought. 'I can't let you stay here,' he said. 'Mrs Corney, for God's sake, this is mayhem.'

The bonfire had been pushed up against the doors of the chapel, and men were pouring out of the building as it began to burn. Behind them, another roar went up. The fire engines had arrived – two bed-posters, low to the ground and shaped like boxes. Someone yelled for a stopcock. 'Out of the way there!' shouted one of the firemen, dragging a leather hose. Someone threw a missile at him, something black and soggy. Four other firemen mounted the engine to work the treddles, while more leaned on the pumping handles. The chief went through the crowd, looking for men to aim the water sprays.

'They won't help them,' said Augusta Corney. 'The chapel's going to burn, and they won't use the hoses. Look!'

It was true. There were men enough to carry buckets, to bring the hoses to the sources of water, to fill the cistern, but none would do it. In all the movement around them, there was the obdurate stillness of refusal. The mob would not lift a hand to put out the fire. Then slowly, from the ranks of spectators standing against the walls came one man, and then another. A standpipe had been opened, and water gushed out onto the street, forming sooty runnels. Mallen saw that Augusta Corney's slippers were ruined. Why on earth had she come out in those? 'We're in the way,' he said, 'we must go.' But she freed herself from his arm, and ran towards the first engine. It took up most of the road, and she pushed a way past it, as if to stand between it and the flames. As it was, they soon became trapped between the firemen and the houses, and were forced up against a brick wall, hemmed in on all sides. Six feet away, in the yellow glow, Simon Greville stared with open mouth. Diet, thought Mallen; he has lost his teeth because of poor diet.

'Where's Samson Rainforth?' yelled Greville.

One of the hoses had begun to work. Mallen kept his eyes on the weak but steady stream of water that fell not on the fire, but on the backs of several rioters. He shook his head. 'Who is Rainforth?' he said into Augusta Corney's ear. She was standing in front of him, so close that he could feel the buttons on the back of her dress, the heat of her body; he could smell the perfume on her neck and something else, almost briny. Pleasure.

'He's a magistrate. Why, do you see him?'

'How can I see him if I don't know who he is?'

She laughed then, in her yellow dress, her head thrown back against his shoulder. 'He's the King's tallow chandler,' she said. 'He has a house in Clare Street.' Her hands had become wonderfully filthy, and a bold line of sweat ran down her neck. Whenever she stepped back, she stepped on his feet, pressed the heels of her small shoes into his instep. She was entranced, and when she turned to look at him, away from the fire, the flames were still there, reflected in her eyes.

Against the wall of a house, his long chin lifted in dogged scrutiny, stood the cripple. He was watching them with the stillness of a cat. 'We're being followed,' said Mallen.

'Oh?'

'There.'

She did not even look. 'His name is Lemuel Prager.'

Mallen was staggered. 'You know him?'

'I know who he is. He follows me.'

'Everywhere?'

'Almost, yes.'

She was extraordinary, this woman. 'Do you want me to tell him to go away?'

'No. He's all right. He'll go of his own accord.'

There was a massive crash just in front of them and suddenly the blaze was almost at their feet, as a flaming pew was thrown across the street at the engines. Instinctively, Mallen pulled Augusta Corney into his arms, and turned her away from the threat. He was aware of the damp line of sweat on her back, and he could feel, to his horror, her heart. 'That's it,' he said, releasing her. 'That's enough. We're going home.'

'Very well,' she said, smiling.

As they fought their way back to the top of Duke Street, a hundred Foot Guards appeared in front of them with fixed bayonets, and drove them back.

6

Again Not Again

1829

Not her. Not her, not Augusta. Again. Mallen left the room. Outside, in an ante-room, the Duke of Wellington was walking up and down, chewing his lip. Barbara Villiers turned as Mallen entered, and took a seat.

'Your Grace.' Mallen made a stiff bow.

'For God's sake, James.' He shrugged. 'You're angry with me,' she said. 'However, I can't help being who I am, and not someone else.'

How could he, even for a moment, have mistaken her for Augusta? Perhaps it was her voice. That note of challenge, always there; the almost musical lilt. It was also true, though, that the Duchess had changed. It was a remarkable fact that, while they might all exist as nothing more than shadows, she had altered. There was some lustre in her face, and a shape to her cheek that had not been there before. 'You look well,' he said.

The Duchess shook with laughter. 'Tell me,' she said when she had recovered. 'What is it that you miss most?'

'You followed us all the way from Hammersmith to ask me that?'

'No, I followed you for another reason. But still, you can tell me.'

'I miss everything.'

'Ah.'

Mallen decided to make an effort. 'The girls, they talk endlessly about food, and there are times when I'd like nothing more than a large plate of oyster loaves.'

She raised her eyebrows and gave him a look that said she had been thinking of something quite different – a look that told him what. Of course she would miss that, he thought. A woman of her great beauty, and countless ways of using it, and countless men to use it on, throughout her life. For some minutes he didn't answer, thinking of his own old instincts, and how much and how often he missed them. 'The oysters are cooked in butter and wine,' he said, 'and then placed in hot rolls.'

She nodded. 'I miss jewellery, I think. And all the wrong things, of course. Power, watching certain men fall from grace. But at this very moment, I should like a syllabub. You must have a proper froth on it – you milk the cow directly into a bowl of ale or cider. There's nothing like it.'

Mallen sat down beside her. Wellington still hadn't been summoned; he was talking in low tones to one of the King's physicians. 'Look at him,' said the Duchess. 'He never gets out of here in less than four hours. The King keeps him waiting, and then won't let him get a word in. He's very clever at turning the conversation from any subject he doesn't like, and at the moment, he doesn't like Wellington's Catholic Bill. Every time the Duke does get somewhere with him, the King's brother interferes and undoes all his work in just a few days.'

Mallen stood up and walked around the room. Wellington, he noticed, smelled of horses. 'You're well informed,' he told her.

'The King's brother, Cumberland,' she went on, 'is a dreadful man, very sarcastic. The King loathes sarcasm, it terrifies him. Largely because of Cumberland, there's no one in the realm at this moment more Protestant than King George. Either Wellington will have to get Cumberland out of the country, or find a reason to throw him in the Tower. The Bill has to go through.'

Mallen was surprised by the strength of her opinion. 'You're not a Catholic,' he said.

'I am dead, James.'

'All the same.'

'No, not all the same. What use would any religion be to me now, or to you? Catholic or Protestant, when we have left one world for another, it is immediately clear that what we find is not at all what we were promised.'

Mallen frowned, and leaned forward over his knees.

'Be that as it may,' she went on, 'if we wish, while we are alive, to worship, then we must have the freedom to do so as we please. So long as it does no harm to anyone else.'

He nodded his agreement. He had studied anatomy; he had cut open more bodies than he could count, and had seen for himself that under the skin they were all much the same. He had brought children into the world, each one a being that needed every ounce of courage, every day, for what they had to do. If they must believe in something, then they must be able to do so according to their choice. It was a matter of reason, and nothing else, that the rights of one were the same, exactly, as the rights of the other. But then it usually led to riot or war, either way. 'So long,' he repeated, 'as it does no harm to anyone else. You and I know that it very often does.'

'Perhaps we should not be tolerant of any religion.' The Duchess smiled, and patted his leg with a fat bejewelled hand. 'I *was* a Catholic, as a matter of fact,' she said. 'I converted.'

'Why?'

'Oh, for the wrong reasons, I suppose. I was a poor ornament, I'm afraid, to any Church.' She paused, and raised her chin. 'I was always loyal to the cause of religious toleration. People forget that. In my day, you could go to prison for your beliefs. Remember, I lived in a time of civil war, and in all the bitter quarrels and resentments, faith and politics went hand in hand. What never ceases to amaze one is the hypocrisy of all the established religions. The moment that faith becomes organised, you find it is full of men who are looking for property and wealth and power. Have you ever read any Locke?'

He was thrown suddenly in a backward leap to the river in Hammersmith, and Julia standing above him on the bank. 'Some,' he said.

'If one man believes that this is the body of Christ, and another that it's a piece of bread, they have no need to fight about it, and it's certainly no business of the state. As for me, when I converted, they all thought it was a ploy to put me in a better position for my next move in the political game.'

Mallen was intrigued. 'Which was what?'

For the time being, she ignored the question. 'The French ambassador was so thrilled, he borrowed an orchestra of violins to play in the chapel.' She turned her face, with a small smile, towards him. 'I was not motivated by deep religious conviction. Let's leave it at that.'

Mallen lifted his head and placed a hand on either knee. 'You never milked a cow, either,' he said.

She laughed. 'Not very well, but I did. Once, in St James's Park. We used to walk there often, with the dogs, feeding the ducks. Charles loved it.'

How strange it must be for the Duchess, he thought, to find herself blown up against the window of the living world, more than a century after her death. Stranger even than for the rest of them. Here she was, in the company of a king and of a queen, one alive and the other dead, in a place where everything was different to anything she had known. She had lived through war and plague, and seen London half destroyed by fire. She had made herself at home in Whitehall and St James's, and dominated the Court with her beauty and her wit. Then death had locked her, pacing up and down in Walpole House for a hundred years, just as it had locked him into the walls of his father's house, and she had walked out into another age and a different place in her seventeenth-century silks. Where she had left open fields with hay or corn, or the dark turned furrows of plough, she had come back to find new straight and open streets, new squares and palaces and churches. She had left a city without bridges, full of serpentine, narrow streets, and returned to one almost twice the size, with pavements and lighting and a tide, from one end to the other, of deafening traffic. And yet, extraordinarily, she was almost as well informed about things as Franny.

'I suppose,' said the Duchess, returning to the subject of faith, 'that you were a good Anglican.'

'Me? No. I was a man of science. I believed in a model of natural order more than in the providence of God.'

'Oh?'

He glanced up at the painted ceiling. 'There was too much magic, for me, in religion of any kind. My work was with disease, and disease, like nature, has no morality, it isn't visited on us by an angry god. I always thought that the causes of hardship must be looked for in nature, in poverty and wars and what we eat, not what we pray to. No, mine was a secular, scientific world.'

'You were very surprised, then, to find yourself here.'

He smiled. 'That may be the work of God, but not of religion. The two, in my mind, are not at all the same.'

'My dear James, what an interesting thought. What, then, is God?'

This made him laugh. 'Honestly? I have no idea. And yes, I was very surprised.'

At that moment, there was terrible howl from the King's room. Something heavy fell to the floor. The door was flung open and the sound from inside became a thin, tormented wail. William Knighton appeared, grim with self-control and jurisdiction. 'Sir Henry,' he said. 'Laudanum.'

The physician who had been talking with Wellington stepped forward. 'Half an hour ago,' he said, 'you were roundly condemning me for giving him too much.'

'Give him some more. Immediately.'

'For the love of God,' said Wellington. 'What's happened?'

Mallen and the Duchess slipped past them into the room. The King was sitting slumped in his chair, his huge frame helpless and shaking. His hands moved over his face, and the bridge of his nose was gashed where his spectacles had broken. Mallen could smell urine. The page stood motionless and gawping in the furthest corner of the room. Of the wraith and Franny, of Dick Grace, there was no sign, nor of the Queen.

'Your Majesty!' said Wellington.

'Arthur –' It was a whisper, a rattle thickened by fear. 'Get her away from me.'

The Duke looked at Knighton. 'What's the matter with him?'

'I can't be certain,' said Knighton. 'Some sort of fit.'

Wellington, greatly distressed at seeing the King in such a state, leaned over him and looked into his purple face. 'Arthur,' said the King. 'I'm quite all right, quite all right. Another attack of the spasms, nothing more. I am very glad to see you. Oh God, get her out of here, the fat bitch. Tell me she's gone. Promise me. Oh God, oh God.'

Mallen ran through oak doors, through gilt and ormolu, through walls and porches, portraits of kings and admirals. He streamed up the Grand Corridor with a wail of fury that sounded, to the living ear, like plovers. He ran through stone. Through the drapes and hangings of empty chambers, through a servants' hall where meat was being carved. Papers lifted as he passed, lists and seating plans and letters. Curtains filled an inch and dropped. He went like a small gale round the yards and orchards until he found them, outside the stables. Franny, in a stable doorway, had her arms crossed over her body.

'What in God's name did you do?' shouted Mallen.

The wraith pointed, without looking. 'Her,' she said, a glint on the edge of her voice.

The Queen was sitting like a crumpled feed sack on a pile of straw. She looked up with wide weak eyes and a defensive chin. 'Oh, oh, oh,' she said. 'Not me. That is only nothing but lies and she was the one, not me. All I have only come to see is how is the poor King, must he suffer with pains and excruciation. I stand always quiet and out of intrusion and nobody hear or see not even this much of me.' She held a pinch of air in her fingers. 'Not even so big.'

'She got him,' said the wraith. 'He saw her.'

'Ah!' said the Queen in a swipe of sure advantage. 'The King is blind. Ha.'

'The King is *half* blind,' said Franny from the doorway. She had not moved, and stood with one hip against the jamb and her arms in front of her. 'And we all know it's the ones with bad eyes who can see.'

'The ones with bad eyes can see?' shouted the Queen. 'Bad eyes can see? Doctor, Doctor –' She made her appeal from the steaming heap of straw, her hands now open in front of her. 'How can these girls torment me with so stupid ignorance?'

Mallen was still stinging with rage. 'You manifested yourself to the King,' he said, 'at the greatest possible danger, given his condition, to his very life. Were you trying to kill him?'

The Queen lifted her elbows, like a table bird. 'The King is blind,' she said. 'How can he see me or any other thing except it is right up to his face like so.' This time, she held a hand flat against her nose.

Mallen could no longer look at her. His eyes fell to the ground at his feet, the cold stones of the stable yard, the sparrow droppings. 'She couldn't wait for him to die,' said the wraith. 'She is going to pounce on him like an old fat cat and get her snivelling revenge.'

'She,' said the Queen, ignoring the wraith and pointing a witchy finger at Franny, 'she say the King can see because the King is blind.'

This, as far as Mallen knew, was true. It was often the case, inexplicably, that people suffering from diseases of the eye, even simple myopia, were more likely to say that they had been visited by ghosts or visions. This was, however, immaterial. Mallen did not for a moment believe that it was only chance or cataracts that had made Caroline take shape in front of the monarch. He had almost hoped, when he agreed to come here, that she might have wanted at last to learn something from the living, to achieve some modicum of insight. 'He will die soon enough,' he said to her.

'Die?' The Queen lifted her voice in a shriek of fury. 'Musten he because he see me die? This man my husband is.' In her fury, her constructions were worse than ever. 'Can I not to him a message bring, or comfort? You, you, you,' she said, pointing to them each in turn, 'you bring me comfort when I in my bed am dying. I know then it is not the end, and I am not all alone completely. Why should the King my husband not know this thing too?'

'Comfort,' snarled the wraith. 'It made him ill just to look at you when you were alive and well. He needed a stiff drink to be in the same room.' Inside the stables, the horses were restless, whinnying.

'Let us not pretend,' Mallen said to the Queen, 'that there was ever any love lost between you.'

The Queen, by now, was almost speechless. 'Love . . . !' she sputtered.

Mallen turned his back on her and walked away across the stable yard. There was nothing to be done. There was no judicial system for the dead, no process of proof of intention, nor means of incarceration. At that moment, he would have liked to lock her up for eternity. The cobbles rang as a hunter was led towards its stable. A man in corduroy riding breeches and a tall hat marched across the yard towards a door in the castle wall. The King's brother, Cumberland. If the Queen had succeeded in frightening her husband into his grave, then the Duke would have been, at this moment, on the point of receiving the news. Mallen was surprised by the force of his own feeling; he had no reason to be concerned one way or the other about a monarch loved by only a few, a man who had grown massive with indulgence and disease, who in his present stupor could only anyway be called half alive.

When he turned round, Barbara Villiers was beside him. 'That was the other thing I wanted to talk to you about,' she said. 'I rather thought that this might happen.'

'She tried to kill him.' Mallen was almost felled by rage and disappointment. 'I thought you wanted to talk about Mrs Corney,' he said. 'I thought you had something to tell me.'

The Duchess patted his arm. 'I'm sorry,' she said. 'No, I came here because I had some inkling, yesterday, that King George was not altogether safe from his wife. One might think that he was too drugged and too fond of his drink to be mortally afraid of anything, but on the other hand, one look at her, and he could drop down dead. He has not, by the way. He's sleeping.'

The Queen was sobbing.

'Not that it is inevitable,' the Duchess continued, 'for a man to expire at the sight of a ghost, but a weak heart might give out for less reason.'

'Quite.'

'Perhaps she did not mean to be so drastic.'

Mallen could smell the heat and sweat from Cumberland's horse. At least we still have this, he thought – the smell, if not the taste, of life. 'Who knows what she meant. I don't think I have any wish to understand her, I only want to be sure that it doesn't happen again.'

Barbara Villiers stepped, out of ancient habit, around a straw-soaked puddle. 'Talk to her,' she said.

But Caroline would talk to no one. Accused and misunderstood yet again, she clamped her mouth firmly shut. She limped back to Hammersmith in a deep cloud of injury. For days and days she hardly moved. At night, when the distillery was quiet, she hid in the rafters with the pigeons.

7

Moorfields

1780

He went straight to Julia's room, taking the stairs two at a time. She was asleep. He sat on the bed and pulled a hand gently through her hair. 'Don't,' she said, without waking. She had pushed off all her covers, even the sheet. One knee was pulled up inside her bed-gown, and her cheek was pink where she had slept on her fist. She turned her face into the pillows and pushed him away with her leg.

For a moment in Duke Street Mallen had thought that Simon Greville was right and that they would be arrested. The soldiers had come up so fast that a number of people, many of them spectators, had been pushed back towards the chapel and seized there. But the magistrate, Samson Rainforth, had recognised Augusta and had given them an escort out of Lincoln's Inn.

He took off his clothes and threw them out onto the landing. He lay on his back in bed, but sleep stayed up near the ceiling, out of reach. He saw Augusta Corney in yellow silk, stepping over a streaming kennel, lifting her skirts in handfuls on either side. He saw her, bedraggled and sublime, feeding the flames, throwing in chair legs and picture frames and cages, not empty but filled with birds, small fists of fire.

When he opened his eyes, his wife was leaning over him, gazing down into his face with a frown of study. He smiled. 'I've been thinking,' he said.

'You haven't. You were asleep.'

'Come for a walk with me on Sunday. A long one.'

'All right.'

His hands still smelled of smoke. The night was over, however, and he was in his own bed and things were normal again.

'James.'

'Me. Yes.'

'There were riots.'

'I know.'

'I had to come home. Louisa brought me.'

'I didn't know where you were.' His body felt dragged down with sleep, and the backs of his knees were damp. 'I didn't know where to look.'

'You looked for me?'

'No, where would I start? The house was empty when I got home, and then I was called out again. There was nothing I could do.'

She let out her breath in a lazy sigh. 'I wasn't in danger,' she said. 'We could see the bonfires from the windows, no one talked about anything else. No one sat down to supper. It was all cold, anyway, and Lady Malcolm made the servants take round plates. Then Charles Grey became worried that they would block off Long Acre, and said we must get home before we were trapped. I must say, I wouldn't live with that man if you paid me. I was in bed soon after midnight.'

'For once.'

'Not to mention the fact that he looks like Lord North, with a potato under his ear.'

'He has a goitre, don't be cruel.'

'At least you're not ugly, James. That's one good thing about you.'

He lifted himself up onto the pillows so that their eyes were level. 'Don't go out again, not until this is all over, not at night, not without telling me where you'll be.'

'It is over,' she said. She was lying on one side, supporting herself on her elbow. He pushed her shoulder and she fell onto her back.

It was all over – it seemed to be. On his way to Bedford Row to see George Corney, Mallen came across a blackened cross, standing apparently unsupported in the air above a heap of embers. He prodded it, and it fell with a thud into the soft white ash. Apart from that, he saw no further signs of disturbance. He checked Corney's bandages, but did not see Augusta. He felt a strong urge, as he left the house, to stay until she returned, but he could not. Julia was waiting for him at home and, not only that, he was under scrutiny from the cripple, Lemuel Prager, who was standing watching him on the other side of the street.

On Sunday, the heat grew steadily during the day. The fields smelled of cut hay, and clouds of flies hovered near the streams. Julia paused on top of a stile, and turned to grin at him. Small burrs had stuck to her dress. The hedges were fat with hogweed, and cows stood in the shade of bulging chestnuts.

'There's a wasp in your hair.'

She froze, then lifted her chin and narrowed her eyes. 'No, there isn't. Listen, James,' she said, turning again and settling her skirts. 'I want to ask you something.' She kept her back to him as she talked, and he watched the tilt of her hat, the expressive sweep of a hand. It was nothing important; something to do with food for a dinner party.

'What's wrong with fish?' he said.

'Fish, yes. Whiting. Turbot *à l'Anglaise*. Mackerel with gooseberries. A large capon, veal with currants, pheasant pie. French beans, artichokes and lettuce from your father.'

'When is this?'

'Wednesday. Charles and Louisa are coming, and the

Malcolms. George and Sarah Fletcher. Come on, I'm thirsty.'

The mud at the edge of the river was strewn with hard, dusty cowpats. They followed a path beside the water, the grass and nettles high beside them. They gave up walking in any one direction and wandered in the fields around Canonbury and Ball's Pond. They took off their shoes and lay with their feet in the river, then dozed for an hour and woke up parched. They played bowls on a shaded green, and ate cold chicken. Tonight, thought Mallen, we will not be shut up from each other by silence or sadness. We will smell of sun. We won't be so tired that we can't keep our eyes open. He traced the underside of her arm with his finger, and made her tremble.

They walked back through Newington Green, keeping to the main road. It was beginning to get dark as they came into London, but Julia was watching high summer clouds. 'James, look,' she said, 'something's burning.'

They were in Moorfields, still almost a mile from home. In front of them, on the corner of Ropemaker's Alley, stood a crowd of people returning, like them, from their country walks. Mallen pushed forward. He could feel the night tip up, and everything slide off it. He saw the flames, and hundreds of people running up and down, throwing themselves on top of one another. They were drinking from casks, and swinging staves and fists. In the alley itself there was another enormous bonfire, another chapel. Lemuel Prager limped steadily towards the opposite side of the road, casting a look towards them over his shoulder. He was, Mallen noticed, not without grace, and surprisingly swift. The crowd let him through as if they were a herd of smaller animals.

He took Julia by the hand. 'Come on,' he said.

'Where?' She stood like a pillar, staring. 'It's awful.'

'I know. Move, come on.'

They walked fast away from the destruction. Somewhere

behind them a man screamed in pain. Mallen lost all sense of direction. He kept going, walking fast, convinced that at the next turn, and then the next, he would know where they were. In the shadow of a windowless wall a shape leapt out at them and Julia shrieked. A dog ran beside them, then vanished again. They turned right and then left, and found themselves on the corner of Drapers Gardens. 'We're walking east,' said Julia. 'We're going the wrong way.'

'We can't be. I don't know how.'

'Because you won't stop to think. Please, James, slow down.'

He looked for something he recognised, for a churchyard, a spire to steer by. The walls shouted with echoes, and dark had begun to come down between them.

'Stop,' said Julia. 'I've got a stitch.'

'Keep walking. It'll go if you keep walking.'

'It won't. James, stop. I can't keep up with you.' The day's heat rose off the stones. The sound of feet was everywhere, like a downpour. 'This way,' he said, pulling her back towards Token House Yard. He was more sure now, and thinking they were almost safe, when suddenly their way was blocked by four or five men, most carrying sticks, all grey with sweat and ashes. 'Woah,' said one. The tallest, of course. 'Just a minute.'

'Let us pass,' said Mallen. *Let us pass*. He sounded plummy and fragile, like a clergyman.

'Passports, then,' said the man.

He knew immediately what they meant. We are going to lose everything for the sake of a bit of blue ribbon, he thought. Everyone else has got the idea today of wearing a cockade, whoever they are and whatever they think. 'Listen,' he said. 'Wait.' For what? The men stood in front of them, toothy and serious. He dug in his pocket for a shilling. They would take everything. He had nearly three guineas on him; they would take it, and the coat off his back, and they would follow him home and break down the doors and burn his books and the bed where tonight, he had meant to make love to his wife.

His pockets were full of grass. 'Wait,' he said again. 'We've been in the country.' This explained everything, it gave them right of way, it was brilliant. He could feel the bones of his skull cave under the Protestant sticks, the thud of their boots in his ribs.

'May the Pope,' said Julia quietly, 'rot in hell.' She took the money Mallen held in his hand and passed it to one of the men.

Mallen heard her, but he didn't understand. He heard the roar from the men, smelled it too, the stomachy fumes. He saw their faces contort. That's done it, he thought, we're dead. The sticks were lifted in the air, a cheer went up and someone slapped a hand down hard on his shoulder. A moment later, the men were gone.

Julia was shaking with rage. At him or at the men, he didn't know. He felt her silence come up like the spread of ice on the surface of water. Her shoulder hardened against his arm, and she said nothing when he spoke to her. But as they walked up Cowcross Street, almost at their own door, she turned to look back, as if the scenes they had just witnessed might have followed behind them at a distance. Then she spoke. 'Extraordinary,' she said.

'Yes. Let's get home.'

But his wife was still staring off in the direction they had come. 'Do you know who I thought I saw?' she said. 'Near the chapel. On the other side of the road to us. I must be mad.'

But Mallen had seen her, too, moving between the crowds and the shadows cast by the flames. Glowing, illuminated. That woman, he thought, is fascinated by destruction. You could even think, looking at her in the burning streets, that she was in her element. She had no sense of personal danger, though it was danger, surely, that drew her. These were the fires of ruin and chaos. He had never met anyone like her.

The magistrates stood by while for four days the mob pulled down houses and chapels and rampaged through the streets. Anyone thought to be a Catholic was attacked with sticks and knives, the clothes torn off their backs, their houses broken into and everything burned. Food and wine were hauled up from the cellars, and there were fierce, wild parties around the fires. The Guards had no orders to fire and were next to useless. The Lord Mayor prevaricated. On Monday, the people who had destroyed the chapel in Moorfields marched through the main streets of the city, carrying the pulpit and other spoils to Lord Gordon's house in Welbeck Street, and burning them in the fields behind. Another group pulled to pieces the house of the King's tallow chandler, Samson Rainforth, and stocks of fats, boxes of candles and other combustibles were carried into the street and set on fire. Rainforth, though not a Catholic, had helped to put down the riot at the Sardinian Chapel, and his name had appeared in the papers as having given evidence against the men who had been arrested. He was dragged out of bed and forced to watch the destruction.

In Moorfields itself, the house of an Irish businessman called Malo was destroyed by several bands of rioters who threatened to murder the people inside if the door wasn't opened immediately. Malo was a natural target because he employed a lot of Irishmen, at lower wages than any Englishman would take. He and his wife and daughters fled over the roof, but the eldest son fainted the instant the mob rushed into the house, and even now his life and intellect were said to be not free of danger. The crowds rose up suddenly and alarmingly, like a river flooding; on the corner of a peaceful street there were suddenly a thousand men, armed with clubs and bludgeons. Newgate had been burned to the ground, as had Justice Fielding's house in Covent Garden, and several others. Many more were said to be threatened, and forty Foot Guards had been ordered to Langdale's house on Holborn Hill, for the protection of his distillery. Langdale was a Catholic, with twelve young children, and his distillery was one of the largest in London.

'Rainforth?' said Mallen. 'Samson Rainforth?'

'Yes. Why?' While Julia was reading from the newspaper, Mallen had been mending his pens. 'No reason,' he said without looking up. 'I think you should go to Kensington.'

'I'm sorry, no.'

'Hammersmith, then. Go and spend a few days with my mother.'

'I can't possibly, I'm staying here. You won't get anything to eat if I go away. Mrs Trent has gone to her family.'

'Ellen can feed me.'

'She can't. I'm not moving from this house, James. I won't go out into the streets, but I'm staying in London. I wish you wouldn't go out, either.'

'I have to.' Mallen, in the middle of all this, had found one reason after another to go back to Bedford Row. He went at dawn, when the streets were wide with light, in the middle of the morning, and then again after two o'clock when, in normal circumstances, Corney would be at Westminster. He went in the warm, crepuscular light of evening. Only twice did he actually go up to see his patient. And when he had walked the street once, he would walk it a second time. Occasionally he saw Lemuel Prager, motionless beside the pump, or limping on the other side of the street; once or twice, he felt like running at him with his arms outspread, and chasing him off like a massive crow.

It was the need to do something that took him there, the need for some sort of action, and then the need to see her without being seen himself. He couldn't get out of his head the sight of her lit by flames in Duke Street or Moorfields, the expression of attention on her face as things around her went to hell. And he knew, if he had not known it before, that he was in the iron sway of a growing obsession. It was an obsession, surely, when he could see the manifest stupidity in what he was doing, and still do it, and let it make him feel happy. If she did see him now, walking up and down the street, then what happened next must be left to fate or chance. He had no idea at all what he might do, or say to her, but just to think of that moment made him feel as if he had never been more charged with life. He knew that this behaviour was idiotic and humiliating, but he could not stop himself. 'I have to,' he said again. 'George Corney is in pain, it hurts him to move.'

'Well, all he has to do is to stay still; he doesn't need you to tell him that. London is going up in flames. I don't want our house burned to the ground.'

'It won't be.'

'I need a piece of chalk.'

'What on earth for?'

'I'm going to write on our door. I'm going to write *No Popery!* in very big letters. Unless you will do it. And I'm going to get up more candles, so that we can light our windows tonight, or they will break them.

George Corney stood behind his chair and tapped the air several times with his finger, as if trying to make a small hole in it. He leaned forward, and cast a worried look downwards, as if he were suspicious of the floor. There was a strong smell of brandy. 'My dear man,' he said, 'how can I help you?'

'I have come here, I hope, to help you.'

'Good, good,' said Corney. 'Sit down.' He swung round in a circle, like an old dog, then stood still again. 'I have just received a most threatening message relating to my own welfare and informing me that they are going to pull down my house tonight. I must find my wife. She must go to Chiswick.' He took a breath and seemed to hold it for too long. 'Although,' he said, 'to be perfectly honest, I've no idea where to look. I wish you'd see if you can find her. If they hurt her, I'll start another war.'

'I received a message that you were in pain.'

Corney waved his arm, revealing a torn seam in his sleeve. 'Not so much,' he said. His face was slack with drink. His eyes were red, and the skin surrounding the wound on his cheek was yellow with bruising.

'First things first,' said Corney. 'We find my wife. Next, a letter to the Commander-in-Chief. Mr and Mrs Corney present their compliments to Lord Amherst, and acquaint his Lordship that the mob threaten their house in Bedford Row, Holborn, and beseech instantly a party of Horse Guards to come to their assistance directly. I'll tell you the problem with that, Mallen. With so many of his regiments in America at the present moment, Lord Amherst is hard pressed, and when he does send troops to a danger spot, the officers in charge can find no magistrate to give them any orders. Judge for yourself what a defenceless situation the military are left in. Excuse me.' Corney began to lift his arm to pull the bellrope, but the movement hurt him too much. 'Holman!' he bellowed.

'Mr Corney, I am your doctor.'

'Of course you are.'

'I should really change the strapping on your chest.'

Corney shook his head for such a long time that he seemed to have no power to stop himself. By the look of him, he would soon be unconscious. I, too, must speak to Holman, thought Mallen. I must know how much opium this man is taking; at the least, he is going to make himself very constipated.

'Holman will find my wife,' said Corney. 'I hear, by the way, that they have burned Newgate to the ground. *No Popery* is nothing but a war cry now; it means very little. They don't even know, half of them, what it is they're protesting about, only that they can smell the stink of violence and of vengeance. The levelling spirit has taken over; it's the rich they're after now. Lord Mansfield's precious library has been burned. Just round the corner! The collection of a lifetime.' Corney looked round the room at his own books and manuscripts, and his face became soft with self-pity and drugged alarm. 'Five people killed outright, and seven others wounded. My servant has been there this morning. Holman!' he yelled again, grabbing the chair for support. He said something else, but the words trailed as he lost the strength to finish them. His face changed colour. Mallen grabbed the bucket of sand from beside the fireplace, and Corney threw up into it.

He met Frank Holman on the stairs. Mrs Corney had gone out in the carriage early that morning, and he had no idea where she might be found.

'I thought –' said Mallen, then he shook his head and carried on down the stairs. The carriage had not, then, been destroyed.

Walking back through Holborn, he ran into Philip. 'Come with me,' said the apothecary. 'Come and look at what's left of Newgate.'

'I'm on my way to see Patrick Bright.'

'You can still see him. I'll come back with you.'

'You've left the shop?'

Philip pushed his hands down into his pockets, and leaned forward a little as he walked. 'I've closed the shop. I've had so much money extorted from me this morning by different gangs, I can't afford to stay open. I'm not in the mood to, not after being threatened with a piece of iron railing this long. For that matter, we're no better off out here in the streets. If you've any money on you, you'd better give it over when they ask for it. Behind every young boy with his hand out, there's a big brute on a horse. They're all armed, anyway, with railings from Lord Mansfield's house. We've applied for a patrol in our street.'

'Are there more troops?'

'They're pouring into London at every avenue. Country boys, bog-trotters. Hyde Park is full of tents and men marching up and down. I've just been there.'

'Will they use force without waiting for the magistrates?'

'They've orders to, but I doubt it. They've never been to London in their lives, probably never had their field pieces loaded.'

As they walked along Holborn, they passed Langdale's distillery on their right, at the top of Fetter Lane. The crowds outside were huge, and very drunk. Langdale himself was standing outside, distributing free gin and brandy in an effort to keep them out of the premises. 'Listen,' said Mallen, 'I really ought to go and see Patrick. I don't like the look of this.'

Dyer's Buildings were on the west side of the distillery, between Castle Street and Barnard's Inn. The orange cat lay sprawled beside a stack of roof tiles, and there was a ripe, hot smell of straw from the nearby coaching stables. 'He's shut up shop as well,' said Philip.

Mallen knocked on the window. Franny's face appeared on the other side of the glass, but was quickly replaced by her father's. Soon they heard the bolts being drawn on the workshop door. 'You've got your topknots on, I see,' he said grimly, nodding at the ribbons in their hats.

'We were concerned,' said Mallen. 'You can't get near the distillery for the mob.'

Patrick led them into the workshop. 'And Langdale,' he said, 'is passing out liquor like there was no tomorrow. Sit down, sit.'

Philip looked around him and chose a walnut library armchair, covered in petit point. Patrick nodded, and he sat. Mallen perched on a stool next to Franny's.

'Last night at the prison,' said Patrick, 'they helped themselves from the cellars and drank it out of their hats. Out of their shoes, and buckets. There was drunken convicts going up and down all night, looking for a blacksmith.'

'Can't you go somewhere?' said Philip.

'No, Mr Little, I can't. Nowhere to go, for a start, and not to mention I won't anyway. Move your backside, Fran.'

Franny jumped off her stool and grinned up at Philip. 'No Popery!' she sang.

'It's not funny, young lady. Go and help your mother.'

'I'm helping you.' She looked up into her father's stern eyes, then turned and went through into the house.

'What I want to know,' said Patrick, 'is must we always have someone to hate?'

No one answered him. Philip picked up a piece of gimp and began to thread it between his fingers.

'Religion,' said Patrick, raising his eyebrows and looking at the neat row of tools on the workshop wall. He shook his head. 'It has precious little to do with religion,' he went on. 'Not now. It might of had, to start with, but not now. It's the poor who've come out now, against the people who have insulted and ignored them all their lives. It's not the Pope they hate. No, it's because the Irish work for Langdale for half of what an Englishman will take, and live off spuds and gin. Why not burn down the prison? Stinking hell den that it was. No, gentlemen, I can't completely blame them. It's only a pity it won't do them any good.'

'What will you do?' said Mallen.

'What can I do? Nothing. Sit tight. Wherever they go, they won't come down here. No reason to.'

'Was there any attack on the Bank?' said Philip.

Patrick shook his head. 'Not that I've heard. There was large bodies of horse and foot soldiers coming past the top of the road last night on their way to guard it. Richard and Franny are at each other's throats today, for lack of sleep and all the blasted excitement.'

'I'll have another look at Richard,' said Mallen.

Patrick nodded. 'Much appreciated. Go on through, they're all there.'

Franny was on the table, barefoot, with her arms outspread, declaiming. 'I will be deep in the cold, cold ground, before I forget this dastardly act –'

'Get down before you fall down, madam,' said Patrick. 'Where's your mother?'

'Upstairs with Michael.'

'And Richard?'

Franny lay flat down on the table-top and peered into the space underneath it. 'Lord Fatty Fartface, Pa wants you,' she said.

'God help us,' said Patrick. 'I don't know if it's worse outdoors or in.'

The prison was still smouldering. Sightseers peered through the twists of smoke, standing apart from each other, chewing bread rolls and saying nothing. The roof was gone, the doors and bars. Some convicts had returned, hungry and afraid, looking for someone who would lock them up again. One man had found the place where his cell had stood, and lay on the charred ground, sleeping. Two or three others, out of their minds with drink, had returned to smash up again what had just been destroyed. As Mallen looked on, he saw the pitching form of Lemuel Prager, curving through the crowd. Then, beyond the cripple, a flash of yellow silk. But that dress was ruined, he thought. She stood so still, and seemed so transfixed, that she might have walked there in her sleep. Then again, he thought, she may have any number of yellow dresses. 'I've seen enough,' he said to Philip. 'We should get back.'

'For what? All your patients have forgotten they're ill and, as for the rest, they need surgeons now, not physicians.'

'You can stay if you want.'

'James, wait, you won't get through that way.'

Their shoes and stockings were covered in soot. Mallen's own heartbeat alarmed him. It gave him physical pain, slamming against his ribs and pushing a hard knot up into his throat. Something's very wrong, he thought; it shouldn't be doing this. 'Come or stay, but I can't wait,' he said.

'What on earth's the hurry? All right, we'll go. I'm coming.'

She looked over at that moment, and saw them. Mallen stopped suddenly, and turned. She was lovely. She was unparalleled, a goddess. 'Just a minute,' he said. Philip ran straight into him, and steadied them both with an arm. 'Wait for me.' Mallen walked straight up to her, and made a bow. 'Mrs Corney,' he said.

She looked calm, even thoughtful. 'It's you!'

'You shouldn't be here.'

She laughed. 'You think that this time I will get myself arrested?'

'I'm afraid that sooner or later you'll get hurt. You can see for yourself, things happen very quickly. Your husband's mad with worry. He's looking for you, he wants you to go home.' Never before, not even with Julia, had he felt so close to lifting a woman's wrist to his lips.

Philip had followed, and was introduced. Mrs Corney smiled and turned, and started to walk slowly over the rubble. 'Where's your carriage?' said Mallen.

'I sent it home. It's not very far, I'm going to walk back. It's dreadful to think, isn't it, that one has lived so close, for so long, to this horrible place.'

'Some of these men here are dangerous.' He could still feel the heat in the ground under his feet. She looked, as they walked through the ashes, like a risen phoenix. All the stink of the prison, the slime on the walls and the rot in its floors had been burned to cinders, and here she was, wandering through them as if she belonged.

She had been watching her feet. She looked up. 'I feel like a ghost, don't you, moving with perfect ease through these walls. Only yesterday they were cells, they were impenetrable. Inescapable.'

'Let me take you home.'

To his surprise, she didn't resist. She took his arm, and smiled at Philip, and they started to pick their way out of the ruins. Lemuel Prager watched them from beside a charred wall. 'That man –' said Mallen.

'I don't mind him.'

'But you must! He is not all there, in his head.'

'He never comes closer than he is now, and he has never said a word to me. He's harmless, Dr Mallen.' Mallen looked back over his shoulder.

'I know him,' said Philip. 'I see him from time to time in Chapel Street.'

'He has a house there, yes.'

'A house?' Mallen had not imagined him to be a man of property. On the other hand, why not. He guided her past a large hole filled with water. 'Will you go to Chiswick?'

She did not answer him. They made the rest of the way to Bedford Row talking about Samson Rainforth and other victims of the violence.

'Lemuel Prager,' said Philip, when they had left her at the door of her house. He kicked a stone into the road, where it landed in a filthy puddle. 'I wonder what that's all about.'

'I didn't know you knew him. Who is he?'

'He was born in Germany. His father was a Prussian general. Prager came over here to live when he was a boy. His mother died, I suppose. Anyway, she was English, her family was. He went into the Army, here, when he left school. After that I don't know, except that he had half his leg blown off in the war, on Belle-Île. John Hunter was there, with the expeditionary force. He patched him up, kept him there for a few months after the island surrendered, then sent him home. He had three or four goes with fever, I think. He used to come to me for salves and paregoric, then he disappeared. I don't know him now, not any more. What's he doing following Mrs Corney around?'

'God only knows.'

8

Glebe House

1830

Mallen went out. Even now, he felt that he had to take only a few more steps, to find his way round one more corner, and he would find her. There was something inevitable in the very air of the cold days of early spring. The moment was so close that it was like something that could be touched.

It was not a question of time. Time swirled round his ankles with all the shape of fog. The present was not a moment but a space the size and dimension of London. In the solid world it was marked by change, it was new mills and Regent's Park and wider, brighter roads; it was new mansions in Lambeth, and villas on St George's Fields.

London was growing, London was always growing. Streets were eternally being torn up or demolished or rebuilt. Every other person was a builder or bricklayer, and the air was thick with clouds of plaster dust. There was a bridge at Hammersmith. Houses had become part of terraces and terraces had become rows creeping northward out of the city. At night, he hid in the bright glare of gas lamps and roamed the streets round Drury Lane, through a litter of wrappings and rotten oranges. He went to the top of the Monument and looked down on the shipping and the church spires, the hospitals, prisons, parks and squares; the smoking chimneys, the distant hills.

He sought out crowds. Mallen became the crowd; he was outside theatres as they emptied, he shuffled with bands of beggars and ran towards every accident, every quarrel. He spent days at Smithfield among the herds of fat oxen, the thousands of drovers and cattle brokers, in the dung and rain and the shunting of pigs. He heard its ghosts, the cries of witches and heretics burned or boiled alive on the site. He watched for fires. He ran through deserted streets until he came to places thick with men and women, where the pavements were full of inordinate life.

The King died. The nation showed almost complete indifference to the news. Shops were shut and church bells rang on the day of his funeral, but there was little appearance of mourning in the streets. Mallen heard the minute guns boom in the Long Walk, but saw no signs of sorrow.

He lost hope again. His certainty turned on him. Wherever he walked, he could smell eggs, overcooked and hard. No one had seen her, no one had heard a word. And so he turned on his heels and went back. He stood for a while in Hammersmith and watched the walls of the distillery, but moved on without going in. He went, once again, a mile beyond it, to the Corneys' old house, in Chiswick.

The house was empty. Different people had lived here, over the years, but there was no one here now, they had all gone, and the rooms were black with shadows and old smoke stains. There were sticks of charcoal in the grates, and small piles of yew berries on the floor, brought in by squirrels. Mallen shut himself in an attic room and lay down in the dark.

During the day, he listened to the language from the river, the buggery bastard yelling of the watermen. He heard birds and carriages, bells and children. At night there was the wind, and the watch. It was not unlike the years he had spent within the walls of his father's house. He settled into the murky cold, he became silt. Up to now, it was as if only hope had given him any form, and now he had no hope, he was like a layer of dust. He felt the stone again, as it came down on his head, and then a second time and then a third. He felt the loneliness of death and the awareness, in those moments, that he was being robbed of his life in the street, with no one there to stop it.

One night he heard steps on the attic stairs. A laden sound, heavy and slow. He listened. The footsteps reached the top of the stairs, and the sound became level, pacing. He fixed his eyes on the place where he knew the door to be. The sound came closer, and paused.

He stood. A thin line of yellow light slipped under the door. He moved through a crack into the room. Two men stood in front of him, casting short and agitated shadows in the light of an oil lamp. Mallen heard the punched-out words of a one-sided argument.

'Triple murder,' said the taller of the two. He was narrow and round-shouldered, dressed in a suit and hat of ginger tweed. The other one Mallen recognised. He had owned the house for a while, though he had hardly ever been there. He was shorter than the first man by six inches, and wore an extraordinary light blue coat, and a pair of soft calf boots. The room was as empty as the others, and the tall man ducked the beams as he spoke. 'I know where it is,' he said, 'and what's in it, and I am going to show it to the world and the courts and all the life annuities people.' As he spoke, he held a key in front of his face, and he beat out the words with it. 'You're going to hang, Connelly. You will never get to France. God! Imagine what they'll do to you when they find what's inside. What is it? Antimony, arsenic, strychnine? Books on how to use them?'

They looked to Mallen like madmen, dancing around each other, jagged with shadows. Their presence here, in this house and at this time, was incomprehensible, and it appalled him.

If the little man was disturbed, he didn't show it. His eyes casually followed a moth caught in the glare of the lamp. Mallen could hear the low *whup* of the wick as it burned, and the sound the moth made as it bashed itself on the glass. Connelly turned to his accuser. 'Oh, go and open the damned trunk, Bluett,' he said. 'Get it out of your system.'

'They won't pay up, you know. They'll hang you. Look at you, where do you get your clothes?'

Connelly pinched his nose between two fingers, and sniffed. Now that the other man had made him think of it, he brushed a gummy cobweb from his sleeve. He looked up into the shadows beyond the light of the lamp and nearly smiled. 'You know this house is haunted, don't you?' he said.

'You haven't a hope in hell.'

Connelly ignored him. 'Why do you suppose it's empty,' he said. 'Why d'you think I moved out, why does no one live here any more? It's the noises, to start with. And then they wake up in the night with such a weight pressing down on them in their beds that they can't breathe and they think that they'll die. Things start moving around of their own accord. Big sharp things, mostly. The place is permanently for sale. What drives them out finally is the smell.'

'Shut up.'

'You can't want money, you know I haven't any.'

'I've seen you coming in and out of here,' said Bluett. 'I know what you've been doing, you horrible little man. Checking your stocks, so you can murder someone else. There's a corridor in hell for men like you.'

Connelly held up a hand to stop him saying any more. 'Did you hear that?' he hissed, one arm raised and arched, one pointing to the side, fingers spread. He looked like a dancer. 'No, nothing,' he said. 'I don't know how you stand it, Jack, coming here to an empty house in the dead of night.'

'I don't come here, you do.'

'I'm made of sterner stuff than you, and I only come when I have to, to escape my creditors. Sometimes, a man has to sink out of sight for a while, even if it means keeping company with ghosts. Ssh!'

Bluett's eyes widened, as if he could use them to hear with. 'I heard nothing.'

'You're right, it wasn't anything. You didn't bring a drop of whisky, did you? Never mind, no.' He brought a flask out of his own coat pocket and unscrewed the top, nodding once or twice to himself. 'She was the wife of a Member of Parliament,' he said. He spoke quietly. Mallen slid all the way into the room and into the shadows behind the two men. He didn't know what they were doing here – he understood none of it, except that the little one was talking about Augusta Corney.

'She found someone else,' said Connelly. 'She brought him back, in the dead of night, to this house.'

'Liar!' Mallen screamed. The sound was like the creak of an old board.

'For months last year,' whispered Connelly, 'it was quiet – they even thought they'd got a buyer for the place, but it's started up again, the sound of tragic weeping in the night, the smell of death, the lost and wandering shape of a woman. I've seen her myself, only a day or two ago.'

Mallen flew round the room, hitting the walls as the moth had hit the lamp. Two days ago! The man was lying. Mallen had been here a thousand times, more than a thousand, and never once had he seen her, nor any other ghost. How did this man know anything? He didn't know: he was wrong, he knew nothing. He slowed down, and hugged the shadows again. The possibility that she had been here in recent days, that they had been in the same house together and not known it, entered his understanding like the news of a tragedy, in pieces. He raised a long wail, a sound that this time penetrated the very walls, and reached the ears of the two men. They stood, rigid and slightly twisted, like trees; there was a tiny whistle deep in the throat of one of them. Then they ran for their lives. The oil lamp caught on Connelly's blue coat. It went over and smashed, and the dust caught fire like a blue and flickering sheet.

The house burned all night. Mallen stood on the grass above the river's edge and watched. Villagers came out, coats pulled over their night clothes, faces thrilled with disbelief. The clock on the church struck the early hours like a knell. The flames, even as they died down, lit the garden and the river; they were reflected in the slow moving water like the flames of a burning ship. Then he saw her.

Had she been there all the time, all night? Where had she come from, why had he not seen her until now? Standing in the crowd with spellbound eyes, a shadow in the creeping dawn, on the other side of the smoke and flying sparks. He tried to run. His legs, though no longer flesh and blood, were like the legs of a man at the scene of an accident. It was an effort like an act of memory to make them work at all, and then he moved with all the difficulty of a dream. She turned, she was going. He stumbled over the edges of the fire, over black-scaled timbers and ashes and flames.

There. On the road behind the house, moving swiftly in the dreary light. He shouted her name, shoving his whole great effort into the sound, which shrank on the air like a bubble of spit. She turned in through the gates of Chiswick House, home to the Dukes of Devonshire, and he followed, and found himself in the grey dawn, circling its walls and flying over the dew-soaked grass of the gardens. Above him, huge cedars stood up against the sky as if they had just crept out of it. There were paths between yew hedges, and the compact shapes of sleeping waterfowl beside a small river. Augusta swiftly trod her way through all of this, through smells of early wood-smoke, and a still morning mist above the water. Did she even know where she was going? He no longer knew her mind. Once he believed he could guess her thoughts, once he had known the direction of all her wishes, but now she was a shape in the dawn that he must follow and find.

There was a steep bridge over the river, and she disappeared underneath it. He stood on its highest point and looked, but there was no sign of her. He climbed down into the water, but she wasn't there. He called her name again, and it echoed on the arching stones. He felt something slip in his mind, and land on the flat, hard edge of fury. He lifted his voice again and yelled, the way that those knocked out by life yell at God. He started running, and moved with a speed that was next to useless, for he saw nothing. In the place where his heart once was, an urgent and hopeless message knocked against his chest. Could she really not know that he was looking for her? Were the ways of this improbable world so perpetually obscured, so difficult? If just once – once! – she would only stand still, and turn around. God knows, she had never made, on this side of the grave, any effort to find him. For all Mallen knew, she had forgotten his very existence. His anger was like small, toothed animals, running up and down inside him. He made himself slow down, swishing his open fists against the flat sides of a hedge. For hours he wandered the grounds, swamped at first by birdsong, and then by growing silence. He looked behind every tree, every statue, in the greenhouses and on all the shaded walks. He stayed there until Franny came, from Hammersmith, and found him and waited until he would come back with her.

9

Langdale's Distillery

1780

There was such a smell of smoke everywhere that Julia kept moving through the house, from front to back, to check that it was not a neighbour's, or their own, that was burning. None of them had slept properly for several nights, and no one was thinking of much else besides the sweeping plunder of the city, the fires, the paralysis of the magistracy, the weakness of the military and all the dire warnings that the Bank, the rest of the prisons, the palaces, the Arsenal and the Inns of Court would be burned to the ground like Newgate. Every last criminal and villain in the city was about to be released, as well as the lunatics in Bethlem, and the lions in the Tower. The streets were full of mad people in swift motion, and all day long they had heard yelling and horses' hooves.

'James, have something to eat.'

'I will, in a minute.'

Even that didn't remind them. Julia had spent the day with the maid, Ellen, trying to make a pudding, but the cloth had leaked and the water had boiled dry twice. Mrs Trent had gone to be with her family.

'There's cold meat,' said Ellen. 'Some bread. Pickles.'

'That'll do. No one's hungry.'

They only remembered at about four o'clock. 'What day is it?' Julia asked the maid.

'Wednesday.'

'God almighty.' She found Mallen in his study. 'Today is Wednesday,' she said.

Mallen looked up from the letter he was writing. 'Am I supposed to be somewhere?'

'Let me just tell you what we have in the house. Some chicken, from yesterday, and cold duck. Malt, flour, sugar, salt. The remains of the beans your father sent, enough for two, at a stretch.'

'You and Ellen have them, I don't want much.'

'Bread, celery, and three pounds of bottled plums.'

'I'm sure we'll live.' Mallen put his pen down. 'We'll find something open tomorrow. The whole of London hasn't come to a standstill.'

'James,' she said quietly. 'It is almost four o'clock. We have invited eight people to dinner. Today, now. With ourselves, that makes ten. James?'

He sat there, turning his pen over in his hands, until she was infuriated. 'James, wake up!' she said. 'For God's sake think of something.'

'They won't come.'

'They will.'

He put the pen down. 'You go and change. Ellen can lay the table and find some silver. I'll be back in an hour.'

He avoided the trouble spots as best as he could, making a tour of the street-sellers between Holborn and Covent Garden. He bought fried fish, roasted ribs of beef, baked potatoes, biscuits, rhubarb and currant tarts; almond cake and cherry pie. In the market, he bought cucumber and cheese. He found three different kinds of grapes; peaches, currants, and a pineapple. It was the tail-end of the day, and he checked them all for rot and bruises.

Perhaps it was the champagne, or a certain *esprit de guerre*, or the fact that Ellen ran herself off her feet, but the meal was a success. They lit candles in all the windows, and the shine off the silver and off the glass made the whole room brilliant with light.

At nine o'clock, Philip arrived. Langdale's was in flames. 'Give me a minute,' said Mallen.

They could see it from the windows, the grey stains of smoke against the evening sky, strange and stormy. Mallen told everyone to leave. He put Julia and Ellen into the Greys' carriage with them. 'Don't come back,' he said to his wife. 'Stay with Louisa, and I'll come and get you. However long it takes me, stay at Percy Street and wait.'

'James!' She was screaming. 'What are you doing, where are you going?'

'To the hospital.'

'The hospital?' said Philip.

'Of course not, no. Come on.'

The heat was furious, and pinnacles of flame were reaching for the sky. The troops that had been stationed at Langdale's had been called off to the Bank, and Holborn was wrapped in fire all the way to Fleet Market and St Andrew's church. There were men and children everywhere; women, street boys, dogs.

And gin. Gin ran in a torrent down the kennel in the middle of the street, unrectified, raw spirit. The stills had burst and overflowed and the liquor was rushing up into the gutters and between the cobbles and bursting into flames. Men and women drank it off the street and came up howling. They lay where they fell, out of their heads with pain. It was pure poison. They drank until they choked, until their throats burned and bled. People were dragged from the cellars on fire from head to foot. They crawled through pools of flame and vomit and over burning piles of furniture; a fire engine played neat spirits onto the flames. From inside the warehouse came the screams and laughter of drunken people burning to death. The two men tried to drag the wounded out of the way of the blaze, but they were beaten back by the heat and suffocation. The noise was like a gale, a roar of flame and massive splinterings. Philip stood spitting soot and beating the flames out on his own sleeve. Mallen grabbed his arm and the big man yelped with pain. They ran together towards Dyer's Buildings. One man took hold of Mallen's coat and peered into his face with an open mouth. Then his head dropped, and he threw up between his own feet. Mallen shook him off, then felt another hand on his.

'Doctor –' He turned, his eyes burning, his vision almost black. It was Augusta Corney. She was dark with soot, and drenched with sweat. 'For God's sake, Mrs Corney!' His voice was hoarse. He punched the words out of his lungs. 'Go home, please.'

'I can't. Even if I wanted to, the streets are blocked. You won't get through, believe me.' She shook her head, and started to walk beside him. As they rounded the corner into Dyer's Buildings, he gripped her wrist and turned her round to look at him. Her face was pale, and she was shaking and dirty. 'What on earth are you doing here? You can't keep putting yourself in danger like this, it's mad.' He was hurting her. He let go of her wrist. 'Stay close to me or to this man here,' he said, indicating Philip. 'There is something we must do, and after that, I am going to take you home. Do you understand?' His throat was raw now. Augusta Corney closed her eyes. She opened her mouth to speak, then shook her head. 'Do you?' he yelled.

'I understand.'

For a moment Mallen could only think of running. He dropped his head and pressed a finger between his eyes. This was what it was like when the world was turned on its head. There was no arguing, only the next thing to be done, and then the next.

People were rushing everywhere, trying to save what they could. At the top of the narrow cul-de-sac, one building had already begun to burn. Lemuel Prager swept past in the light of the flames, and disappeared. Mallen wiped the sweat out of his eyes. He turned to look for Philip again, and ran smack into Patrick Bright. He was carrying a chair, half-covered with brocade, and Mallen felt the back of it slam into his ribs. Patrick turned a circle, looking both lost and furious. Mallen took his elbow, and steered him back towards the house. Franny was standing outside, with Robert and the baby; Hannah had gone upstairs to make bundles of clothes and bedding. Mallen sent someone to get her, while Philip went to the coaching stables to find some means of getting them all out, but either the horses had been moved away from the fire or they had already been hired out. Carriages had been leaving London all day.

Mallen stood thinking, his eyes on the ground.

'We can take my carriage.' Mrs Corney had to tell him twice before he heard her. 'It's not far from here. If we go together, we can get through.'

They had no choice. Philip picked up the children, one by one, and passed them to the adults. Patrick stayed. 'I won't go,' he said. He turned a circle on his own doorstep, and went back into the workshop. There was no arguing with him, and no time for it.

Their passage through Holborn was appalling. They struggled through twisted faces, rigid shoulders, open mouths and running eyes. They lost each other in the clouds of smoke, and tripped on iron cask-hoops. Mallen fell once, stumbled and righted himself, and when he looked, he could no longer see which way he was going. His eyes burned, and his chest felt staved-in. Suddenly, he couldn't see Hannah or Franny; they had been taken off in unknown directions by the bullying surge, and a bolt of fear went through him that they were trampled underfoot. He tried to turn, hemmed in on every side, and shouted their names until there were tears in his eyes. Then someone had him by the arm, and pulled him to his right. It was Mrs Corney, and they were in Brownlow Street. 'Wait, stop,' he gasped. The child in his arms was silent and still, and Mallen suffered a moment of certainty that he had killed it, had smothered it against his chest. 'Michael,' he said. 'Michael.' The child looked up into his face, and away again. He hoisted him higher, and started to run. Mrs Corney, miraculously, had Hannah and Franny by her side.

The coachman looked as if he had put a whole peach in his mouth. Corney's horses were jumpy and kicked at the poles and threw back their heads. 'Where are we going?' said Franny. It was the first time anyone had asked.

'Hammersmith.'

The house was dark. They all climbed out of the coach, crushed and dry-mouthed. The children were white-faced and pathetic with exhaustion. Franny's eyes had coins of dark beneath them.

His parents were country people, they had been in bed for hours. The kitchen was ticking with silence and the cooling stove. The dogs sat in front of it, old and useless and sweet to strangers. His mother went upstairs and opened chests and presses and made up beds. Hannah went with her. Through the floors, Mallen heard the quiet murmur of their talk and the low snap of sheets. Franny sat at the kitchen table, swinging her legs.

'I'm going to take Mrs Corney home,' Mallen said to his father. Nicholas put a poker into the stove and riddled the ashes. His face and arms were brown from the sun. He pushed a new log onto the embers, and straightened. A bubble of water spat under the kettle.

'I'm only going to Chiswick,' said Mrs Corney. 'It's less than a mile. My coachman will take me.'

'No, I'll go with you,' said Mallen. Franny looked up and gave him a long, level look. Her chin stuck out like a small promontory, and the inside of her lip was caught between her teeth. Then she straightened her back, and sighed.

'Hungry?' he asked her.

'I don't know. Where's Pa?'

'He's at home, looking after things. Can you make toast without burning it?'

Her elbows slid along the top of the table. 'No,' she whispered. Mallen saw something move under the bodice of her dress. Wilkes. He winked at Franny, but her face didn't move.

His mother, when she came down, brought out bacon and bread and a white cheese. Augusta Corney sat at the kitchen table as if it was what she was used to, and ate with dirty hands. Every time Mallen looked at her, he felt Franny's eyes on him. A fox barked outside. When they had finished eating, Mallen stood. 'I won't be long,' he said. Franny looked up at him; there was bacon grease on her chin. Mallen cupped her face in his hand and wiped away the smear. Suddenly, he felt close to tears. 'You must wash your face,' he said. She shrugged. 'I mean it, Fran. All of you. You've soot in your eyes, and it'll hurt if you don't. Bathe them well, and your hands, too. Look at these paws.' He lifted her hands and placed a kiss on each of them. 'Disgusting,' he said. 'I won't be long. When I get back you'll be asleep.'

Franny nodded her head up and down, then shook it side to side. 'I'm waiting for Pa,' she whispered.

'I can go to Chiswick,' said Philip. 'I don't see why you should.'

'No.' Mallen jumped at his own sharpness. He looked at his friend and tried to smile. Philip was sweating. Part of his sleeve had burned away. 'You're hurt,' said Mallen. 'I'll find something to put on it. Finish your drink.' He turned to his father. 'You go to bed,' he said. 'I can let myself back in.'

Nicholas rubbed the bristles on his chin. 'I don't know if I should let the carts go into town,' he said.

'I don't know, Father.'

'Have to, I suppose.' He looked his son up and down and made a face at him. 'Better take some of my clothes when you get back. You're black.'

The only light came from the lamp on the outside of the carriage. In the hedges on either side of them, the fat heads of cow parsley loomed and vanished. Mallen and Augusta sat and stared into each other's faces without turning or speaking or wondering who might see them. Their features leapt with shadows and the uneven road. Mallen's exhaustion had gone. Something big and flickering filled his chest and tapped the back of his ribs, but the children were safe, Julia was safe, the fires and the roasting bodies were six miles behind him. He opened his mouth to speak, but instead found himself coughing out his guts.

'Spit,' said Augusta Corney. It was the first thing she had said since bidding his parents goodbye. His head was almost between his knees. He looked up at her, baffled. She was holding out a handkerchief. 'You're full of soot,' she said. 'Spit.'

The handkerchief was a tiny square of lace. He leaned forward and hawked out of the window. Whatever he had been about to say, and whatever might have come of it, was gone. 'Where are your children?' he said. He hadn't realised that he knew she had any.

'In Dulwich. I have two boys, they are at school there. They'll be safe.' She looked out of the window as she spoke, onto the jolting dark. He thought he saw loss in her face, something grave and sad and, as it raised his compassion, it renewed the fear in him, made his heart swell and knock.

'Thank you,' he said. 'If it wasn't for you . . . without this carriage, I don't know what we would have done.'

She wasn't interested in his thanks, though, and waved them away. 'I watched a man burn to death,' she said.

Mallen's pity reached even deeper. They shared, in the rattling silence of the carriage, the terrible human thing that they had seen, and Mallen knew he would soon reach out and touch the mark that it had left on her.

Dear God, he thought.

They turned into a short drive that curved around the front of the house. His eyes were stinging again, and he wiped them on his sleeve, pressing his face into the crook of his arm. When the carriage stopped, Augusta Corney didn't move. For a long time, she sat looking at her hands. Then she seemed to decide something, and Mallen helped her down.

The door was opened by a servant. Augusta looked up as she mounted the steps, like someone leaving everything behind. Mallen thought she was going to turn and walk down again – he even put out a hand to stop her. 'James,' she said.

Now he understood his fear. He knew that all he had to do was to suspend all thought, to step outside its region and act on instinct alone. He was in a world gone mad, after all. Everything he knew about her crowded his head, and with it all his own stability, all his loves, the long, extraordinary ribbon of life in front of him. He felt her hand take his, and heard the breath stammer in her chest. 'Go in,' he said.

'James!' It was a cry, a whisper. It was choked with soot and longing. It took away his strength, it ran through his limbs and made him fold. 'Go in,' he said again. She moved her hand to his face, and made him look at her. In a few seconds, he thought, our whole lives can change. Fate had even provided him with a solid threshold. He saw himself step into the house, the thin light of a few candles, empty rooms.

He knew how his hand would scoop her waist, how his lips would find her throat. He saw destruction and outrage drop away with their clothes, as he pressed his face against her skin. Now, he thought. Now his hand reached out, now he felt her cheek beneath his palm, now the row of buttons on her spine. Then he looked down at his hands, and saw to his wonder that they hadn't moved at all. He lifted her fingers to his lips, then turned and went back down the steps. She said his name again. Mallen could see nothing. He walked away from the house, the gravel loud under his feet.

Part Three

I

Fever

1783

Mallen went slowly up the stairs to his study. He was followed by his small son, William. It was ten in the morning, and he had just come back from attending a long labour in Piccadilly. As he sat down at his desk, he tried to remember if he had ever thought this through, the fact that he would never get the sleep he wanted. He pulled a sheaf of bills towards him and picked one off the top. It was still a mystery to him, after all these years, why Philip never did proper bills in March. Whichever way you looked at it, there was no reasonable answer. The man had been married for almost a year, but it had made no difference to his paperwork.

William tucked himself into a corner of the window seat, and propped himself on his elbow while he dug in a pocket for something. Mallen put the bills back down on his desk and rubbed his eyes. He doubted he would ever get used to having his own son, his own children. We shall have to move soon, he thought; the house is too small, and there are too many stairs.

It was three years since the riots. When they ended, London had been full of soldiers, so that it looked like another city, somewhere else. Its hospitals were filled with wounded. Three hundred people had been killed, and four hundred and fifty prisoners rounded up and put in sheds in the ruins of the King's Bench and in St Paul's Churchyard. A hundred and sixty men were brought to trial, and twenty-five were hanged.

At night, when it was over, there was no noise, anywhere, only a profound stillness. Most people still didn't know what had hit them and, because they didn't know, they worried that it would happen again. They remembered that they were sick or nervous, and feared they would give birth to monsters. Mallen was run off his feet. He bought himself a new carriage. With great effort, he put Augusta Corney out of his mind, although for several months he went from one place to another in a mood very similar to grief. He had to remind himself, over and over, that nothing had happened, that his life had not changed. Equally, he had to tell himself that his sudden moods of elation, of feeling that anything might happen, were made out of nothing. It had been a time of danger, and it was over. In January of the following year, his mother died and was buried in Hammersmith. He felt exposed by her death, as if he was suddenly more open to the sky.

Julia had not even known that she was pregnant. She was never sick, and in the chaos of the riots and in the weeks before and after them, she had not observed the changes in her body, and if she had, she put them down to other causes. At a time when they had been closest to despairing, though, she had already conceived. As she grew, Mallen began to feel the joy that he had taught himself to feel no longer, but still it was as if the greater part of his heart had been made smaller and sadder. What was worse, he found himself irritated by his wife's growing beauty, by the way she gazed into space, and her sleepy accommodation of everything. His feelings for her were clouded by ambivalence and inattention, just at the time when they should have been pure.

William had his nose against the window pane, and was trying to make out the shapes below him on the street through the thick distorting glass.

Somewhere, at some time during that year, his unhappiness

had vanished. His son was born five months after the rioting ended, and now there was another one on the way. Franny Bright came every day to help. She was fourteen now, tall and open-faced and full of illogical wisdom.

Outside, it was a bright April day, with fleets of high cloud in a blue sky. He leaned forward over the desk and found what he had been looking for. Then he stood and picked his son up from the window seat. 'Come on, you,' he said. 'You're going downstairs. I have to go and see someone.'

'Who?'

'Mr Little, if you must know.'

William peered into his father's face from a distance of three inches, with a stern look, then slid out of his grip to the floor. 'Me too,' he said.

Very soon, thought Mallen, I am going to stop giving this boy every last thing he wants. 'Go and find something to put on, then,' he said.

Then, one day, he was summoned to Bedford Row. He was shown up to the drawing room on the first floor, where George Corney was pacing up and down, dressed to go out. Gout and piles, thought Mallen; he walks like a crow. He suddenly felt irritated by the urgency of the summons.

Corney shook his hand. 'Dr Mallen,' he said. 'Thank you for coming. It's very good of you.'

'Not at all. You don't look well, I must say.'

Corney frowned, and turned. 'This way,' he said. He led him out of the room and down a corridor. Mallen assumed that he was being taken to the library, but before they got there, Corney paused outside a door, and knocked. 'Augusta?' he said. Mallen felt the strength leave his legs.

The room was dimly lit, curtains drawn, oil lamps turned down on the dresser and beside the bed. A young woman, a maid, was folding something in one corner. She looked up as they entered, put what she was holding into an open drawer and left the room. Mallen's throat was thick and dry. He put his medicine bag down on the floor.

She was lying with her eyes closed, her face pale and strained. Her hair was loose, and damp with sweat. Corney said her name again. She frowned, and opened her eyes. 'This is Dr Mallen. Do you remember? He saved Holman's life when he poisoned himself. He looked after me when I was attacked.'

She moved her head on the pillows to look, not at Mallen, but at her husband. She remembers at least that he was never attacked, thought Mallen. He understood, quite suddenly, and without wishing to, how much Corney adored his wife, and how little she gave him in return. Even his lies were lost on her – and they were for her, all of them. 'Mrs Corney,' he said, leaning over the bed. It made his heart ache to see her like this, and it was all he could do not to lift her up and hold her to him. 'I'm sorry to find you unwell.'

She looked at him then, and the expression on her face was almost the same as when he had last seen her. Pain. Why on earth hadn't they called Dr French? 'I remember,' she said. 'Dr Mallen, of course.' She closed her eyes again, and Mallen knew she was going to say nothing. His own head was a storm of memory. He reached over and pulled a chair to the bed. 'Tell me what seems to be the matter,' he said.

She knew what he needed to hear, and told him when she had first begun to feel unwell, how it had started with a headache and shivering, and then pains in her back and her limbs. She had felt a sense of weight and uneasiness, and was thirsty all the time. Yesterday she had been violently sick, and the pain had got worse. He quizzed her on what she had eaten, how she had been sleeping, and whether her bowels had been regular. As she spoke, he watched her for any other signs of fever or inflammation. He noticed with dread the small petechial spots like flea bites on her arms. 'You should have called me before this,' he said, addressing her husband.

'Dr French came out last night,' said Corney. 'He gave her these.' He went to the dresser, and handed Mallen a couple of medicine bottles. The emetic was almost as strong as the one he had given Holman three years before, the other was a sudorific.

'He took a lot of blood, too,' said Corney.

'What did he diagnose?'

'He didn't.' Augusta tried to sit up on the pillows, but sank back again. 'The pain is better, but it's coming back, and the vomit –'

'He has made her fifty times worse,' said Corney.

Mallen took her wrist, and felt the pulse. 'This rash –' he said.

'It's everywhere. It started here.' She placed a hand on her chest.

Corney had left the bedside and was pacing again. Mallen pulled the lamp a little closer to the bed. 'Do you mind if I look at your tongue?' he said.

For a moment she looked confused, then she opened her mouth. Mallen leaned forward. He fought the urge to run out of the room in tears, to bang his head against the bedpost and rail against God. 'Good,' he said. 'Thank you.'

Typhus. He sat back in the chair and pressed his hands against his knees to stop them trembling. He could feel something very cold between his shoulder blades. 'Mrs Corney,' he said. 'I'm afraid you have contracted spotted fever. Dr French should have been able to tell you that; I don't know why he did not.' If I find him, he thought, I'll kill him.

She closed her eyes. Corney, at last, had stopped pacing.

He looked utterly lost. There was a sound, from the street, of a carriage door slamming shut and a yelp of laughter. Corney sat down on a stool at the foot of the bed and put his head in his hands. 'I take it,' he said, 'that you have some experience of treating this disease.'

Mallen didn't answer him. 'You won't need these, at any rate,' he said, taking the bottles and putting them into his pocket. 'Violent purging will only weaken you. As for any further bleeding, that's out of the question. Nature is the one who is going to do all the work. We must simply do what we can to help it, and to make you comfortable.'

She opened her eyes again. 'I will die,' she said.

Mallen could not bear the defeat in her voice. 'If you make up your mind to give up,' he said, 'then there's practically nothing that I can do, or Nature either, for that matter.'

'Dr Mallen!' Corney's head swung round, leaving his hands like an open book where his face had been.

'I'm going to have some physic made up for you, something for the pain, and to lower the fever. The one thing in favour of Dr French's treatment is that it will have purged the system, and we may start straight away on the correct medicine. This room should be kept cool and clean – I want to see at least one window open all the time. Your bed clothes should not be too heavy and must be changed frequently. The floor should be washed once a day, and sprinkled with vinegar. I don't want anyone to come in here who does not absolutely have to. A nurse, myself, no one else. Your meals can be left outside the door. You must have plenty of cold drinks, and a light diet.'

'Thank you,' she said. Mallen put his hand on her forehead. He could not resist at least that. He traced the line of her eyebrow with his thumb. She looked at him in surprise.

As soon as he left the house, he began to shake. Something was wrong with the tendons behind his knees. All his abilities had deserted him, as if someone had pulled them off his back like a coat. She was going to die. Delirium, lethargy, death. Everything that he had made himself forget about her had returned to him in a rush, and he felt, alongside the present fear for her life, that same inexorable longing that he had felt three years before.

He went to see Philip. These days, he usually found the apothecary working on a cure for melancholia. 'This is nine parts gin,' Mallen told him.

'It is not. Juniper, yes. That's what you can taste. No liquor, though, or hardly any.'

Mallen raised his eyebrows. 'It's disgusting, I'll give you that.'

'Good, thank you.'

Behind them, Philip's apprentice yawned deeply as he filled bottles. 'Although,' said Mallen, 'there's nothing to beat an antimonial vomit. You have to get it out, one way or another.'

Philip leaned back in his chair, and Mallen waited for the crack of breaking wood. 'This has antimony in it. Here, swallow. A single draught, two fluid ounces. The same tomorrow, and thence for a week.'

'But I'm not melancholy.'

'There's something the matter with you. Have you just lost a patient?'

Mallen shook his head. 'No. I don't know. I need a few things from you, though. Spirits of vitriol six drams, tincture of castor and cardamoms. A febrifuge. Can someone take them round to Bedford Row when they're ready?

I want her to start tonight.' Suddenly, he needed to say her name.

'I remember her,' said Philip. 'Of course.' His business was doing well. He lived, nowadays, in the rooms above the shop. He had a staff of four, who worked in the room behind it, and an apprentice. Eighteen months ago, he had met the daughter of a Spitalfields engraver, a pretty, intelligent woman who barely came up to his chin. He was still besotted, and they were expecting a baby at the end of the year.

'How is Elizabeth?' asked Mallen. Philip's face broke into a beaming smile, and he rocked his chair back. 'In English, please.'

'She's well. She's gone to Borough Market. She keeps asking if we can afford you, when the time comes.'

'You'll be hard pressed.'

Behind them, the apprentice made several noises as if he were about to sneeze, but did not. Philip gave him a quick look over his shoulder. 'Don't lick your fingers,' he said. 'Mercury,' he explained to Mallen. 'I don't want him to become paralytic. He finds it tasty, my clap remedy.'

Mallen looked at his hands. He had stopped shaking. 'I must go,' he said.

'I hope Mrs Corney isn't dangerously ill?'

'She has spotted fever.'

'Ah, Christ.'

For a week she lay shivering and sweating, drifting in and out of delirium, losing strength. Mallen went every day to Bedford Row, though there was nothing that he could do. Soon she would either die or begin to recover. The maid had been replaced by a nurse, and George Corney never seemed to leave the house.

He forced himself to go to the hospital, to the theatre, to church. When anyone spoke to him, he had to fight to make any meaning of the words. Another week went by, and he began to hope. Then one day he was shown into her room to find her sitting in a chair by her window. The nurse was making up the bed, and dust flew in the planks of sunlight. Augusta would not turn, and did not speak, her attention fastened on the world that she had almost left, the hazy light of the tree-lined street, the high and peeling flight of swifts over its roofs. Mallen's relief was so great that he almost forgot himself, almost wept. At the same time it struck him that now he would have no more reason to come and see her.

She was still very weak. Her convalescence would be prolonged and slow. 'She can't stay in London,' he told George Corney. 'As soon as she's well enough to travel, she should go to Chiswick.' It felt like a sentence he was passing, not on her but on himself.

Corney had thought of this. 'But what about you?' he said. 'I don't want anyone else, any other physician, I mean, to see her.'

Mallen opened his mouth to remind Corney that his wife now only needed rest – good air, fresh food. A careful regimen and strengthening tonics. A nurse, a cook, servants. She had no more need, day-to-day, of a doctor. 'Of course,' he said, 'I shall see her as often as is necessary. Chiswick is no distance, and I have a carriage.'

Lemuel Prager stood leaning against a waiting coach on the other side of the street. He watched without moving as Mallen descended the steps from the house. That man knows as much about her as I do, thought Mallen. He knows that she has been ill, when the fever started and the moment that it broke. He turned left, and began to make his way to Fetter Lane. Before he had gone half a dozen steps, he caught up with Frank Holman. Holman was carrying a parcel, tied with string. 'Mr Corney's riding boots,' he said.

'I've just come from his wife. The worst is over, I think she'll make a full recovery.'

Holman nodded. 'Thank God for that,' he said.

'Are you going to Blandford's? I'll walk with you.'

They fell into step, and made their way through a narrow alley onto High Holborn. Mallen dodged a pile of horse dung, heaped beside the road. 'What do you know about Lemuel Prager?' he said.

Holman looked at him, and shifted the parcel under his arm.

Mallen tried to gauge the man's expression. 'I ask because I'm Mrs Corney's physician. He follows her everywhere. He's outside the house at this moment. She says she doesn't mind him, but I think it must become oppressive, at some point, and I don't want her under any extra strain.'

Holman nodded, but he said nothing. For a moment they were separated as he stepped round a gathering of street boys. Mallen knew that if he waited long enough, the other man would speak. He was a physician, he spent his life asking questions, but he also knew when to hold his tongue. Holman seemed to come to a decision, and began to tell the story quietly and coherently as they made their way along Holborn towards Snow Hill. 'He's German,' he said. 'He was sent to London at the beginning of the Seven Years War. He was fifteen.'

'His father was a general?'

'In the Prussian Army, yes. His mother came from Lincolnshire. When the boy was twelve, she died of a fever. Not long afterwards, his father went off to fight. Prager was put on a boat, and came to live with his aunts in Castle Street.'

This much, Mallen already knew. Then Holman dropped

a thunderbolt. In 1760, when Augusta was seventeen, and Prager a year older, they had met and fallen in love. Lemuel, at least, was besotted.

'He wanted to marry her?' said Mallen.

'They were engaged.'

Mallen looked at him with his jaw open, like a fish cast up on the shore. 'Mrs Corney was engaged to Lemuel Prager?' he said. His voice was high and baffled.

'She wasn't Mrs Corney, then.' Holman apologised, with a dip of his head, for stating the obvious. 'The date had been set. The house in Castle Street was stripped from top to bottom, and done up with everything new. He spent a fortune on it, but then he had the money.'

'They never did marry.'

'No, he went to war.'

Prager was in the Army, waiting for his commission. England and Prussia were allies. His father was already something of a hero, having beaten back the French at Minden, under Prince Ferdinand. Prager himself hoped for a posting in Germany, or even North America. In fact, he was sent to France. He sailed with seven thousand other troops, to take Belle-Île, off Quiberon. They left Portsmouth in March 1761. There were ten ships of the line, eight frigates and about eighty other ships, as well as a covering squadron off the coast at Brest. The garrison that opposed them had less than three thousand men, but the island was protected by rocks and strong currents, and the first landing failed. Reinforcements were sent, and after a long blockade the French surrendered. During the fighting, Prager took a bullet in his shin, which shattered the bone. When it eventually mended, his left leg was two inches shorter than the right, and the foot was twisted. The troops remained on the island for about a year, but Prager was sent home as soon as he was well enough to travel.

Augusta wouldn't look at him. She wouldn't speak to him, or let him into the house. He had come back a cripple, and she didn't want him any more. Belle-Île had been a victory, but he had not come back a hero. She tore up his letters, and sent him away.

'That I find very hard to believe,' said Mallen. He was finding it all hard to believe.

Holman turned down the corners of his mouth. 'It was more than twenty years ago. Who knows what was possible then.' By his tone, however, it was apparent that Holman had no difficulty in accepting this part of the story as true.

'He's been following her all this time, for twenty years?'

'No, not all the time.' A year after Prager's return to London, Holman told him, Augusta married George Corney. Prager disappeared. He went back to Germany. His heart was broken, and his aunts feared he might kill himself if he stayed in England. To all appearances, he forgot Augusta and lived a normal, if solitary, life. Then, two years before the Gordon Riots, he turned up outside the Corneys' house, and since then he had shadowed her almost everywhere she went. 'Though so far as I know,' said Holman, 'he's not there every minute of the day, or even every day, and he's never spoken a word to her.'

'But why does she let him do it?'

Holman shrugged. 'She shouldn't, in my opinion. If he's not all there in his head, then neither is she.' He looked at Mallen suddenly, his eyes wide with horror.

'It's all right. You can say what you want to me.'

Holman shook his head.

'Frank, no one will ever know that I have spoken to you on the subject. I need to hear what you think. No one else knows the first thing about it.'

'I sometimes think she likes to have him there. It appeals to something in her, Christ only knows what.'

Mallen was struggling. 'I don't understand. He was away for a long time. Why come back, why then, and not before?'

Holman shook his head. What was there to say? They were outside Blandford's now, the boot-makers. The sun had come out from behind a bank of low cloud, and the street was pale with summer light.

'His aunts, are they still alive?' said Mallen.

He shook his head. 'No, dead. He's alone there, in the house, except for a cook, and his German manservant.'

This, at least, made sense. 'You know him, the manservant?'

Holman drew his shoulders back, and sighed. 'Quite well, yes. Between you and me, Dr Mallen, he thinks the man is raving mad, although only when it comes to Mrs Corney. In everything else, he's as sane as you or me. He orders his household like a normal man, and eats and drinks, and makes reasonable conversation. He has few friends, but only because he hasn't the time to make them. He's not interested in anyone else.'

Mallen looked at the ground, then stretched his neck.

'He also says,' Holman went on, 'that Prager wouldn't hurt a hair on her head.'

'He still loves her.'

'Well for God's sake, Doctor. In my book, it's something more than love.'

Mallen found himself staring at the wheels of carriages as they passed, the dizzy spin of their spokes. London itself seemed to be going round and round, fast and busy and indifferent.

'He's like a dog,' said Holman. 'You can throw stones at him, but he won't go away.'

Mallen looked at him. 'You've thrown stones at him?'

Holman managed a smile and shook his head. 'It's him I feel sorry for,' he said. 'Whatever happened to him, it goes very deep. He does it because he's alive, and it's what he must do. He's a man, not a dog, but he will follow her until he drops dead.'

The door behind them opened, and someone came out of the boot-maker's shop. They were both reminded of Holman's errand, and Mallen put a hand on his arm. 'Thank you,' he said. 'I'm very grateful.'

2

St Anne's, Soho

1831

It was early summer, 1831. The distillery was thick with dust and vapours. 'The King is dead,' said Franny.

'I know,' said Mallen. 'I'm sorry. However, the King has been dead for more than a year now, can we not drop the subject?'

'By all means.'

In fact no one spoke, any more, about King George. His spirit, it seemed, had not taken up lodging anywhere near or accessible to them, and he had, to all appearances and to Mallen's great relief, been forgotten. The Queen had moved on. She had turned her attentions instead to Alderman Wood, the man who had supported her throughout her trial and who had marched, with his sons, up and down outside Brandenburgh House, armed to the teeth against assassins.

'He is a chemist and a hop merchant,' said Franny.

'I'm sorry, who?' Mallen, since Glebe House had burned down, had been lost in gloom. He was out of touch.

'Alderman Wood!' she yelled. 'Listen.'

'I'm listening. Sorry.' Mallen settled himself on one of the rafters in the vaults above the grinding hall.

'He has been Lord Mayor, twice. Very radical. A strenuous supporter of the Whigs.'

'And do we have any reason to believe that the radical Wood is also about to expire?'

Franny shuffled up next to him, her legs hanging down beside his. The machines had all stopped, the belts and wheels, and the distillery was calm. 'He's old, but no. The Queen is simply looking for crumbs, now. He was the only one who ever seemed to like her, and old people reminisce: she wants to hear him say nice things about her.'

'Which,' said Dick Grace, 'so far, he has not.'

'Sadly,' said the wraith. They had appeared together, hand-in-hand, from downstairs. Far below them, on the ground floor, they heard the night-watchman open a door and slam it shut again.

Dick Grace had not turned out to be a wholly reformed young man after his experience on the gallows. He was, in Mallen's opinion, a sort of spectral recidivist, frustrated by his inability, most of the time, to actually shift physical objects in the solid world, and by being unable to profit from it when he did. Small things went missing from the pockets and sideboards of various magistrates or from the wives of jurymen, and he threw a few books around now and then. He haunted the courts and picked up the gossip, as well as prison slang – he had taken to calling Mallen *Splodger*, and the distillery *the drum*. Sometimes, when the grief at losing his life so uselessly and so young became very great, he could be seen by the living, weeping at night on Newgate Street. The wraith always found and consoled him: she took him off to the usual drinking places to find William Calcraft, the executioner, and they would follow him home, wailing and keening and making horrible choking sounds.

It was Dick who pointed out to the Queen that Thomas Connelly was due to appear before Alderman Wood in the Midsummer Sessions at the Old Bailey.

'For arson,' said Mallen, 'or murder?'

Dick Grace shook his head. 'Forgery. Converted his Navy Five per Cents. Didn't like living on the income, so he forged some signatures and ran off with the principal. They're at Newgate now, the men from the Bank of England, having a talk with him on account of how public feeling is running against the capital penalty for forgery, and they don't want his blood on their hands. They'll bring on some other charge instead and write it off. Case closed.' The young thief spread his arms. 'Five thousand pound,' he said. 'The likes of me get to hang from a rope for five pounds' worth of swag, and he gets a slap on the wrist.' He pulled the wraith into his arms, and danced with her round the grinding hall. 'As for murder,' he said, 'not enough evidence. And they never got him for the fire. Too bad.'

Franny stuck her legs out in front of her, then swung them under the girder again. Behind them and on either side, dunes of grain waited to spill down into the grinding hall. A long drag of sorrow pulled its way through Mallen, sorrow and waste and fault. He took one of Franny's hands in his own. The distillery was like a ship, pulling them evenly across the night. They heard its creaks and spills, the quiet scrabble of its rats.

'He always brought his lovely tochter with him,' said the Queen, rousing herself from a long and dreary period of reflection. 'Many hours we played, at my house.'

'Alderman Wood,' explained the wraith, as she glided under the young thief's upstretched arm.

Mallen nodded. 'And his lovely doctor?'

'His daughter.'

'Ah.'

'He is the only one who is fine and upstanding in all those times. He is the only man who is gone to Italy to find evidence that the King is wrong and I am not disgusting and a slut. When the old King died, he met me at Montbarde in Burgundy to come with me back into England, and sat by my side to come into London. He said to me come live in my house and never worry, my dear.' The Queen found a corner for herself, up amongst the girders, and subsided again into thought.

*   *   *

Mallen had no great wish to return, yet again, to Newgate, but Thomas Connelly had burned Augusta's house to the ground, and she had seen it, and there was every chance that she would be at the Old Bailey to see him convicted, even if he was not on trial for arson. He took Franny by the hand and they slipped from the metal rafters and down through the dusty halls. The others, all of them, followed.

He had missed the season changing. The fields on either side of the road were busy with stooped figures pulling up vegetables, and with stooks of hay stacked like tiny houses. The road through Kensington was lined with buildings that looked as if they had been polished. House-martins swooped under the eaves of the cottages, and the small gardens shouted with colour.

As they crossed the eastern end of Hyde Park, the Queen suddenly stopped. Her eyes were fixed on the ground in front of her, and Mallen thought that she must have seen something in the grass, something small and either puzzling or precious. She remained like this for some time, then lifted her head and looked, through the trees, towards the rooftops of Park Lane. 'But no,' she said quietly, and with a peculiar certainty.

Mallen was not the only one to sense that it was, for her, a moment of some significance. The others, too, all stopped and waited, standing in a half circle behind her. But if it was such a moment, the Queen, it seemed, could not hold on to it. She shook herself and moved on.

They never reached the Central Criminal Court, however. In the churchyard of St Anne's, Soho, it was the wraith who pulled up short. The churchyard was almost empty – only a few old parishioners drifted, long dead and indistinct in the early sun. A couple of thrifty-looking Huguenots whispered tirelessly in French behind a tombstone.

'Charlotte –?' The voice was upturned, like a face towards the light. Expectant, startled.

'Not me,' said the wraith. 'Not my name.' She turned as she spoke, her mean little face ready with compassion.

The man sat with his back against a headstone. He wore a black silk coat and white neck cloth. His white hair, very short, stood out round his head like a haze. He looked with sightless eyes in her direction. 'No,' he said. 'A mistake, forgive me.' His smile – sad and thin – missed her cheek by inches.

'Somebody else,' said the wraith.

The old ghost nodded. The arm that had been raised to halt her now waved briefly in front of him, and came to rest in his lap. 'I mistook your voice,' he said. 'For a moment I thought you were my daughter.'

'Charlotte.'

'Yes.'

The wraith craned forward to peer into his face, while his eyes remained where she had stood. She knelt on the grass beside him, then stuck out her feet and sat down.

'Though the truth is,' said the old man, 'you don't sound like her at all. There's Wapping in there, somewhere, isn't there?'

'In where?'

'In you, your voice.'

'Bermondsey.'

'Ah.' He nodded, corrected.

'I've seen you here before,' said the wraith.

'Oh . . . quite likely.' He lifted his head and gazed up through the branches of a yew tree as if he could see the filtered blue between them. The clock of St Anne's made a flat, thin sound as it chimed.

'You come and go,' said the wraith. It was a question, probingly asked.

He chuckled. 'Someone told me once,' he said, 'that if you put a man down in the desert and set him on a straight path in any direction, he will inevitably – without compass or the aid of the stars – find himself back where he started, having walked in an almost perfect circle.'

'No!' said the wraith.

'Quite true. Even while he's convinced, in his own mind, that he is following a direct line from one point to another, he will wind up in the place where he began.'

'He can walk straight, can't he?'

'Apparently not.'

'Drunk?'

'No, no.'

'He's stuck there, then.'

'It would seem so.'

'Alone and lost.'

The old man shrugged.

'The sun beating down without mercy, the last drop of precious water gone, his lips black and broken –'

'Oh, here we go,' said Franny. 'Vultures, camels, the French Army; despair, hope, death.'

'Tuh.' The wraith spread her hands. 'He's lost,' she said, pointing with her chin to her new acquaintance. 'And blind as a bat.'

His name was Hugh Franklin. Since the day he had been run over by a coach on Fulham Bridge and killed outright, he had been trying to find his way back to his home in Blackheath. All his efforts had so far brought him, always and with tedious certainty, back to this spot, though it was a place, as far as he knew, to which he had not the least connection, not now and not ever, and to which there was no string that tied him, no beginnings, no end, no significant act.

'But what were you doing in Putney?' asked the wraith. Mallen, watching her from a distance of a few feet, could see in her face a quiet diligence, a pursing of her small, keen features.

'Buddleia,' said the old man.

Hugh Franklin had been all his life a cultivator of plants and shrubs from all over the known world. In his garden in Blackheath he had nurtured fuchsias, alpine primroses and eucalyptus. He had grown delphiniums from St Petersburg and roses from revolutionary France. He had raised gladioli, pelargoniums and ixias from the Cape of Africa; magnolias from Bulls Bay, South Carolina, and the spice bush and sweet gum from Virginia. Azaleas from Russia, and Chinese chrysanthemums. A camellia from Chusan Island.

'But how do you know, how can you see what they are?'

'I don't know, not always. I have to be told.'

The point confirmed as a valid one, the wraith nodded, and crossed her arms. 'And who tells you?' she asked him.

'One of the gardeners. Or Charlotte, my daughter.'

Franklin's daughter, he told them, had almost as much knowledge of vegetation as all the botanists in England put together and could grow out of doors plants considered by anyone else to be too tender. Together they had managed to raise plants and shrubs and trees from parts of the world which they had never seen. They had planted walks, groves and small enclosures, had raked and hoed and seeded and pruned. On summer evenings, when the air was still and warm, the fragrance of mignonette and lavender was like another dimension. Franklin had gone to Putney in search of *buddleia globosa*, with its balls of orange, honey-scented flowers. During the hour he spent at the nursery, his coachman had disappeared from the face of the earth, and with him the coach, and Franklin had been stranded.

'Drunk,' said the wraith.

'I'm afraid so. Most probably.'

He had started walking, out of anger more than anything

else, leaving the plants to be collected. A stranger took his arm
and led him for a while, though not in the direction of home.
He felt the air change as he approached the bridge, and heard
the sound of hooves and wheels on timber. Something like
light entered his heart, suddenly alone, with the bright breeze
off the river and the swerving call of gulls. He felt lavish and
improvident. He decided to go to William Dancer in Fulham
Fields and get a fruit tree off him – several. And tobacco stalks
and wood soot, to spray for aphids. Afterwards, he would
hire another coach and go home to Blackheath. He gave his
halfpenny to the toll collector, stepped onto the footpath on
the east side of the bridge, heard the beat and rattle of the
approaching coach –

Mallen stepped forward. Someone living had recently
walked this way, and he could smell the sharp, high stink
of trodden weeds.

'We'll get you there,' said the wraith. 'We know the way
to Blackheath. We can get you home as easy as that.' She
snapped her fingers, soundlessly, in the air.

Franklin smiled, then gave a light and fluttering sigh. The
Queen piped up now. 'My dear man,' she said to him. 'I lived
in Blackheath. For many years I know this place like the back
of my hands. People come every day from London to see me,
even the King.'

'He did not,' said the wraith.

'Not that one, his father. The old one. Disaster. He seize
me in his arms and throw me on the sofa and near to ravish
me only the sofa have no back on it, and I can jump off the
other side.'

'The point being –' said Franny.

'I only say I know how to get there to Blackheath. I was
back and forward all the time.'

'In a coach. Driven by someone else.'

'But I can see with my eyes where I am going. London

Bridge and so on.' The Queen set her wig straight on her head and prepared to move off.

'Oi!' yelled the wraith. 'What about Alderman Wood?'

The Queen turned. 'Ah,' she said. 'Yes. No.'

'Well, which?'

'This I will later explain. I have, when we are coming here, made up in my mind that it is not so good to go to Sir Matthew Wood. It come to me in Hyde Park when we are walking, that it is not so wise or clever. Actually, an utter waste of time.'

The wraith did not speak, but she pushed her little face right against the Queen's until the older woman was forced to say something more. She spoke slowly as she marshalled her thoughts in the strange new effort of insight. 'It is true,' she began, 'Sir Matthew, he was kind, for sure, and give me both amusement and bare necessity, he put a roof on my head and give me moral support. Everything is true. But it is not for me myself. He have all my gratitude, and I do not forget, never. But it is for his own gain, always, he do these things. He want for to put his name in the paper and have status and rouse indignation against the government and the King. He look all the time for enrichment and some fame. For me, my dear child, this was great benefit and good, but it was not love and affection. It is all over and done and gone,' the Queen went on. 'In any cases. Finish, finish. Find something to do. For now, I am going with this man to Blackheath, back to his dear tochter, also Charlotte, like mine.'

The wraith waited for more, but the Queen had said enough. 'Close your mouth or a fly will go in it,' she commanded, taking Franklin by the arm.

It was at this point that Barbara Villiers found them. 'It wasn't as difficult as you might think,' she said. 'I thought you would all be at Newgate. I have spent the morning there.'

Dick Grace leapt to her side. 'And?' he demanded. 'They let him off, didn't they?'

The Duchess turned a comprehending smile on him. 'They did not,' she said. 'Transportation. Two counts of knowingly and fraudulently demanding and endeavouring to have transferred, assigned, sold and conveyed a large sum of money which, at the time, did not belong to him. Connelly is to be taken to the hulks at Portsmouth, and will sail for Van Diemen's Land before the end of the month.'

'For life?'

'Yes, life.'

Dick Grace took her hand and kissed it, as if it had been she, and not the judges, who had passed sentence.

'Come on, then,' said the wraith. 'Let's get going.'

The Duchess came over to where Mallen was standing, and took his arm. 'You were on your way to Blackheath?' she said.

He shook his head, and looked askance at her. 'No. Not at all . . . I was on my way to the Old Bailey.'

'Whatever for?' She looked surprised.

'Connelly burned down her house –'

The Duchess dismissed this with a movement of her hand. 'I assumed you would be going to Blackheath. I thought you might already know.'

'Know what?'

She put her hand on his arm, and used it to steer him round beside her. 'Let's walk together for a bit,' she said. 'We can catch up with the others later.'

They turned their backs on the churchyard gates, and moved again through the graves. The quiet calling of the doves above them was like purling water. 'I have found something out,' said the Duchess.

Mallen nodded. 'Tell me.'

'Mrs Corney had two sons.' It was not a question, but she turned her face to him as if for an answer.

'Yes,' he said. 'I never met them.'

She traced with her hand the back of a toppled stone. 'The elder one I know nothing about. He was fifteen when his mother died. Arthur, the younger one, was eleven. It must have been very hard on him, even if he hardly ever saw her. Are you all right, shall I go on?'

'Yes, go on.'

'He was in the Navy, he was a captain. In 1798, he was with Nelson, at Aboukir Bay. It was, I gather, a crushing defeat for the French. He came home and got married, but she was much younger, and they fought. He started to gamble.'

'How do you know all this?'

She took no notice of the question. 'I suppose he went back to sea, I don't know. Some people say he was at Trafalgar, though accounts differ. Others seem to remember that by then he had been court-martialled for stealing Navy silver, but if he did, he must have got off.'

Mallen couldn't help interrupting again. 'What people, who?'

'Ghosts, James. Remember, once upon a time I could find out anybody's business. In the early 1800s he was stuck at home, on half-pay. He was in his thirties, now, and had bought a house in Blackheath. I don't think he knew what to do with himself. From what I gather, he was liked by half a dozen people, and no one else. He spent huge sums of money. As I say, he gambled.' She paused at the end of a gravel path, and turned. 'In 1795, the Prince of Wales had married Caroline.'

Mallen sank down onto one of the graves. The stone that covered it, even in the sun, was cold. The Duchess sat down beside him. 'You know what happened next, to Caroline. She stayed with George for two years, then moved to Blackheath. She held a lot of parties, and there were affairs –'

'Arthur,' said Mallen.

'Yes. I wouldn't go so far as to say that he was in love with her. None of them were, but he stayed the course longer than most. They were living almost next door to each other, and he had nothing else to do. I'm sure he didn't mean anything to her. There was a string of naval officers going in and out of that house, it's common knowledge. However, I think in fact he was a bit mad by then. Stupidly, he gave her a lot of money. This much I found out from an old ghoul at the prison, who used to work at White's Club. Arthur Corney had almost nothing left by 1813. He was barred from the club, and just about everywhere. One thing he did still have, the only thing, was the house. His wife died, and he stayed there on his own, owing more and more money, and hardly seeing the light of day. Caroline had seen him off by this time, and in any case, a year later she had left the country. Needless to say, he never got any of his money back. She got rid of him without much ceremony, I think, and made him look stupid. She could treat men very badly, that much is true, but then she had been treated very badly herself. A woman like that is hardly likely to crush a man, but she can make him angry, and if he is a shallow person, the injury might get blown up in his head. Some men, particularly I think if their mothers never loved them, take that sort of thing very badly. In any case, he didn't come out of it well. The rest can be told quite quickly. He went to pieces, and ended up in Newgate, for debt. His trial was set for April 1819, but he died in prison before it came up. Gaol fever, I believe.'

Mallen looked up into the branches of the yew trees above them. He could feel a chatter, like teeth, in his chest. 'I knew none of this,' he said.

'Of course.'

'Otherwise –'

'Otherwise you would have known why she spent so much time following the Queen. For several years after she died,

Augusta went nowhere. She was walled up inside her house, just like you. She came out when the rest of us did, and she followed Caroline until her death, and made sure her bones were well and truly buried. After that, it seems she began to look for Arthur's ghost. When you saw her at the Sermon for the Dead, it was not the first time she had been to the prison. My friend from White's had seen her many times.'

'And since?'

'No, no sign of her since then. She has moved on again, apparently.'

'To Blackheath.'

'It's more than likely. It's my guess that she's looking for him, to make up now for what she never gave him before.'

'What can she do for him now?'

'Well, then. To ask him to forgive her.'

The tears were pouring down Mallen's face, though it was not sadness that he felt; it was something further out than that. 'But why,' he whispered, 'why in God's name has the Queen not said anything? It's not a common name, it must mean something to her.'

'The Queen, James, is an old bitch. You mustn't under-estimate the selfishness of a woman whose reputation was a lot less than it should have been, and who has, at least once, been called a whore. They do not give up their secrets.'

She was on her own ground there, he could not contra-dict her.

'On the other hand,' she said, 'it's perfectly possible that she has forgotten all about him.'

'She can't have done!'

'I don't know. It's astonishing what the dead can forget.'

3

Recovery

1783

The drive to Chiswick was dusty but green. It was late summer, still warm. At Hammersmith turnpike he passed one of his father's carts, laden with crates.

She was up, and walking in the garden. 'I've been reading all morning,' she said. 'I needed to stretch.'

Mallen smiled. 'Excellent! You look much better.'

'Thanks to you.' From the look on her face, he could see that she really thought he had saved her life. She trusted him, he was her friend. 'What were you reading?' he said.

'Cowper. It's yours, I must give it back to you. I've got your Swift, too. Should we go in, do you think?'

He would not be able to come here any more. It was over. There would be no more driving to Chiswick in the long light of the afternoons, no more looking forward to it, like a madman. She was almost well, and it was over. 'Not unless you're tired,' he said.

'I'm not tired.' She sat on a bench that had been placed on a small rise above the river. Mallen remained standing, looking out over the water. Until today, he had always found her in bed or sitting in a chair in her room. Corney had employed a local nurse, and in front of her and the servants he was as cool towards Augusta as he could manage – a cold fish, like William Hunter. He made himself solemn and precise, and kept his hat on at all times. When he had the rare chance to be alone with her, he sat with his legs stretched out in front of him, his hat on the floor, while they talked about whatever came into their heads. He brought her periodicals, which they read together, going through the accidents and spectacles, the gardening hints, the lost and stolen. More than once, he had found himself wishing that her convalescence could go on for ever.

He sat down on the arm of the bench. Such peace and quiet. The old house, the lawns, the line of yew trees and the river; the sound of blackbirds and boatmen. Mallen had never felt so fully conscious as he did now, so aware of each word and sound, alive to the feeling that everything surrounding him was full of charm or danger.

'Tell me I can go back to London soon,' she said. 'Tell me I can, or I'll throw myself in the river.'

He grinned. 'You're the worst patient I've ever had. You've no idea how difficult you are.'

'I will, I'll throw myself in the river!' She stood, and walked the few feet to the water's edge, where she turned and leaned forward, her hands on her knees. 'I can't swim,' she said.

'And you can't do anything you're told.'

'You're a monster.' She threw herself onto the grass below the bench and sat with her feet tucked under her skirts. 'One day they'll find me here, my hair white, my teeth gone, and they'll come looking for you.'

'I'll be dead by then.'

'No, there's no hiding. They'll dig you up.'

'I'll deny everything.'

She leaned back on her elbows, and lifted her face to the sun. 'It's terrible to be weak,' she said, suddenly serious. 'The world feels like a great ship that's going on without you. I've been listening to it for weeks, and sometimes I've felt that I would be left behind for ever. It's like being a ghost.'

'That's all over now. You're almost well, look at you.'

'Yes. But sometimes I think that perhaps I deserved it.'

'What are you talking about? No one deserves to be ill.'

A coot swam into the shallows, and paddled off again. 'If I go out in the rain and the cold with too few clothes on, I may catch pneumonia.'

He couldn't help seeing her, then, in a real downpour, wearing only what she had on now. 'True, but you wouldn't. Anyway, that's quite different. Disease is not a punishment.'

She was quiet for a moment, thinking. 'Perhaps not,' she said. 'It seems like it, however.'

'How could it be! What on earth have you ever done?' Mallen saw her look of surprise; he must have been shouting. He turned his face to the river. The light on the water was fractured, and bright chips danced on it. 'I saw Lemuel Prager. He was by the gates.'

'Yes. He's often there.'

'But where does he sleep? Where does he find his food?'

She pushed a loose strand of hair behind her ear. 'He does have a home, you know.'

'I wish he would spend more time in it.'

She shrugged, and looked up into the sky. Mallen wanted to lean over her and take both her hands in his. It occurred to him briefly that perhaps Holman was right, perhaps Augusta did not simply tolerate Prager's presence in the background of her life, but somehow thrived on it. However, he did not want to think about Prager now. 'Where are your boys?' he asked her.

'With their aunt. She's taken them to France. I miss them. It seems so strange that you haven't met them. They're very big, now. They make me feel ancient.'

'You will never be ancient; you will live for ever!' He strode away from her, down to the water's edge. Small, humiliated fists banged in his chest. *You will live for ever!* It was a declaration, and it rang up and down the river. It was time to leave, to go home. This, then, he thought, is how things change, how in a moment something happens or is said, like an accident, and there is no going back.

'You know, I do feel tired,' she said, behind him. 'Just now, suddenly.'

He ran back up the slope. 'Here, take my arm,' he said. He lifted her gently from the grass and they walked back between beds of bloated roses and past a straggling border of sage and lobelia. The house, when they reached it, felt empty, though he heard a door close somewhere, and the sound of feet. On the stairs to her room, she held the banister while Mallen came up behind her. He watched her as she climbed with surprising strength in front of him, saw her body sway with each step, the tendons at her heels. He felt the rules break all around him, and the air fall away in pieces.

'Where is Nurse Steadman?' His voice was not steady.

'Oh . . . somewhere. I am not, these days, her only patient.'

In her room, she lifted herself onto the edge of the bed, and leaned forward to take off her shoes. 'Oh!' she exclaimed, sitting up again. 'I can't do it.'

He knelt on the floor to help her. The shoes came off easily. Silk damask slippers, with a ribbon over the toes. She wore no stockings, and for a moment he held her naked heels in his hands. His face almost touched her knees; he could have buried his head in her skirt. He smelled the dusty lavender scent of cupboards, and something sharper, deeper. He placed the shoes on the floor beside the bed. 'You've overdone it, I suspect,' he said, standing. There was a shiver in his voice like riddled ashes. She lifted her legs up onto the bed and sat back on the pillows. Mallen leaned forward, put a hand on her brow. Then he took her pulse. 'You'll live,' he said.

She laughed, a bright shout that made him jump, and sent a fork of pleasure through him.

He sat down on the edge of the high bed, one foot tucked behind his shin, and took off his hat. She was better. It showed in her face, in her brown, confident eyes. She was, he suddenly understood, not even tired.

'James –' she said.

His throat ached with gratitude. He leaned forward over her, his whole body alive with trembling. She frowned, and lifted a hand to his face. He slipped the shawl from her shoulders, and ran his finger over the skin below her throat. He kissed the hollow of her neck, held her chin and kissed her mouth. There was a breeze on his face from the open window, and he heard the high, breezy *tswit* of swallows outside. He ran the back of his hand across the inside of her wrist and tasted it with his tongue. She pulled him to her, her breath full of small sounds, her teeth on his lip. This was the moment that his life, his heart, had curved towards for years, for ever.

There was a tap on the door, and the nurse let herself into the room. Mallen became completely still. The room went very dark, as if he had swallowed it. The nurse yelped, either with fright or laughter. He lifted his head, slowly. His weight was forward on his arm, and it began to shake. He looked into Augusta's eyes and saw – what – anger, curiosity? 'You know Nurse Steadman?' she said.

He spoke without moving. 'Indeed. How do you do, Nurse Steadman.' He leaned a little further forward, and placed an arm behind her neck. 'No,' he said, 'don't move.' He lifted her head, pulled out another pillow, and placed it behind her shoulders. 'There,' he said. 'Better.' He sat up, and turned to the nurse. 'Mrs Corney is much improved,' he said, in his coldest, fishiest voice. 'But she has tired herself out.'

The nurse said nothing. Her lips were invisible.

'No more long walks.'

Augusta rolled her eyes.

'I want you to go to bed for at least an hour in the afternoons.'

'I'm going back to London,' she said. 'In a few days.'

'We'll see.' He stood, with difficulty, and straightened. He saw the smoke stain on an oil lamp, a knot of dark polished wood in a bedpost. 'For the time being, I want you to stay here. Rest. Have as much as you can to eat, and only gentle exercise.' She was looking at him with her mouth curved open, her lower jaw protruding slightly. 'I'll leave another prescription for tonic.' She closed her mouth and lowered her eyes and would not speak to him.

On his way back to London, he had a curious sense of something like elation. He felt both sodden and noble with love, and cheated of it by the intervention of fate, but he was aware, too, of an almost giddying sense of deliverance. His horse twitched its ears, and shook out a snort. I have been very ill, he said to himself. He had not been ill, but his heart had come very close to wrecking for ever his peace of mind. How astonishing, how fragile it is, he thought. It is not only the young who are ready to throw their lives away, who can be reckless with everything they have. He closed his eyes and lifted his face and saw the shadows on his retina of passing trees in the evening sun.

He had been set back on a course with all his old navigational instruments. Home, family, wife. One word of what he had done, if he had done it, and all the gates of his professional citadel would have closed against him instantly. He would never work as a physician-midwife again, and Julia would be destroyed. It only amazed him that during all these weeks of Augusta's recovery he had known exactly what it was he was heading towards, and had more than half believed that he was not being a lunatic. Not only that, but he had put himself at the greatest risk, at the start, by traipsing in and out of her room while she was still in the grip of an infectious fever. Himself, his wife, his family. He reined in his horse, leaned forward in his seat, and put his head in his hands.

*   *   *

Julia lay on a sofa, beached and exhausted. Her face looked raw. The baby was not due for three months. 'Where have you been?'

'Islington.' His lies were easy, and he hated himself. He had not even told her that Augusta Corney was ill; he had lied so that when the chance arose, or the time came, he might have a certain freedom to betray her. It had been in his mind, all along. 'And also to Chiswick,' he said. 'Mrs Corney has been very ill. Fever.' There.

It had been in his mind all along, and yet it had not happened. Suddenly all his relief ran out of him. A vital part of his life had been taken from him before he had lived it. It was not enough, what he had. It did not reach high or wide enough, and all he could hear in his heart was the same sound of footsteps going up and down the same stairs, every day. All that was sublime or bright was with Augusta, and he had left her, he had run away and he would never, ever, be able to go back. 'I'm going to get something to drink,' he said.

'Ellen's downstairs. I'd like something, too. Water.'

There was a clawing ache in his chest that wouldn't go away. She had said his name, and he had seen in her smallest movement all the outward signs of passion, and he had been forced to stand up and walk away. Wherever he went, even in his own house, he saw pain. In the streets, he was desolate. He found himself looking for her everywhere, even though he knew she wasn't there.

The next he heard of her was from Philip, two days later. They were in the coffee house in Fetter Lane, going through a pile of prescriptions. Philip, as usual, had the paper open in front of him. 'Concentrate for a minute,' said Mallen. 'Spirits of wine and spirits of rosemary, two ounces each.'

'And twelve of camphor. I can do this in my sleep, James.'

'And something for the cough.'

'Balsam of Gilead. Two drams.'

'Good. Mrs Glover.'

'Mrs Glover, flatulence. Aloes and canella bark, two doses.'

'And make up some more hartshorn for Thomas Monroe. He took an emetic last night by mistake that I gave to one of his maids, so put a proper label on it.'

'I will. How is Mrs Mallen?'

'Huge.'

'You should come to Ranelagh with us tonight, the two of you. Have some supper, listen to music. We won't be late.'

'I don't think I could get her out of the house.'

'She can't be that big.'

'I mean,' said Mallen, pointing his coffee-spoon at Philip's chest, 'that she doesn't go out these days. It's an effort.'

'Well, ask her.' They went through the rest of the prescriptions, though it was Mallen and not Philip who couldn't concentrate. 'By the way,' said Philip, when they had nearly finished. 'The tonic. Are you going to take it, or shall I send someone round?'

'Tonic?'

'For Mrs Corney. Bedford Row.'

'But Mrs Corney is in Chiswick.'

'No, James. London. Frank Holman came in yesterday.'

4

Franklin's Tendency

1831

Blackheath was a windswept tableland south of Greenwich Park, on the road to Canterbury and Dover. It was a matter, from Soho, of seven or eight miles, of which they had so far covered a little over three. All the way from London Bridge, the wraith had been walking with her eyes tight shut.

'What are you doing?' said Franny.

'I'm blind.'

'I see. And have all your other senses become uncannily alert by way of compensation?'

'Not yet.'

'Never mind. You're hardly likely to fall over anything, and if you do, you won't hurt yourself.'

'Not the point. Where are we?'

'You tell me.'

'Great Dover Street,' said Hugh Franklin, who was yards ahead of them, walking with Mallen and the Queen. 'On your left you will soon see the Bricklayer's Arms. In your case perhaps not, but it is there.'

The wraith sighed. 'What,' she whispered to Franny in a tiny voice, 'does he need us for, exactly?'

'It was you who suggested it.'

'He was stuck in a bloody churchyard! I thought he couldn't find the way.' She was almost shouting now.

In front of them they heard Franklin chuckle. 'I know my way, I never said that I did not.' The old man waited for them to catch him up. 'I've used this road countless times,

I remember it well. It's only that recently I haven't known how to stay on it.'

'Not since you met your horrible end,' volunteered the wraith.

'Quite. Not since then.'

The Queen had her arm in his, and was tilted queerly to one side, leaning at an improbable angle of about forty degrees. 'I have one answer to this problem,' she claimed, looking upwards and aslant into his face. 'If I may say, Mr Franklin, you have a . . . tendency.'

'A tendency?' said the wraith, flicking the word like something repellent.

'To the left,' said the Queen. 'Like, I think sometimes, some horses.'

The wraith, whose eyes were still screwed shut, sighed. 'Yet again it is going to take us forty minutes to find out what she means.'

'Oh, quiet, you hussy. He have a tendency all the time to go to the left. Somebody have to keep him straight or he goes off down the wrong way. May be this is why he walks like in a desert and always go back to Soho. May be something get bashed in his head when he was trampled and run over to death.'

It became clear, as they put this to the test, that the Queen was right. If left alone, Franklin would veer off to one side, and even now seemed inclined to divert up Bermondsey New Road. Though the drift was gradual it had some force, and the Queen had already prevented him from doing this – hence her own tendency to lean in the opposite direction – a number of times.

Why? Of all of them, it was naturally Hugh Franklin who found this question most poignant. Throughout his lifetime he had never listed either to one side or the other. He had learned painfully and over the course of years to make his way independently – listening, counting, feeling, asking. He had broken his shins, his knuckles, his shoes, his chin against countless unseen obstacles and yet he had never got lost for want of a straight course. It was only since finding himself in St Anne's churchyard that he had begun to walk in circles. Mallen agreed that there might be something to be said for the effects of severe trauma occurring moments before death, though an organic cause seemed far-fetched; this explanation, anyway, did not sit right with Hugh Franklin. 'If there is a reason,' he said, 'I shall no doubt learn it one of these days.'

'Damn!' cried the wraith, who had walked straight into the toll gate and was now swinging backward on it.

Soon they were out in the country, under leafy chestnut trees that lined the road. The dust thrown up by passing riders smelled of sun and earth, and the fields on either side of them were high with wheat, or green with market gardens. The Queen, holding fast to Franklin, talked to him at length about her own garden in Blackheath, where eminent men had admired the beautiful order and careful cultivation of even the most insignificant spot, and the judicious combination of the useful with the agreeable. 'Vegetables,' she informed her new companion. 'I have neat borders of some flowers,' she boasted, 'but only small, because I grow many vegetables.'

Franklin had lived in Blackheath for forty years. The house that Caroline spoke of had long since been demolished, but he remembered it.

'Demolished?' said Mallen. He hadn't even thought to ask. He threw a look of query behind him at the Duchess, who shrugged. It did not, after all, mean that Arthur Corney's house was also no longer there.

'Workmen,' said the Queen, moving in a reflective sweep from the garden into the house. 'Stupid as posts, but we build a dining room and a new library, and also I have a tented room *à la turque*. Yes! This room have been inspired by Sir Sidney

Smith, who have captured all the French siege artillery one time against Napoleon. He begave me a pattern for the room in a drawing of the tent of Murat Bey which he have brought with him from Egypt.'

'He begave you a lot more than that,' muttered the wraith.

This being true, the Queen sank again into thought and recollection, and soon had fallen back to bring up the rear.

It might have been thought that the wraith – with her eyes still glued shut – was not the best person to lead Franklin at that point, but she did, and between the two of them they managed to take the entire party off the main road at New Cross and into Deptford.

'Excellent,' said Franny.

'Never mind,' said Franklin. After all his struggles, all his circling, he was now almost home.

The town smelled of timber, pitch, tar and hemp. It rang with the sounds of foundries and ropewalks. Coopers sang filthy songs in their yards, and laid-off men sat on ruined casks. Franny took over from the wraith, and led the blind man through the lanes and alleys, along the side of the creek, past a sailyard, and under the shadow of the church. Then down through the same lanes and alleys, along the side of the creek again, past the same sailyard and under the same shadow of the same church.

'It's no good,' said Franny. 'I can't do this. We'll end up in Soho again.'

So Mallen now took Franklin's arm, and they turned south and east again towards the heath. The sky grew dark with dusk and clouds. They passed an oyster-seller, heard the scrape of her knife in the shell. They slid past reeking drink shops, and an old dead-house where the drowned were laid out on a shelf. They were on the river; they had gone north. They turned again, and night came up over the water with dark sheets of rain. They turned once more, but the river was still beside them, and the black mud of its banks. They were all caught, it seemed, in Franklin's tendency.

They found themselves a-hover on the rain-pierced surface of the water, and blown like skirts by a chasing easterly wind. They turned to left and right, and faced the same way still. Borne back to shore, they fetched up in the Naval Victualling Yard, between the high walls of storages stuffed with ship's biscuit.

'I can smell rum,' said the wraith, wrinkling. 'Where are we?'

The yard was lit by oil lamps. A door slammed, and a commissary came running out of one of the officers' houses with a cape held over his head.

Barbara Villiers paced up and down, up and down, on the cobbles. Franklin began to pace with her, up and down, but soon went wayward and coasted towards the forage bins. They had come so far – further by miles than the old man had, since his death, ever managed – and now it seemed that Deptford would not let them go.

Franklin was becoming weary of bumping into things. He found himself somewhere to rest on the step of a roasting shed. 'Tell me,' said the Duchess, sitting herself beside him. 'Were you blind all your life?'

'Ah, no.' The rain turned the dust of the yard to mud. In the offices above them, the last of the lamps went out. A purser came out onto the steps of one of the buildings and knocked his pipe out on the wall.

For the first twenty-seven years of his life, Franklin had been able to see anything and everything. He worked, travelled, married. His father was a merchant, who played golf on Blackheath and had a fine study full of books. When he died, Franklin continued to live in the old house with his wife and mother. In 1804, he fell ill with a fever which left him blind. His world, suddenly, became very still. It became smaller, too, no bigger than the house, and the large shambolic garden that surrounded it. Nothing much had been done to the garden for years. One night, his wife came out to find him digging. To her astonishment, he had pegged out a perfect square. The following day, she took him all the way across London to buy roses from Lee & Kennedy.

'What happened to your wife?' asked Franny.

'Oh, she died. Many years ago.'

The wraith had become strangely quiet. Suddenly, and for the first time in hours, she opened her eyes. 'She must lead him,' she said, pointing at the Queen.

'It's a miracle,' said Franny. 'She can see.'

'She must lead him.' The wraith's voice seemed to come from somewhere out in the rain. It brooked no questions, the voice of a small and bedraggled oracle. Barbara Villiers stopped pacing. The Queen stepped forward and took Franklin's arm again.

They left the Victualling Yard and followed the river to Greenwich. The Queen kept Franklin straight and true, and they did not falter once from their path. They cut through the Seamen's Hospital, where pensioners and the ghosts of pensioners walked the wide corridors, peg-legged, missing arms or, like Franklin, blind.

'When I am come to England,' said the Queen, 'and am disembarked here, I think all Englishmen have only one arm or one leg.'

'It wasn't funny then and it isn't funny now,' said the wraith who, all the same, began to affect a bad limp.

They came out, on the other side of the hospital, into Greenwich Park. Trees dripped onto the empty paths and avenues, their outlines hard and dark against the sky. Under a row of Spanish chestnuts Mallen saw the shapes of standing deer. He chose this moment to confront the Queen about Arthur Corney. The look in his face made her retreat behind the inadequate form of Dick Grace, but she quickly rose to her own defence. 'How can I know Arthur Corney, of course I never did! I never heard that name before I am dead and you say it to me. Mrs Augusta Corney who follow me to my house and Westminster and round about and get on the boat and go to Brunswick, she is the only one I know.'

They would get nowhere, the Duchess decided, so long as she had her hackles up. 'My dear,' she said, and then, because she really had to pull out all the stops, 'your Majesty. Arthur Corney was a captain in the Navy. He had a house very near to yours in Blackheath. He was with Lord Nelson at Aboukir Bay –'

The Queen shrieked. 'Arthur!' she yelled. What came next was incomprehensible. It was largely in German, with some French and a little English. 'Arthur,' she whispered, in a sudden diminuendo. 'But that was not his name, not Corney.' She bit the side of her cheek as she cranked up her mind to think. 'Really, that is quite extraordinary. Arthur Corney. Yes, perhaps I think so.' Her face began to clear as it was swept by memory. 'Not a nice man, I am afraid to say. Awful. He come to my house sometimes and we dance and do the other thing, but he have no respect for me. Dreadful liar. No wonder I have forgotten him and not remembered even his name since that time. Really, he was a disaster. Never mind he look fine in his uniform.'

The wraith had her hands on her hips. 'You can't even remember the names of the men you went to bed with!' she said. 'You're disgusting.' To her horror, however, the Queen began to weep.

'There, there,' said the Duchess. 'It was all a very long time ago.'

'I bet *you* remember,' said the wraith. 'And that was longer ago.'

The Duchess did not confirm or deny the truth of this. 'The Queen has had other things on her mind,' she said. 'However, what we need to do now is to find his house. Perhaps she will be able to help us do that.'

The Queen sniffed, and then brightened. 'I know his house. I can go to there with my eyes shut,' she said.

'Not you, too,' said Franny.

'Oh, be quiet. You know what I mean.'

Franklin accepted another diversion with equanimity. 'By all means,' he said. 'We are not short of time.'

Mallen, at last, felt that he was near to his goal. Somewhere just beyond where they stood, on the other side of Shooter's Hill and the long green swathe of the heath, was the place where she was bound, now, to be. His certainty was like a silver shaft down the length of his spine. The rain had stopped, and the night was clear and warm.

'This way,' said the Queen, setting off with a strong and confident stride, and dragging Franklin with her. 'Actually, no,' she said, turning. 'This way.'

Owls called to each other across the heath. Beneath their feet, small creatures scratched and trembled in the ground. They reached the outskirts of the village, and made their way through winding alleys and small gardens. Very soon, they were in almost as much trouble as they had been in Deptford, though not for the same reasons. The Queen's sense of direction had deserted her and, her own house having been razed to the ground, she could not get her bearings. She remembered only that Captain Corney's had been set back, behind trees, and away from any other buildings. The night became ever darker, and Mallen's frustration grew. Without her help, they hadn't a chance. With it, they were apparently doomed.

'Better start from the beginning again,' said the Queen,

whose spirits were not dampened. It was a small village. They got to know it well. Eventually, when they had been up and down the same part of the same road six times, the Queen stopped. 'Here,' she said.

There was nothing. A stand of trees, a plot of land. The small, dark leaves of strawberry plants. The feathery stems of asparagus. 'This is *not* it,' said the wraith.

'Definitely.'

'There's nothing here!' said the wraith. 'You mad old crow. You have been marching us round like the Duke of York for half the night, and now you point to a vegetable patch and say that it's a house.'

The Queen did not allow this outburst to affect her composure. 'Absolutely definite,' she said. 'This is where it was. Like mine, they have knocked it down. No surprise, it was ugly and completely rotten. I know for sure because there is that tree.' She pointed with the hand that was threaded through Franklin's arm. 'Hit by lightning after I lived here six years. Big storm, very frightening, everybody hide.'

Mallen, distraught, wandered over the beds in the dark, along the careful rows of burgeoning green. Although he had half expected it, he found it hard to believe that the house was no longer there. He left the others standing beneath the stricken tree and walked, again, the length of the village. There was nothing, he could feel it; he knew in his heart that she was not here, and never had been. He felt lost and empty, and he wished that death would take him again and make him into something perfectly still in the walls of his father's house. He wished that time would leave him still and silent, with only the distant sounds of life.

The Duchess found him walking back towards them on the road. 'Come,' she said, 'let's take Mr Franklin home.'

*   *   *

Franklin's garden was everything he had said it would be. Dawn came up over cobwebs, drenched and brilliant.

'What colour is the sky?' the old man asked the Queen.

'Blue.'

'What kind of blue?'

'Like a cup.'

This, Mallen thought, was vague, and yet she was right – it was translucent, a china blue. Waterfowl flew over them towards the marshes, and the garden rang with the sound of birds. It was a bright and quiet place, intricate and varied, with borders and shade and hotbeds and frames. Gravel paths led from terrace to pond, to bench to flower beds, to a grove of pines, or a thicket of vine and juniper. The Queen had not let go of Franklin's arm, and they were walking on a narrow, curving path. Mallen followed them under trellised roses, down paths lined with long-stemmed lavender, past beds of overflowing colour. Franklin was guided at every turn by scents and echoes, and gently steered by the Queen. Everywhere they could hear water, the breezy splash of fountains and the play of hoses as the gardeners watered the beds. The place was a map, a web, a universe of scents. Mallen closed his eyes, and the scents became colours – dark pepper greens, flat and endless yellows, the ancient purple smell of sage. The perfume of golds and carmines, and strange tangy colours that smelled of sea and forest and the green sides of barges. This – all this – had been Franklin's life, and Mallen found it almost shocking, the achievement and the tranquillity.

Franklin's daughter worked with the gardeners, a wide hat on her head to keep off the sun. Her face, like Franklin's, was strong and handsome; her husband, a Scot, strode past the ghosts in his merchant's coat and sturdy boots, carrying trays of alstroemeria.

Hours came and went, and then days, like the slow rise and

twist of fish. The wraith and Franny lay side by side, squinting into the sky. At night, they looked like moths against the moon. Mallen watched the Queen as she moved through the garden, watched her bend to look at something with an ease and grace that he had not known her capable of until now, her arm still laced through Franklin's. She has forgotten us, he thought.

He saw – suddenly, and for no reason – his wife, pressing her face to a window pane, the tip of her nose flat and white against the glass; a rose of moisture where she breathed on it. He saw the curve in a road, and recognised where it was, but not why he should think of it. It used to be, he thought, that all our memories lived within our heads, inside a crown of bone. Now the same thoughts have only shadows to occupy, and vanish in great numbers and then return again, as if they had been somewhere else. They return like pigeons, with both grace and agitation, and in a great swoop. And still they cannot be seen by anyone but ourselves; even when there is nothing to lock them in, they are shut away from the sight of others. Even someone so clever as the Duchess cannot find them out.

His love for Julia had been enduring. Enduring because it had survived, and because, at times, it had been something that they had had to bear. It was a love that they had struggled with, and made strong, a love that brought their children into the world. He missed her with a feeling that is only known in death, a sense of loss and grieving that has more space to roam than loss or grieving ever does in life. It was not a regret for passion or the sublime, but for the one thing that had been everlasting in his life, for a companionship that was almost miraculous.

There is day and there is night, but there is no time. We think or hope that death will be like sleep and forgetting, and it is true, we do forget, but not everything, as we might have expected, and not for ever. Much is lost, but not because it is useless or because it has no meaning now. If that were true, we wouldn't remember the things we do: bits of road, a misted window. The lymphatic system, John Hunter's ducks – things that might have had importance once, or never. What changes in the world is that after a time there is no one else remaining in it whom we knew or loved or had to rub shoulders with. We no longer visit them as they lie in their beds peacefully sleeping. Sometimes the houses where we lived no longer remain. If they are still there and we can go back, the people who live in them now never think of us, or even imagine our past existence in the same place. We wander from one place to another, searching and, as with nearly everything on this side of the grave, the reason is almost always something left over, something that was never resolved in our lifetime, the same injustices, griefs and stupidities, or the legacy of those things. They may make us pace up and down for centuries. And if it is the getting of insight that will in the end settle any one or all of these things, that can take for ever. Those who died young, they have often nothing to resolve but their youth. Death can only take them so far. Perhaps even death has pity; or equally, perhaps it has none. If some of us exist as ghosts, and some do not, who are better off? Nobody knows, not here. Sometimes it seems, reflected Mallen, that anything would be better than this.

All our lives we are looking, he thought. We look for one thing or another, for courage or vitality or cleverness, God knows. As often as not, we look for it in other people, in those we revere or love. We become besotted with what we have not so far found in ourselves, and we will follow it to the ends of the earth. And it is within us, whatever it is, all the time, if only we understood, or turned the other way to look. Sometimes it stays undiscovered, even when we die, and is the source of sad and bitter feelings at the end. It never occurs to us that this thing for which we search might follow us beyond the grave, but it does, it can. Even then, at the end of our lives, we haven't understood what we truly possess.

He felt the stone come down on his head and send a running crack through his skull. He experienced the same confusion, knowing that he was going to die, but not why, or at whose hand. The terrible dismay at being slain by someone he could not see. His spirit curved over the pain of knowing that he would never do those two or three important things, whatever they were, that he had vowed to do before he died. He could feel the meaning drain from his life with his blood, until the only significant thing that remained of him was this briefly extraordinary fact of being killed. The pain turned yellow and infinite, and he was suddenly terribly thirsty. He remembered lying there for hours before he was found, and the sound of the wheels underneath him as he was taken for burial to Hammersmith.

'Those two do not leave each other alone for a moment.' Barbara Villiers was beside him. She looked offended, as if she had asked for one thing in a shop and been given something else.

'Naturally,' said Mallen.

The Duchess made a sound of rattling contempt, and began to pace. 'He was constrained to walk in circles, and now he is not,' she said. 'It has nothing to do with her.'

'No?'

'James, you will believe anything.'

She turned, and paced again. Then turned, and paced. Mallen began to count. Seven steps, then seven steps, up and down. These are the dimensions, he thought, of the room she paces in Chiswick. Seven and seven. It seemed, for the Duchess, a step backwards. She was still, after all, pushing the same boulder up the same hill, and it was still her beauty, still the same mourning for passion and her body. And for nothing – there was no more language of bodily things, only of shadow and spirit; all the arts of glance and touch were gone. There was no more thought of physical love. It was like getting old, but a thousand times worse, and then a thousand more. Yet there was transport, after all, eventually. Mallen only had to look at the Queen to see it. Her face had a bloom on it now like the bloom of the fruit on Franklin's wall, a flush of secrets and discovery and bliss. She had found what the Duchess so far had not – an equivalent, a corresponding joy to the ones they had left behind. Who would have believed it? Not Barbara Villiers, at any rate. She watched the Queen and Franklin with a look that swung between scorn and desolation. Mallen took her arm, not out of affection or even pity, but out of some probably useless instinct to hold her down, morally, to where she had come so far, to stop her falling away again.

'You don't know, James,' she said, her voice so quiet that he strained to hear it, 'what it is like to have had beauty, and to lose it.'

He was suddenly furious with her. They had all lost something, every one of them. They had lost, most of them, more than just their looks. His anger passed in moments, though, and his voice when he spoke was calm. 'It seems to me,' he said, 'that we have as little use for beauty, now, as we have for religion, or for syllabubs.'

Her eyes flashed. 'Don't be flippant.'

'I'm sorry.' He turned her off the narrow path and onto a small paved terrace. 'It's true, I don't know what it's like. I never knew what it was like to have beauty in the first place, besides which, I am a man. But what I don't understand is how you can be so completely oblivious, apparently, of all the things that you have *not* lost.'

She raised an eyebrow.

'Your mind! You have an astonishing mind. Your soul shines out of it still just the same as it must have done when you were twenty. You can still enchant people. Who else is as well-informed about a hangman born a hundred years after she herself has died, a man who keeps rabbits, and fishes in the New River? Who else knows the ins and outs of the current government, about the status of Catholic relief, and the fact that the King despises sarcasm? Who else but you could have found out what you did about Arthur Corney?'

'Franny, quite probably.'

'Not even Franny. You have vitality, and you have wit, and a clever mind, yet you have spent a hundred years walking up and down in the same rooms, grieving for something you no longer need.'

She puffed out her chest and sighed. 'It was not as if I had any choice, James.'

This he acknowledged with a hand on hers. 'But now –' he said.

'Now I should get a grip on myself and use my time in other ways.'

He smiled, and led her back towards the fountains.

And then, one day, they were all – as if alerted, like birds, by some alteration in the air – on their way back over the heath towards Shooter's Hill.

All except Hugh Franklin, and the Queen.

'No, but it is not possible,' she said. 'With such a tendency as this, he will only go to stray. I am sorry to say, he is useless. Without me I only dread to think what he will do.'

'She can't just stay here,' said the wraith.

Franny swung down from the branches of a small Douglas pine. 'She can, we can't. Come on.'

*   *   *

The Duchess walked beside Mallen on the way back. 'You know, she does have a point,' she said.

'Who has a point?'

'The Queen. It does no harm to go back to the beginning.'

He raised his eyebrows.

'Augusta Corney used to walk up and down on Chiswick Mall. I saw her frequently. You never believed me when I first told you, but it was true.'

'Her house is no longer there.'

'No, but the road remains.'

5

George Corney

1783

They sent the apprentice to Bedford Row with the tonic. He returned, an hour later, to the coffee shop. 'For you,' he said, handing Mallen a letter.

It was not from her. It was a note, scribbled by George Corney. 'He wants something for gout,' said Mallen. 'And he thinks he has a fever.'

'Thinks?'

'One of us will have to go and see him.'

'I don't mind.'

Mallen had already reached for his hat. 'Let me think about it,' he said. 'In fact no, I'll go. Anyway, you're going to Ranelagh.'

'So are you.'

'Another time.'

George Corney was ill, but he wasn't going to die. His foot was bandaged, and he had chills and a low fever. Mallen took his pulse and smelled his breath. He had already been taking something, laudanum probably. It was the first time they had met since Augusta's recovery and Corney was abject in his gratitude. It was as if someone had placed an envelope in front of him and, opening it, he had been overwhelmed by its contents.

'I gather she's back in London,' said Mallen, aiming for a tone he was at pains to reach. 'She's made an excellent recovery.' He moved across the room to retrieve his medicine bag. They were in the library again.

'And a swift one,' said Corney.

'Swift?' He hadn't expected that.

'Not many people would be up on a horse so soon.'

'She *rode* back to London?' Mallen experienced a wave of professional fury, not to mention plain astonishment.

'Not to London. I'm talking about yesterday, when she went to Hyde Park.'

The man was making things up again, he was mad. For God's sake, she had only ventured into the garden two days ago. 'Is she here now? I could have a look at her.'

'I don't know where she is.' Corney leaned forward over his knees and breathed out through pursed lips. 'She has a will of her own,' he said to his feet. 'And a hot temper, for that matter.'

Mallen shook a medicine bottle and held it to the light. His hands, he noticed, were shaking. 'I can give you some wine of colchicum now, for the gout. I want you to take a vomit this evening. Nothing to drink afterwards, except for three half pints of warm water. Tomorrow morning, a rhubarb draught. I'll write it all down for you.'

No one seemed to know where she was. In his mind, he moved her around. He put her in France, in an empty house without servants. Then he moved her to Italy, standing upright against a black sky. He saw her lit by the flames of a large hearth in the mountains. There were times when, from one source or another, he knew that she was at Bedford Row, but he never saw her, and then she would be gone again. He had not seen Lemuel Prager either for months. At the beginning of December, his second child, a daughter, was born. Annie. He showered his wife with flowers, perfume, cushions, lace, until she broke down and yelled at him. All I've done is to have a baby, she shouted. She began to cry, and sobbed for hours, until she was raw and humming and her teeth chattered.

She became hollow-eyed, and stiff with panic. Whenever she picked the child up to feed her, she started all over again. Their nights were ghastly. She seldom slept, and when she did she dreamed of accidents and death. As soon as she was strong enough to travel, he sent her to Kensington to be with her father and out of the way of William. He sent for her sister, and found a wet-nurse.

At home, Franny took charge of William, with the help of an Irish nursery maid. Ellen and Mrs Trent managed everything else. Remarkably, there was food on the table, clean clothes, soap, coal.

George Corney's condition grew worse. 'I don't know what's wrong with him,' Mallen told Philip. 'I've tried everything.'

Philip nodded. 'Go through it again with me.' The list of symptoms went on and on. 'What's he taking?'

'Nothing. I've taken everything away.' Mallen frowned, and rubbed the side of his nose. 'Wine of colchicum.'

'Colchicum.'

'He's got gout.'

'I know. What dose?'

'Half a dram.'

'That shouldn't hurt him.' Philip rubbed the side of his nose. 'On the other hand –'

'If it was the colchicum, he'd be dead. He's been taking it for months.'

'Then it's chronic and not acute. He's been taking more than you told him to, and less than enough to kill him outright. You ought to get him off it, James. Keep him in bed, warm drinks, something for the pain.'

The weather was awful. Banks of blue-grey cloud promised snow, and brought rain. William rampaged round the house. Franny took him to the menagerie in the Exeter 'Change, and for a week afterwards he insisted that he was a capuchin monkey. Twice, Mallen found him under his desk, wide-eyed and piteous and chattering incoherently to himself.

He went to Kensington. The road had turned to mud and stone and mud-filled ruts, and the trees were bare and the hedges black. Septimus Neville met him in the hall. Mallen had the impression that his father-in-law had been waiting there, perhaps for hours. He looked miserable and cold. 'I've brought something for her,' he said.

Neville twisted the cork out of the bottle. 'It smells like gin.'

'Juniper berries.'

He re-corked it, and gave it back to Mallen. 'Anything I say to her is wrong.' Neville scratched the neck of his dog, a large grizzled hound that smelled like a pond.

'Offer me a drink,' said Mallen. 'It's been a long day.'

'Why isn't she happy?'

Mallen steered him out of the hall. 'The mind of a woman who has just given birth . . .' He found a decanter, and poured two drinks. 'They live in another world,' he said, 'and you and I will never understand it.' They were William Hunter's words, almost. 'It won't go on for ever.'

It was not her fault, but he found it hard to be kind to his wife. He spoke to her with a fixed smile and his voice was thin and remote. He sounded like her doctor. Julia herself was torpid and self-absorbed. She forgot instantly anything that was said, and looked at him with a lack of interest that bordered on scorn. She was careless with the objects in the room, picking them up and staring at them until they stared back at her. He found her sister intolerable.

'Nature will sort it out,' he told Septimus Neville. Counselling patience, and itching to get out of the house.

It was dark when he left. The harness was greasy and his hands were freezing. The rain turned to snow, short avenues of dancing moths in front of the lamps. The thought that he might never love his wife again made him weary and afraid. He jogged on, half sleeping, half awake, aching with cold. Then suddenly, near Kensington Gore, he heard other horses, the thud of exertion in front of him, the din of wheels. He saw lights come out of the snow, leaping with speed. His own horse snorted with panic and leapt forward, breaking a strap. Something hit them with a massive crash, and his jaw slammed shut. His seat tipped under him as the wheels slid sideways, and the carriage pitched to one side. He rolled onto the forward brace and felt it bang into his breastbone. He heard an argument, fierce but brief. A man's voice, the coachman, and then a lot of strong language from someone else. For a moment, less than a moment, he saw a face in the carriage window. 'Prager!' he shouted.

Then the carriage was gone, vanishing behind him, and Mallen listened as the road returned, slowly, to silence. He got down to look at the damage. It wasn't bad – a lamp smashed, the strap broken, and a long scratch in the paintwork. He led his horse out of the ditch and the carriage righted with the bruised creak of springs and leather. It could not have been Lemuel Prager. Prager might be mad, but he wasn't a lunatic. He rubbed the back of his hand over his mouth, and it came away bloody. It wasn't Prager. It was the cold and the night, it was exhaustion and his own wild thoughts. Mallen held his horse's head and looked back along the road, but all he could see was snow and the dark.

When he reached home, Franny saw the blood on his mouth, and the beginning of a black eye. 'What happened?' she said.

He felt the inside of his cheek with his tongue. It was pulpy and raw. 'It's nothing,' he told her. 'An accident.'

She was sitting at the table with William, having toast and eggs. There was tea, too. The nursemaid poured another cup and pushed it towards him. She wasn't much older than

Franny, with huge dark eyes under huge dark brows, her face ethereally pale.

'You're soaked,' said Franny. She pushed her chair back from the table. 'I'll tell Ellen to put some water on.'

'Please.' He leaned over William's shoulder and took a piece of toast from his plate. 'Your mother sends her love,' he said.

'It's snowing,' said William.

'Yes.'

'Can I get down?'

'No, finish eating.'

The nursemaid put another piece of toast in front of the boy. He poked a finger in the melting butter and licked it. 'When we get down, can I go out?'

'I don't know.'

'But can I?'

Mallen studied his son. 'Ask Franny,' he said.

'You've been out all day,' said Franny. 'Eat up, and I'll see.'

On the way to the door, Mallen turned. 'Fran,' he said, 'do you know Lemuel Prager?'

'The cripple,' she said, without looking up from wiping William's face. 'Sort of.'

'He follows Mrs Corney around.'

'I know. It's because she broke his heart and he lost his mind. He's got a house in Castle Street and a castle in Germany, and fifty servants and a park.'

'Steady on.'

She grinned. 'He has! He lives and breathes for Mrs Corney, but he knows he can never have her, and when you talk to him, he doesn't sound mad.'

'You've talked to him?'

'No.' She reached for a spoon, which she used to stir the tea in her cup, peering into it as if waiting for something interesting to surface. 'I've heard him. He hasn't got an accent.'

Mallen frowned. 'If she did break his heart, it was a long time ago.'

'She did.'

'Why didn't he come back before?' It still puzzled him.

She gave him a look that suggested he had not thought it properly through. 'He was in an asylum,' she said.

'He was not.' For once, Mallen decided, she wasn't strong on her facts. William started banging his boots against the legs of his chair, and Franny told him to stop. 'Just wait,' she said. 'Your father and I are talking.'

Mallen tried not to smile.

'He was in an asylum, and he escaped.' Franny was insistent, tapping out the facts on the table with a finger. 'He escaped, and dressed up like a peasant and limped from Berlin to the coast. He isn't dangerous. He wouldn't hurt a fly.'

'And what about the castle and the servants?'

Franny scowled over her own contradictions, as if they were a bowl of porridge. 'He lived in the castle before he was put in the asylum. It's grown old and crumbling waiting for him to come back, and the servants, too. If he went back now, they might lock him up again, so he . . .' She had run out of steam. 'He's waiting,' she concluded.

'For what?'

She shrugged. 'For someone to tell them he isn't mad. But he is, so he's stuck.'

'And how do you know all this?'

She spread her hands. 'I do.'

She was making things up. Mallen went to his room. Ellen brought hot water and he washed and changed his clothes. After that, he couldn't muster the will to do anything else. William ran in and out of the room while he was supposed to be getting ready for bed, and at one point he heard Franny reading him the Riot Act. Just as well that someone does, he thought. At half past seven, Philip was shown up. 'Put some clothes on, you'll freeze,' he said. 'What have you done to your eye?'

'What do you want?'

'It's George Corney.' His face said the rest.

Mallen wadded a towel and threw it into a corner.

'They couldn't find you. They sent for French.'

'And?'

'He took sixteen ounces of blood. Said there was nothing he could do.'

Mallen shook his head. 'Have you seen him?'

'Not French, no.'

'I meant Corney.'

Philip nodded. 'Holman asked me to look at him. He came and got me. I've given him some ipecac and salt water.'

Mallen walked across the room and stood by the window, where he looked out onto the falling snow. He let his breath out, and the glass misted. 'Franny didn't tell me,' he said.

'There was no one here.'

Suddenly, he was furious. He pushed past Philip and went out onto the landing. 'Franny!' he shouted.

'James, listen to me –' said Philip.

Franny appeared from the children's bedroom, her face white. 'What?' she said.

'Where were you this afternoon?'

'Out. Vauxhall Gardens.'

'In this weather? Where was Mrs Trent? And Ellen?'

Franny's chin was trembling. 'Ellen was off,' she said. 'Mrs Trent went to Borough Market.'

'All afternoon?'

'It's a bloody long way!' She smacked a hand over her mouth. 'Sorry,' she said, through her fingers.

'Frank Holman was looking for me.'

'I would have said. I didn't know.'

'All right.'

'I would have said!'

Mallen rubbed his face in his hands. 'I know you would, Fran. I'm sorry. You've done nothing wrong. I shouldn't have shouted. Go on and get them into bed.' He turned back into the room, picking up a coat from a chair by the dresser. 'Who's at the house?' he asked Philip.

'No one. Holman, the servants.'

'I'll go there now. Come with me.'

Philip held up a medicine bottle. 'Holman gave me this.'

'Yes, it's the colchicum. I told him to stop taking it.'

'He's been drinking it like water.'

Mallen thought they might lose Corney before morning. He gave him something for the pain, and sent downstairs for warm water bottles. Holman moved in and out of the room with bowls and towels, grey with worry. The night became deep, and then quiet, and when the watch went by outside, they could hear the stiff creak of his boots on the snow. Eventually, in the early hours, Corney started to drift in and out of sleep. Philip also nodded off, in a chair. At around five, Mallen decided to go home. 'If he wakes up before I get back,' he said to Holman, 'ask them to make up some gruel. If he won't eat that, try white of egg.'

'Don't give me eggs.' It was a gravelly whisper. 'Don't even talk about them.'

'It's only –'

'I mean it.'

'All right. No eggs.' Mallen picked up his hat and left the house.

He slept for two hours before William woke him up. It was only just light. William galloped down the stairs and out into the snow. The back door banged about eight times before he decided to get up. His fire wasn't lit, and his room was freezing. He went straight back to Bedford Row, and sent Philip home. It was now just a question of waiting, and getting Corney to eat what he could. He was out of the woods, and Mallen told him so.

'I'm dying.'

'No, you're all right.'

'I'm dying, my feet are cold.'

'There's an inch of snow outside – my feet are cold.' Mallen looked round for his hat, and found it underneath a chair.

'Where are you going?'

'Downstairs. I want to talk to Mrs Vance. You're going to need building up.'

He got as far as the hallway. Augusta was standing there, pulling off her gloves. 'James!' she said. 'How . . . what a surprise. What on earth have you done to your face – you look like a Mohawk. Let's find a room with a fire.' Her face was flushed with the cold, and she looked, in her high fur collar, radiant and smart, and staggeringly lovely. As she let the housemaid take her coat, Mallen found that he was shaking.

She took him upstairs to the drawing room. 'I know what you're going to say. It's my fault, I've been away. I've only just now come back from Chiswick.' Her eyes flicked over her shoulder, at the door, then she dipped her head and smiled. 'I'm so glad you've come. I haven't said . . . I haven't even thanked you. James, I –'

Mallen stopped her. 'I came here,' he said, 'because your husband is ill.' Her face registered nothing beyond the fact that she had been interrupted, and he told her again.

'Yes, yes, I know. I received a message.'

'He's not at all well.'

'There's nothing wrong with him! He always says there is

when there isn't, and everyone believes him.' She looked into Mallen's eyes, and something collapsed in her face. 'Where is he?' Suddenly, like a cat, she twisted on her heel and ran out of the room. He heard her opening doors along the passage. He followed, slowly, and found her sitting on the bed beside her husband. 'George,' she said. 'What is it, what happened?' She put a hand on his arm and he howled with pain. She started back in terror. 'What have you done?' she whispered. Mallen stood back in the shadows. For the first time, he wondered if it was possible that Corney had known all along what he was doing; could he really have gone so far as this to get her attention and her sympathy? Augusta turned. 'What's wrong with him?'

'He's been taking too much of his medicine.'

'I can't even touch him!'

'His muscles are still tender.'

'Why – *why*?' She got up from the bed and moved around the room, bumping into the furniture and wringing her hands. Extraordinary, thought Mallen; people really do that. She heard Corney groan, and went back to the bed.

He opened his eyes. 'You're here,' he said.

'I'm here, yes. I didn't know, George, I had no idea.'

He lifted a hand to touch her hair. 'Where are the boys?'

'They're at school. Do you want them? I can send for them.'

'No.' His breathing was rattled and heavy. 'Stay with me.'

'Of course.'

Watching them, Mallen thought how little he knew her; and yet he knew everything, all there was to know, all her life and her being. He listened to the murmur of their voices, and thought, with a great crash of pain in his chest, of the summer, of easy talk beside open windows, the pearly rise of her laugh.

Corney closed his eyes again and held his wife's hand. His head, on the pillows, looked suddenly small; when he spoke, it was as if he was summoning his last strength. 'It isn't so bad,' he said.

'It is bad, it's very bad!'

Mallen thought he saw a smile cross Corney's face, but it was hard to be sure. In any case, it soon turned into a twist of pain. His eyes found Mallen. 'I think I need to go again,' he whispered.

Holman appeared from the gloom like a spectre, with the chamber pot. Under his bed gown, Corney's legs were like sticks; they were white, and almost hairless. His stools were like rice-water still, but there was no blood in them. When they had finished, Mallen found Augusta in the drawing room again. She was sitting in an armchair near the fire, leaning forward over her knees. He felt a furious impulse to kneel at her feet and howl, to hold her chin and weep into her face and demand to know why she had let him go and where she had been all this time. 'Wine of colchicum,' he said, 'is a known remedy for gout. It reduces inflammation and relieves pain. In large doses, anything above three drams, it is poisonous and can be fatal.'

'How could you let him take so much of it?'

'That wasn't me. I prescribe frequently, and in small amounts, but I can't watch every move of all my patients, and I can't stop a grown man going against my instructions.'

'He wouldn't do that!'

'He was in a lot of pain. No doubt he thought that the more medicine he took, the less he would suffer.' He wanted to ask her why she had ever married George Corney, someone so . . . solid, so fixed to the ground, so defeated. Compared to her, he was lifeless, a sandbag. She was full of vibrant attachment to the world, and he was a weary casualty of his own lack of fire. A man who had to lie to make himself interesting.

She got up, and stood by the fire. 'I shouldn't have said what I did. I'm sorry.' She put a hand to the corner of her mouth. 'Is he going to die?'

'No. He'll be well in a few days.'

She looked up, absently, into the mirror above the mantelpiece. 'Does he know this?'

'I've told him, yes.'

She nodded. The light in the room was strangely ashen, even though it was no longer snowing outside. 'You saved his life.'

'That was Philip Little. He's an apothecary, you've met him. They sent for French, but he did nothing, and I was out of town, I didn't get here until later.'

'Well, I'm very grateful. So will George –' She stopped, and shook her head. 'Will he sleep now?' She was watching him, and her scrutiny was grave.

'I hope so.'

'I'll go to him. This is a nightmare.'

At the door, she paused. She looked out into the passageway, then stepped back into the room and closed the door. 'I have thought of no one else but you, no one, for months,' she said. Her voice was quiet. 'I have been everywhere I could think of, to Rome, to Bath, to Norfolk, and I have not, for one moment, stopped thinking of you.'

Mallen felt a bark, like laughter, in his throat; he pushed it down, and tears sprang into his eyes.

'I know now isn't the time, but I must say it. I think about you. I think about no one else. Listen, please. I find myself wishing that I was ill again, just so that I could see you.' There were tiny marbles in her voice. 'Every day, it was all I looked forward to: to seeing you and hearing you, and talking to you. I used to get up early and wait for hours. All I wanted was to get well, to look like a human being again, so that you wouldn't hate the sight of me. And then

I got better, and you had gone and I could do none of those things.'

He stood staring at her for a few moments. The house was very quiet, as if they had just found each other here in the middle of the night. 'You look human again,' he said.

She bit her lip, and frowned.

'I love you, too.'

She sighed. Her arms swung round her body. 'I don't know what to do.' It was a whisper.

'No. Nothing.'

She looked briefly round the room, into the corners below the ceiling. 'I don't think that's possible. I don't think I can do nothing.'

He placed his hands on the back of a chair, then pushed himself off to stand beside it. He could not take his eyes off her.

'Tomorrow,' she said. 'Come to Chiswick.'

'I can't. I have . . . I can't.'

She stood in front of him, and he held her fiercely. They kissed. His lips touched her dry cheek, her mouth. 'You have no idea,' he said. 'Ever since I first saw you, in this room. Years ago . . . years.'

'Ssh.' Her tongue slipped over his, and they clung to each other, and then she had turned, and was crossing the room to the door. 'Tomorrow,' she said. 'Please.'

As soon as he left Bedford Row, Mallen was called to Welbeck Street, where one of his patients was in labour. It was easy walking distance. He could hardly believe that it was still daylight, that in fact much of the day was still in front of him. He could feel the ache of a stupid grin at his jaw. He had no idea of his normal demeanour, of how slowly or how quickly he normally walked, or whether, on a normal day, he would feel that London was his, and that he cherished every part of it, every freezing, mud-covered stone. He turned off Oxford Street, his shoes stained by a low tide of slush.

It was late when he got home, and William was in bed. Franny was curled in a chair in the parlour, in almost complete darkness. The only light came from the fire. 'You could go home occasionally, you know,' he said, putting his hat and cane down on the table. 'While your mother and father still remember what you look like.'

'You're back.'

'After a while, people begin to forget the faces of even those they love.'

'I'm not dead!' She looked up at him, grinning. 'Are you hungry?'

'No.' He threw himself into a chair. 'I came back along Oxford Street,' he said. 'It was almost deserted. Hardly a soul, from one end to the other.'

'It's late, it's cold.'

He pushed off his shoes. His stockings were black, and wet. He rubbed the stubble on his face.

'What's happened to you?' said Franny.

'Nothing. A black eye.'

'It's not that. You look mad.'

'Well, thank you. I look mad because I have a black eye. Someone drove me into a ditch, if you remember. Mrs Corney said that I looked like a Mohawk.'

'Ah.'

Mallen kicked himself for even saying her name. He was going to have to be more careful than that. Franny was silent. She pulled a leg out from underneath her, and stretched it. 'How's Will?' he said.

'He's well. Asleep. He knows what he wants to do when he grows up.'

'The Army?'

'No. He's going to live in Hammersmith. He's going to grow things with your father.'

Mallen made a face.

'He could do worse. He loves it there, and one day it'll be his.'

Mallen leaned back in his chair and smiled. 'You mean to tell me that he's worked that out already? I hope he's not impatient; I'm afraid it might be a long wait.'

'Will you ever go and live there?'

Mallen had sometimes thought about this. 'We might,' he said. 'I hope so. One day, when we're old and grey. Perhaps before then, I don't know. I could practise in Hammersmith. I don't think I want to be in London for ever.' He got up and poured himself a drink.

'Your wife will be home soon.' This sounded, to Mallen, like a warning. He was taken aback but he was too exhausted and too used to Franny's shattering insights to feel any real surprise. 'Yes,' he said.

'She loves you, you know. I don't think you have any idea.'

This time, he did feel surprise.

She squinted at him, screwing her nose and making a purse of her lips. 'And I think, by your own lights, you love her, too. Just remember, she isn't blind.'

He opened his mouth to speak, but there was no point in pretending he didn't know what she meant. 'I wouldn't do anything to hurt her,' he said.

Her look was level, and motionless. 'Things are bad enough.' She leaned forward in her chair until her face loomed over her knees. 'You need sleep.'

He nodded. 'Go and see your parents tomorrow. Give them my love.'

6

Walpole House

1831

It was a fine old brick house on the river, facing the water and the waving reed beds of Chiswick Eyot. It had been a private home and a boarding house and, since the start of the century, a school. Its dormitory windows looked out over the quiet road that passed the old iron gates, over the path and the river and the eyot – a small, slug-shaped island twenty yards from the north shore – to the hills of Putney and Richmond. Strangely, the only person who was not with them was the Duchess. It had been her haunt for years, and now they were here and she was not. She had brought them here, from Blackheath, and Mallen had feared that soon they would hear the tap, tap, tap of her mournful pacing. But they had not. Within days, the Duchess had slipped off out of the house again, and vanished. No one knew where she had gone, no one had seen or heard of her.

It was not, these days, the perfect place to seek eternal rest. It was home, if one could call it home, to thirty boys between the ages of twelve and seventeen, who chatted like starlings and banged their desks and rang loud bells. First lesson, second lesson, break. Classics, reading and arithmetic. At night, Mallen watched from the windows, out over the road. He saw the ghosts of fishermen and ancient clerics and their wives, but nothing of Augusta. Not yet.

They had arrived at the house in the moon's third quarter. Now the moon was full, and the tide was high. Down by Slut's Hole, the road was already several inches deep.

The boys were at supper. Dr Turner sat at the high table, while a senior boy read, over the clatter of spoons, from Deuteronomy. This was no seminary, but Turner would not allow the boys to talk during meals, and he could not bear to hear the sound of their eating without something else to listen to. It did them no harm to associate the Scriptures with physical nourishment. '"He that is wounded in the stone,"' read the boy, '"or hath his privy member cut off, shall not enter into the congregation of the Lord."'

'Are we sure this is suitable?' asked Turner's colleague, Mr Franks.

Dr Turner silenced him with a look. He was not an approachable man at the best of times, and at full moon he was detestable.

'"There shall be no whore,"' read the boy, '"of the daughters of Israel, nor a sodomite of the sons of Israel."'

A kitchen maid came in and approached the high table, standing at Dr Turner's elbow. 'Message from Mr Rathbone, sir,' she said.

Turner was suddenly furious with himself. He could not believe that he had let this happen. Fool, fool, fool. He knew what was coming, and there was nothing he could do to stop it. '"When thou comest into thy neighbour's vineyard, then thou mayest eat grapes thy fill at thine own pleasure; but thou shall not put any in thy vessel."' That had torn it, and what with all the talk of whores and sodomites, the little mutts had their ears on stalks. It was September – every orchard between here and Hammersmith was groaning with fruit. At a very rough estimate, that put between twelve and twenty-five of his young gentlemen over walls and up trees in a matter of hours, stuffing their faces and yelling holy scripture at anyone who tried to get them down again.

'Sir –' said the maid.

'Whatever it is, it can wait.'

' "When a man hath taken a wife –" '

'No, Ashworth, stop, stop! Chapters thirty-three and thirty-four, not twenty-three and twenty-four, for the love of God. As a matter of fact, go and get yourself some supper. Give that to me; I shall read during the rest of the meal.' He placed his knife and fork together and passed his plate to the maid and told her to take it away.

'Mr Rathbone says –' She was new, and young, and terrified.

'Later!'

'Yes, sir.'

Meanwhile, downstairs, the kitchen was filling with water. The wraith, Dick Grace and Franny sat on a high shelf and watched the level swiftly rise. Cook had found a soap-box, and was standing on it as she ran a sharp knife up and down a square-baked apple tart. The surface of the water, as it rose, was rippled with the light from the lamps, and swam with leaves and reeds. A small eel bobbed its head, repeatedly, against the base of the dresser. The school porter, Rathbone, waded up to his shins, lifting sacks of coal and other stores out of the way of the flood. 'They'll drown,' said the wraith.

'They will not,' said Franny.

At that moment, Cook's soap-box went out from under her, and with a low moan she swayed in the air, then fell and hit the water. There was a hard, flat sound under the splash.

'I don't think I can believe in God any more,' said the wraith.

'It's only river water,' said Dick.

'Never mind the water, I don't think I can.' She paused, and leaned out into the dark above the stove.

Mallen appeared at the top of the stairs. 'Tch,' he said. 'Who is that?'

Cook was in two and a half feet of water, and howling with pain. 'Cook,' said Dick.

'If God created heaven and earth,' said the wraith, 'then what does he call this?' She spread her arms, with her palms upturned.

'It's a spring tide,' said Mallen.

'No, not *this*,' said the wraith.

Rathbone, old and creaky as he was, had ploughed his way across the room in a series of long and difficult strides. He got behind Cook's head, and plunged his hands down into the water to catch her underneath her arms. This he did, and Cook peeped with shock. 'Don't!' she cried. Then, with the water going into her ears, she yelled at him to save her. She was waterlogged, however, and he could not lift her; instead, he floated her round to the stairs, and anchored her, by her elbows, to the third-to-bottom step. Then he went up to find out if there was a single person in the building prepared to lend a hand.

'What, then?' Dick asked the wraith.

'Here. Where we are now. I don't know what it is, Dick, I don't know where we are.'

Dr Turner appeared on the stairs and was faced with a scene of drifting vegetable matter and a soaked and groaning female. There was little room to manoeuvre, but with the help of Mr Franks and Rathbone, he got Cook up the stairs and onto dry land. She had broken her hip, and the process was very painful for her. Mr Franks sent one of the older boys to find a surgeon.

'We are where we are. We can't know everything,' Franny said to the wraith. Even to her own ears it sounded commonplace, and she pulled in her shoulders and scowled. Mallen, by this time, had settled himself on the long deal table, his legs hanging over its side into the water. Above them, they could hear the racket of benches being pushed back as supper came to an end.

'Yes,' said the wraith, in a low and sorry voice, 'but is this all there is?'

'That's what my mother used to say,' said Dick. 'Every day, all her life.'

'"And the waters returned,"' said Dr Turner, '"from off the earth –"'

'And left a bog and no one to get breakfast,' muttered Rathbone. The waters had not, as yet, returned, though they were beginning to go down. Mallen shifted himself from the table to the mantel above the range. He closed his eyes. For a moment, his lids danced with the red scar of lamplight and then he saw, instead of two feet of muddy water, a door that opened in front of him. He found himself walking out into a white and shimmering light, and felt a sun-warmed wooden step beneath his feet. In front of him, somewhere, was the sea. There was strength in his legs again, and a lift and movement in his heart that shot him with astonishment. He felt vigour in his limbs, as if they were still flesh and bone, and the trembling promise of sturdy movement. Steep wooden steps led down the side of a cliff, and these too were warm, and weathered to grey, and grained with sand. He made his way down them, and as he did he was conscious of an eager hope and the staggering smell of salt air. He felt the rough edge of fescue grass on his shins. A slice of fear split his body evenly in two, but at the same time, or a moment later, he was aware of feeling consoled, as if a hand had come down over his face, his mind, and smoothed it out.

'Doctor?' said the wraith.

Lamps guttered and died. The candles had burned down,

and no one could find new ones. The kitchen was dank and the range had gone out. He did not know if he could answer her question. In life, there were things beyond the discovery of reason that were matters for faith alone. In life, belief in what death would bring was based on so-called revelation, and taken on trust. They had never known that it would come to this, and now they could not know what was to come next, or what they should believe. They had no more certainty in this life than before – only hope, and the imagination to expect something beyond their present existence. Without that, they might stay here for ever.

A surgeon was found; he arrived soaking wet and extremely muddy and roaring drunk. Having grabbed the schoolboy's private parts and made filthy eyes at him from under the brim of his hat, and having yelled blue murder at Cook, whom he seemed to take for a poxy, shitten-faced turd-brain whore when he saw her, it was necessary to disable him and put him to bed. The disabling, never spoken of in so many words, was done by Mr Franks, with one solid blow of the leather-bound Bible brought up from the refectory. Cook, meantime, wept with the pain. 'Go and find another one,' Mr Franks told the poor boy who had found him in the first place. 'You're soaked already, you may as well.'

Mallen went downstairs. The wraith was still swinging, in the kitchen, from the high shelf. She was stuck. She had a great horror of water, ever since her father had tried to drown her in a tributary of the Fleet when she was three. She had only managed to stay calm, when they were blown onto the river at Deptford, by virtue of the fact that she had had her eyes clamped shut.

'Shut them again,' said Franny.

'I can't. Oh, lord.'

'You're a ghost,' Franny reminded her. 'You are dead and

insubstantial and have nothing to fear from a few inches of water.'

'It's no good reasoning with me.'

'We'll have to stay here, then.'

So they sat there, chatting into the night about life and death and the coming of steam. The wraith, it seemed to Franny, was becoming at last, in some respects, philosophical. 'Whatever happened to Mrs Augusta Corney?' the wraith suddenly said.

'You'll never know.'

'But the doctor . . . *he* will never know. Not if he never finds her, he won't know who it was who whacked him on the head and did him in.'

Mallen, listening, lifted his face in the dim room. He did know. He knew the identity of his killer, and the reason for his death. It had come to him in this strange and noisy place; he had seen it as he looked out over the road, and over the river, with its thoroughfare. It had been there all the time, in his own mind, the answer. For nearly fifty years he had shut it out, in the very act of searching for it. And with it had come the recognition that he, too, had been responsible for Augusta Corney's death.

He went out into the night. Chiswick Mall was under water still, and small boats ploughed through the dark and bobbed against the railings in front of the houses. He sat on the stern of one of them as far as Hammersmith, where he slipped off and walked up to the old house. He crept through a window, and saw his father, moving around the front room on stiff legs, bending to see what it was that he had dropped. The man muttered something, and a dog lying in front of the fire lifted its dark eyes like a clerk, and settled again. No, it was not his father, it was his son, William. Fifty years old, grey and whiskered. His wife sat at the table with a ledger in front of her. Plums, walnuts, cherries, roses. Geraniums, the last of them, the bill for the seed still outstanding, how did that happen?

Nothing seemed to have changed, not the furniture, not the threadbare rugs, nor the cobwebs on the bell-pulls; the house even smelled the same. William looked up at a wall-mounted clock, checked it against his pocket watch, and sat down opposite his wife. My son, thought Mallen. He had been such a stranger as a child, as if he had come from the other side of the world. Now, it was Mallen who was the stranger. Suddenly he scented death, and his heart swayed with pity, but it was only the dog. It was on its last legs, eaten up by worms. He left the house, and wandered back towards Chiswick. The river had gone down, leaving a thin mat of silt over everything. He stood for a long time, looking out over the water, the small blades of moon on its surface.

7

The River

1784

Augusta sat in front of a fire that she had lit herself. The servants were downstairs, or had gone to bed. 'At last,' she said.

'We can't do this, it's impossible.'

'You're here.'

It was April. He had not seen her for over a week. He was staggered at how happy she looked. Her face shone with light. 'Lemuel Prager is outside, near the stables,' he said.

'I know. He's all right.'

'It's pouring.'

'He's been out in worse.'

He frowned, and shook his head. 'We can't do this.'

'Please, don't talk about it now.'

He leaned down to kiss her. 'You smell of fire.' He sat, his legs stretched out beside her. 'I mean it,' he said. 'We can't.' He took her hand and turned it over in his. 'I'm supposed to be at the hospital. I'm up to my eyes in work.'

'Send some of your patients to other doctors.'

'– And every time I come here, it's a risk. It won't take much; a word here or there.'

She leaned away from him and frowned. 'Would that matter so much?'

'I would lose everything.' He could not look at her. A log broke in the fire. When he came here, he had to close his eyes to everything else. When he came here, he had to hope to God that no one he knew would see him, and

261

that he would remember, when he went home, his own lies.

She stretched her back and smiled. 'Do you know what I saw today?'

'No, what?'

'I saw a balloon go up. In the fields behind the Foot Guards at Knightsbridge. Moret tried it there, two years ago, do you remember, but he never got off the ground. The balloon caught fire and he ran off with the takings. I was there. The crowd went mad.'

He was gazing at her. He had no idea what she was talking about.

'They tried it again today, in spite of the cold. You wouldn't believe the noise it makes! It was another Frenchman, Rodier. He went up . . . oh, high, I don't know how high, above the trees, the houses, everything. There were hundreds and hundreds of people there. The men in the basket hung on for dear life, you could see they had never been up before. Only Rodier, who waved his flag and leaned out like a madman.'

He loved her. He loved her with his heart, his life. She was like no other woman, no one in London, no one in England. He thought of a patch of green on the edge of the city, gently receding as they rose above it. A distant pink in the sky, perhaps. Sunrise, or nightfall. Augusta holding his waist, a coarse and happy shout from the crowd. He groaned. This is the sort of infatuation, he thought, that can make us imagine almost anything.

She was watching him. 'We can go away,' she said.

'Don't say such things –'

'Why not?'

It had already happened; she had thought it out. Toulouse, Rouen, Ravenna. As long as they were in London it would be like this, hours taken here or there from his work, the constant fear of discovery. Eventually, even for her, the risk would become dreary. She was right, there was nothing else for them to do but to go away.

'Why not?' she said again.

'My work, my family. Your family.'

'You can work anywhere.'

He raised his head and saw the fine, hard set of her jaw. 'It's not –' He spread his hands.

'Then don't work!'

His face felt like paper. Paris, or Lieden. He imagined setting up in a foreign town, making a name for himself again. He saw himself treading narrow streets between high buildings, heard the sound of his own feet on the cobbles. He saw them, the two of them, in a room in the rue Conté, or walking through St Peter's Square. He saw their trunks being carried through the streets of Philadelphia or Massachusetts. Curiously, he saw them as strangers, not only to the place, but to each other. 'We can't,' he said. 'How can we? It's impossible.'

She leaned forward and hit him, on his shoulder. It felt as if he had been kicked by a small horse. He took her arm and held it, but she twisted round and hit him again with her other hand. Then she pushed herself onto her knees and slammed her open fist into his chest. He fell back, hitting his head against a chair leg. He felt her mouth on his, the curl and hunger of her tongue. They fought as they kissed, hurting each other and tearing clothes. She pulled his shirt open and bit the flesh at his waist, and he lifted her skirts up over her legs. They made love half mad and half-dressed, tangled in silk and firelight. Only when they were lying quiet again did she lift a tender hand to his cheek.

'Gottingen,' he said. Had he been asleep? Perhaps, for five minutes. 'Or Vienna.'

'I have friends in Linz.'

'They're building a new hospital in Linz.'

'All we would need is a roof over our heads. We could be there by June.'

He dozed as she talked, spinning plans. Her voice was like the firelight, flickering.

It was light when he got home. Julia was eating breakfast with William. She had come home after Christmas, though the baby was still in Kensington. 'What's wrong with you all?' he said. 'You look as if someone has died.'

'It's Franny,' said Julia. 'Where on earth have you been?'

He turned on his heels and left the house again.

She had a high fever, headaches, a rash. She was sleepy and could not bear bright lights. She never woke up properly, it swept her up in hours. Mallen didn't leave her side. It was as if a massive dark had rolled up over him; in one moment, she had slipped into something unfathomable, the grip of fever, and the falling away. He gave her everything he could think of until Hannah took his shaking hands in hers and begged him with tears streaming down her face to stop. They could not help her. The room was in the middle of nowhere, cut off from the rest of the world by pain. Franny drew away from them like something precious but beyond reach going out to sea. She could not hear her name when they spoke it. They waited as if she might come back, but she could not. Even when she had gone, Mallen refused to be sure until he held a feather to her lips. The days that followed her death were full of trodden grief and the smell of lilies. He all but lost the power of speech. When they had put her in the ground, he could not move from the spot where he was standing.

May lifted fists into the sky. The days were swept by squally rain and sudden shouts of sun. Julia spent hours with William; he wouldn't let her out of his sight. Mallen wrote to Augusta, but did not go to see her.

Two weeks after the funeral, Julia told him to put on a coat. They walked up Gray's Inn Lane to Bagnigge Wells, where they tramped past the fish ponds and the fountains, and bought buns in the bun house. William shrieked at the fish and threw raisins at them over the chain-link fence. Julia took Mallen's arm. 'He talks like Franny,' she said.

'You must find someone else, if you want to.'

'I will. I'll do it when the baby comes home. Until then, I'm all right.' She turned her face to him. 'I am all right.'

'I know. You've been extraordinary.' She had. She had done everything. She had managed the house, William, the servants, as if the past few months had never happened. It was she, and not Mallen, who went every day to see Hannah and Patrick Bright.

They crossed onto a formal walk, between box hedge and holly. Julia looked behind her, for William, and went on. 'I want to say something to you,' she said.

'Now?'

'Yes.'

Mallen nodded. A blackbird exploded out of the hedge beside them.

'You seem to think that I don't know where you have been going, and who you've been going to see, but I do, and I want you to understand that it must stop. If it doesn't, you're going to destroy my life, and the children's, too. I think you may be under some kind of spell; I think you have begun to forget who you are, and I don't know what to do. You don't have any will any more. You're never at home, and when you are, you're like a stranger in your own house. This is your family, James. William thinks you are the greatest man on earth, and yet there are times when you look at him as if you didn't know him, as if you don't know what he's doing there. I love you, James. At the moment, my heart's too angry and afraid to feel anything else but anger and fear, but I do love you. If you don't stop this thing, though, then a great wall will grow up between us, and I will shut my mouth and I will never speak a word to you again, or show any outward sign of feeling towards you. You're going to have to choose.' She was not looking at him as she said this, but somewhere into the air. 'You're going to have to choose,' she said again.

Tears poured down his face, cold in the wind.

There was a constant knot of pain at his jaw. Franny's death had become like a dark lining to everything he did. He sat down at his desk and wrote a letter to Augusta, in which he made it clear that he would not see her again. He heard nothing from her, not a word. He went from house to house, from the hospital to the coffee house, and from there to the next place, and then the next. In all the dark silt of his pain, he knew that there was no choice, that his life with Julia was the greater kind of love, that his children were his very existence.

He took William to see the skeleton of the giant, Charles O'Brien, in John Hunter's museum in Leicester Square. Hunter himself was there, fussing over other exhibits recently moved from Earl's Court. 'This place is chaos,' he told Mallen.

Mallen lifted his chin towards the eight-foot skeleton. 'It's brown. Why?'

Hunter peered at the small boy. He was miles away, in another country, looking at glass jars. 'Had to boil the flesh off it,' he said. 'In pieces. For reasons of speed and secrecy.'

Mallen remembered the whale, and the copper cauldron in Hunter's cellar. 'Secrecy?'

'Long story. Everybody wanted him. I had to part with five hundred pounds and smuggle him home in a hackney.' Hunter pulled out his watch and consulted it. 'I have to go,' he said. 'But take him through and show him the paintings. Eskimos,

Indians, that sort of thing. A rhinoceros by Stubbs. Quite good.' The famous anatomist clapped a hand on Mallen's shoulder, and vanished.

Outside, it was grey, raining. Mallen debated whether to walk or to find a hackney. He lifted his face to the sky. It was only drizzle. William had got down on his haunches to examine something on the pavement. He looked like a squirrel. 'Get up,' said Mallen. He leaned down to take his hand, but stopped, and straightened again. His eyes went up and down the square, until he found what he knew he had seen. Augusta's carriage was parked twenty feet from them. She was watching him, from behind the window, her face framed by the curtain. He stood transfixed. There was not even a flicker of surprise in her face and he knew from her expression that she had looked for him and followed him. He scooped William into his arms and walked, fast, back to Holborn.

The following day he was in the coffee house when a messenger came to tell him that one of his patients had gone into labour. He sent off a couple of notes, and went home to get something to eat. As he turned out of Fetter Lane, he saw Augusta's carriage again, waiting by the pump. On his way home that night, she was behind him all the way from Haymarket to the house.

Yet again, Philip had failed to give him a bill for March. He went to Cursitor Street, and found him sorting dried roots. There were no customers in the shop. 'Someone's made a hell of a mess, here,' said Philip. 'I turn my back for five minutes –'

'Not getting enough sleep?' said Mallen. The baby had been born in January. A boy, the longest baby Mallen had ever seen.

'Oh, we give him half a cup of gin at midnight; he sleeps right through.'

Mallen's jaw dropped.

'Joke, James.' He brushed his hands on the front of his coat, and came round the counter. 'Let's sit for a minute,' he said. A thin shaft of emerald light fell through one of the glass vials in the window. 'Have you seen Patrick Bright?'

'Once or twice. I'm on my way there now.'

Philip nodded. 'I wish one knew what to do for them.'

He didn't know that he was going to say it until it was out of his mouth. 'Pray.'

Philip leaned back in his chair. Mallen narrowed his eyes. 'Don't do that,' he said. 'It's bad for the chair.'

'You haven't prayed since you were a boy.'

He put one hand on top of the other, over his knee. 'Not often, I suppose. But there are times, don't you think, when you do it whether you mean to or not. What else is there? It's what you do.'

'By nature?'

Mallen thought for a moment, his eyes on the floor. 'It seems to be involuntary, and therefore, yes, instinctive.'

'Your mother taught you to do it. Hands together and eyes closed.'

'A learned instinct, then.'

'If you say so.' He yawned, stretching his arms. 'I never prayed much until I fell in love,' he said. 'I wonder what that says about me.'

'And now that you have a child, you're never off your knees.'

'Praying for sleep.' Philip grinned, and stood up. He went to the door, which was standing open. 'But you're right. One does pray for the little ones.'

'How is he?'

'Fat. Loud. But healthy, thank God, touch wood. The apple of our eyes.'

'You haven't given me a bill for March. Again.'

'James, it's only May now. I'll get round to it. I'll do it this evening. I'd hate to upset your bookkeeping.'

'You upset it every year.'

'So you say.' He put a hand to the back of his neck. 'Is that woman ever going to come in, or not?'

'Who?'

'Mrs Corney. She's just sitting out there in her carriage.'

Almost everywhere he went, from that point on, he saw her. Outside the coffee house, outside the houses of his patients. She never got out of the carriage, she never tried to speak to him, and if he made any move to approach her, she drove off. It was all he could do not to throw himself at the carriage door, to leap up into it, moving or not. He became exhausted with expectation, waiting. He began to think that he could tell the sound of her wheels apart from any others. Sometimes, occasionally, she was on foot. He saw her at the far end of a street, or on the other side of a bridge. He could have picked her out of a crowd of a thousand. Then one day, when he was walking home with Julia and William from the livery stables, he turned to see her not more than twenty feet away. They had all been to Kensington to see the baby. On the way back, they had been singing William's favourite songs, songs that Franny had taught him, at the top of their voices. All down Oxford Street, yelling like a mob. They were happy and hungry. When William got tired of walking, Mallen lifted him up and carried him, and the boy hung round his neck, blowing little bubbles of spit into his face. 'Stop it!' he said, and turned, for no reason, to look behind them.

He got them inside the house, and ran back down the steps. She was there, on the corner, in the dusk. He sprinted after her and caught her up and grabbed her wrist. 'No!' she shouted.

'Don't yell. What are you doing?' He could smell her perfume. 'You have to leave me alone,' he said.

'I won't.'

'You will, you must.'

'Or you will . . . do what, James? Do you think that one . . . one *letter*, a dozen words . . . Oh, God, look at you.'

He needed to keep her moving, to walk fast, anywhere. He had to get her away from here, from his family. He pulled her down Charles Street and into Hatton Garden. 'You have to stop this,' he said. 'For your sake as well as mine. You'll drive yourself mad. You'll end up doing something awful. I don't love you. I did once, but I don't now.'

'You do!'

'No. I want you to stop . . . haunting me.'

'I can't –' She was crying. She swung her head from one side to another. 'I can't,' she said again.

He put his hands on her shoulders, and then her elbows, then her wrists, holding her together. 'I'm sorry,' he said. 'I can't tell you how much. I don't think I know what to say.' She continued to shake her head. Tears fell onto his hands. 'My choice is very clear. It always was. I was mad.' She looked at him with such hurt in her face that he cursed himself for saying it. 'Where's your carriage?' he asked her.

She seemed completely lost. She looked one way, and then the other. 'There,' she said, pointing with her chin towards the thoroughfare of Holborn. He was still holding her wrists. He let go of them, and took her arm: two people, walking through Hatton Garden as the evening drew in. They found the carriage, and he handed her up into it.

'Please,' he said. 'No more.'

John Hunter wrote to him, asking him to lecture at the museum. It crossed his mind to say no, but he knew that he couldn't, and every spare moment for several weeks was spent in trying to put words down on paper. During that time he saw Augusta often, either in her carriage or walking, but he never made any sign that he had seen her, and tried to forget that he had. The effort to sit at his desk and write was almost beyond him. There were times when he was inclined, more than anything, to get up from his chair and walk off through the streets, and keep on walking until the streets ran out and he was in open country, without any fixed idea of where on this earth he might end up, but he brought himself back every time by listening for the sounds in his house, or looking at the words in front of him, or the objects on his desk.

One night, two weeks after the lecture, he was called to a house on the river, at the bottom of Surrey Street. As he approached it, he heard the quiet knocking of boats moored to the wall. He had been thinking about Franny; sometimes he seemed to swim through her scent, the smell of clothes and lemons. At night, on the edge of sleep, he would hear her say his name, with a tone of caution or admonition.

His patient, an old man with cancer, was dying. He had eight children; Mallen had brought two of them into the world himself. The house was full of quiet, managed sorrow and the smoke of untrimmed lamps. He did what he could for the man, without actually killing him with physic. Then he talked for half an hour to the two older daughters, and left.

Augusta was standing at the top of the steps to the river, leaning against a low wall. She pushed herself off it as he came out of the house. She was a shadow in the dark, but he knew her. This time, he felt something break. She was going to go on doing this for ever and ever. Wherever he went, she would be there, and she would force him, always, to think about her, wonder about her, to miss her, pity and dread her. He was still trying to find the words to say to her when she hit him.

This time, she hit him on the jaw. Blood filled his mouth. She hit him again, a fierce swipe, like a cat.

He put up his hands to fend off the next blow. 'Stop it,' he said. 'Calm down.'

'Come with me!'

'No. Where?'

'Linz. Vienna.'

'No.'

She raked his face with her hands. He grabbed her wrists, and she twisted her head to bite him. 'Stop it,' he said again, 'you're going to hurt yourself.' She sank, and he caught her waist and held her.

'I can't live here any more, I can't spend the rest of my life like this . . . I have to go away.'

He touched her face, and pushed a lock of hair away from it. 'Listen to me,' he said. 'I can't leave. Neither can you. This is difficult, but we must do it, and try not to look back. For ourselves, for our children.'

She threw her head to one side. 'My children hardly know me.'

'Go home.'

'No!' It was a wail, and it rose out over the water. She freed herself from his hold and started to smack his face, one side and then the other. The blows were solid; they hammered his cheeks and the bridge of his nose until his eyes filled with tears. She was strong, astonishingly so. Already, his face felt bruised and huge. He stood there, hands at his sides, waiting for her to exhaust herself. He remembered her propped in a chair at Chiswick, too weak to lift a pen; he saw her close her eyes over an open book. Her hands formed fists, and she punched him in the throat and on his shoulders. He tried to grab her arms again, to hold her and force some calm into her, but she slipped away, every time. 'Stop it!' he shouted. 'Stop.'

Suddenly, he felt a massive blow on his back. It was as if he had been hit by a tree, or a boat, and he tottered forwards under its force. His body filled with astonishment. The back of his chest felt staved, and there was no air in his lungs. His feet would not obey him.

He saw everything before it happened. He saw her face turn flat with shock. He watched his hands as he raised them to save himself. He felt the impact as he crashed into her, and the dark space in front of him as she staggered. His hands met her chest, her shoulder, air. She twisted at the top of the steps, and her feet scraped the stone. In the meagre light beneath the houses, he noticed the worn-down heel of her slipper. Why does she always go out in those, he thought. Then all he could see, in the break of the wall, was a light on the far shore, a lamp in one of the timber yards in Lambeth. There was a moment when everything was suspended, the night and all of life, then the sound of struck wood as her head hit the side of a boat.

Another blow landed on his back, and he foundered and fell to the ground. Who was it? A madman, someone very strong. A pattern of mossy slime covered the stone under his face. He crouched, struggling at once to get to his feet and to protect himself. He pushed his knees straight under him, and stumbled towards the wall. He looked down into the darkness. Nothing. The night was printed onto the river. No outline, no shape, nothing but the low slap of water and the sound of rocking boats.

This time, it came down on his head. A stone, or a brick. It opened a line across his skull, and his head filled with a pain that spread like red light over the world. He saw the wall in front of him, and the gap in it at the top of the steps. Then he knew, with the prescience of the lost, that Augusta was already dead. He was alone. A cry hollowed out the cave of his chest, but there was no one to hear it. The stone came down on his head again, onto broken bone, and his thoughts, his memories, and the things that he had forgotten until this moment, collapsed together in another field of pain. That he would never know the reason, or the identity of his killer, filled him with a searing sense of cruelty and sadness. Why was he lying here, the blood pooling under his ears, the pain like a huge sheet of sound, the teeth loose in his jaw? For moments he was willing to turn over and die of his own accord, if he could only know who it was, and why. The thought of his children gave him the strength to struggle, made him want to cling to life and run away, but the madman was too strong, and what was more, he was behind him still; he could not see or reach him. Through all his pain, he felt tears. He did not know if his eyes were still in his head, and yet he felt himself weep. The third blow killed him, and while his soul raised its hands flat against the panes of his life, he no longer had the strength to fight the engulfing calm.

8

Leaving

1832

The wraith swung her arms and quietly mouthed her thoughts. Trees swayed gently over their heads, and chestnuts exploded at their feet. In the distance, London lay under a thin cobalt haze. To the east, a fire in Streatham Vale sent smoke into the sky, and on Wimbledon Common volunteer soldiers were lined up for review. They were on their way back from a long day out at Epsom, walking on the Downs.

Dick, between the high hedges, whistled. They passed through small farms, setting off chickens like Chinese crackers. They did not know, yet, where they were going. Franny, walking in advance of them all, struggled with the feeling that something both strange and disquieting had happened, or might. The future was not where she had always imagined it to be. It was neither in front of her nor behind. Memory fell like cards on either side of her, and she saw Dyer's Buildings and Hammersmith and the frigate in the bay at Harwich. She saw streets full of people, a scaffold, the dusty halls of the distillery. She thought of the Queen, and Franklin, and realised that she did so in the way that the living think of the dead. The sky was streaked in the west by patterns of cloud and the sinking sun. She looked behind her for the doctor, but could no longer see him. A sound that she had never heard before escaped her lips, and it seemed to her that her heart had shouted. At the foot of the bridge, she stopped and turned, and waited for Dick and the wraith. As night drew in, they crossed the river at Battersea.

*   *   *

Mallen closed his eyes. He felt the warmth of wooden steps under his feet again, and heard the sea. He saw the wide, open light of the sky. The branches of tall pines moved in a coastal breeze. Someone said his name, and he opened his eyes, but there was no one there. He was alone in the dusk on Putney Heath.

Lemuel Prager. He had followed her to the river. He had stood back in the darkness, waiting; he had seen them struggle and heard her cry, and thought that Mallen was trying to kill her. He had watched him plead with her, and hold her shoulders and her wrists to make her stop. It had been there all the time, the answer, flat on the muddy bed of his mind.

He heard her cry, and ran at Mallen like a bull. It was not an accident, it was an act of fury. Nothing less could have made him run like that. In the dark, by the river, he had heard her voice and seen her lifted fists.

Mallen felt the force of the blow on his back, again. He saw Augusta's face turn flat with shock and recognition. His hands went out in front of him, and he cannoned into her. She went down without a sound, over the steps and into the river. Behind him a cry went up, a long, cracked howl. Had Prager meant to kill her too? No, he had been trying to save her; he was coming, he thought, to her rescue, and he saw her stagger and fall. Perhaps it was grief as well as rage that made him pick up the stone and smash it into Mallen's head. Perhaps it was love, of a sort. He had killed her, anyway. In much the same moment as the third and fatal blow came down, she had slipped unconscious between two boats and drowned.

He might be anywhere, now. The streets were full of ghosts like him, men who in a matter of moments had changed, without knowing they would, or meaning to, the lives of other people, and their own; who had crashed into a sudden hell, and altered everything. Men like Mallen himself. All that remained to them, when they were dead, was as much as they understood, and their morality. If they suffered, they suffered for centuries. Their remorse was like the sound of wind in the early hours. He should not have been there, of course. Someone should have stopped him, long before. Someone should have sent him home.

No one had even spoken to him. Holman was right: he was not a dog, but a man who, because he was alive and breathed, must act as he did until he was made to stop. Augusta had known only that he loved her, and she had worn his devotion like a cloak. She never even questioned it. He had followed her through flames, and she had felt herself privileged by his suffering. Mallen, as far as he had ever understood what happened between them, had been too blinded to take it properly into account. He had disregarded everything in her that was self-interested and cruel. He had been too much in love with her, with who he had imagined her to be. He lifted his eyes to the darkening sky. If he had only got to the bottom of it, if he had only stopped longer to think. He had done too little, and too much wrong, and in the end he too had been instrumental in her death. She had burned very brightly, and they had put her out, he and Lemuel Prager, in the waters of the Thames.

His love for her had been hard and bright, but at the moment that he had been forced to make a choice, it had begun to die. In its place was left a resonating pain that stayed with him in the timbers of his father's house, in every street he searched. An open pain of regret and grief, and of what they had left undone. She was everything that he was not, and yet together they had blown up their lives and the lives of the ones they loved, and when she perished she was still in the full, mad flood of her pursuit of him. He had never stopped to think what that might mean. He had written her a letter; he had thought it would be enough. He had let her love him and then, when he had to make the choice, he had gone away and left her with nothing. It had been, on his part, a long infatuation. He had never even known her. He had allowed it all to happen, and then he had failed to pick up the pieces. When he had understood what he must do, he had wanted it to be like the straight clean cut of a surgeon's knife. He could not imagine anything else. When it has been done, there it is, it is done. The pain can only be endured, there is nothing else to do with it.

She had looked for him everywhere, and followed him, and it had led her to her death. Her search for passion had turned on her, destroyed her, and in death she herself had turned, to look for something else. For what, he would never really know. She had followed him, but only as far as the grave. At the moment of his death, and hers, she had forgotten, it seemed, the reasons for her pursuit of him.

He could see the lights of London, now. Churches, houses, market squares. The lamps, like strings of light, on the bridges over the river. Above him, the stars were coming out. He had lost sight, completely, of Franny. They had gone on, all of them, though he did not know where. As for him, he would not go back, he knew that much. Not to the old walls of his father's house. The sound of waves was loud in his ears, now, which was remarkable, as Putney Heath is several miles from open water. In his whole life, he had never been closer to the sea than the Firth of Forth, but now he heard the slip and run of shingle under the waves. As if he were familiar with the sound, as if it were something he had always known and lived with, but only now recalled.